PHANTOM EFFECT

Also by Michael Aronovitz

Novels

Alice Walks

Collections

Seven Deadly Pleasures

The Voices in Our Heads

PHANTOM EFFECT

MICHAEL ARONOVITZ

NIGHT SHADE BOOKS
NEW YORK

Night Shade books may be purchased in bulk at special discounts for sales promotion, corporate gifts, fund-raising, or educational purposes. Special editions can also be created to specifications. For details, contact the Special Sales Department, Night Shade Books, 307 West 36th Street, 11th Floor, New York, NY 10018 or info@skyhorsepublishing.com.

Visit our website at www.nightshadebooks.com.

Library of Congress Cataloging-in-Publication Data

Aronovitz, Michael.
Phantom effect / Michael Aronovitz.
pages ; cm

ISBN 978-1-59780-846-0 (softcover : acid-free paper)
1. Serial murderers—Fiction. 2. Psychic ability—Fiction.
3. Future life—Fiction. I. Title.
PS3601.R657P48 2016
813'.6—dc23

2015013629

10 9 8 7 6 5 4 3 2 1

Print ISBN: 978-1-59780-846-0

Cover design by Diana Kolsky
Edited by Jeremy Lassen

Printed in the United States of America

To Ursula Dabrowsky, whose filmatic style of pure grit and astonishing beauty stood as the ongoing influence for the writing of this book.

THE MATRIARCH

I ain't scared, asshole.

It's not like I ain't changed a tire before, right? It's just that the bulb light is shot and I got so much shit in the trunk I can't find the jack. The cold rain is blowing in from the left across the median in dark wailing sheets, and I'm reminded of Jesse James, this little black guy who works in the warehouse moving pallets. We break his balls 'cause his mama named him Jesse, and he ain't even no sports player like Milton Bradley or Coco Crisp. But mostly we give him shit because he uses these old-school sayings like "stop coming at my neck," and this is some sweeping, machine-gun, Forrest Gump rain, coming right at my *neck*, Jessie-boy, and all down my back, straight through to my drawers and I ain't laughing now, brutha.

I got an empty box for a hubcap in here, a dented toolbox, a fly reel, an old mini-stepladder missing a stair tread, and a blanket with a design of mooses and an elks on it. My mama got it for me when I was like seven, and for some reason I dragged it around all these years. My mama was Lenape Indian. She used to tell me I had the spirit of a warrior, but my feminine side made me cautious. She said this blanket had my dreams wrapped up in it, and that someday I was gonna make some powerful woman happy.

I work for men. I'm six foot five. I got a granite jaw and deep carved lines around my mouth like judgments. I fix gas compressors, slab saws, and power tools. I keep dirty magazines under my workbench, and I wear a blue canvas monkey suit with my name stitched in an oval on my chest.

A truck is coming; I can tell by the drone. Eighteen-wheeler. International cab-over shitbucket with a 6V-53, most probably. The lights sneak over the ridge and wash across, and when I look down to the side I see the reflections in the long black puddle snaking along the edge of the breakdown lane, rain making needle dashes in it. He can see it too, I know he can, but the hillbilly-fucker roars right on through, sending up a sheet of gutter flush and road grit.

Prick!

I stalk out to the middle of the highway shouting into the roar of his back-spray. I put up both middle fingers and almost hope he screeches those Firestones, fishtailing and halting there like a ghost-ship on a black sea, exhaust making twists and threads in the air like serpents and omens.

He does kiss the brakes actually, but I ain't scared, asshole. Rearviews distort but don't lie. He don't want no showdown between the slick reflection of his tail lights and my long, slanted shadow, this big silhouette standing out here on the double yellow, arms hanging down, long black hair sketching patterns of rage into the driving rain. No thank you, right? Safer up in the cab there, ain't it, brutha?

I'm back at the rear of my vehicle, wind rising and moaning, black clouds cutting across the moon, and I see that it's not just the back left tire that's pancaked, but the right one as well, pulling a monkey-see-monkey-do, starting to belly down and bulge like some pregnant little immigrant. I only got one spare, but I ain't scared, asshole. I can ride that bastard for at least a few miles before it's sunken down to the rim like its twin, maybe a bit after that. Enough to get off Route 476.

Hopefully.

I lean back into the trunk and force myself not to start throwing shit around. Last time I had the jack out, I think I threw the tire iron back by the dented tin that once had three types of popcorn in it. I should have tucked the little black bitch away in the triangular leather pouch that goes in its place under the false-bottom particle board covering the tire well. But I didn't, and it was irresponsible. That was my nickname growing up: "Irresponsible." Through dark magic and psychological power of attorney, Mama appointed it godfather to my chores, my hygiene, my attitude, my study habits. I have tattoos that brag of convictions, but I don't believe them. I have trust, but it's an old corpse. I have a soul, but I loaned it to the church. I hear they keep it in a basement cage to contrast the robed and polished ivory standing behind the first floor podium.

I lift the particle board and have to put my back into it, considering all the parts stored under the blanket with the mooses and elks on it. Stuff shifts and tumbles a bit off left making muted sounds in the rain, and I paw around in the dark recess. No pouch. Only what feels like a catcher's kneepad, a gas can lid with old caterpillar webs caught under the lip, and a moldy Garfield toy I won at the Dillsburg Community Fair three years ago, tossing wooden rings into bowls slicked with Wesson Oil.

I ain't scared though, asshole. I am going to have to drive this shit-can as it is, bumping along the dark highway—just the three of us, a pancake, a pregnant immigrant, and one drenched soldier, pressing forward like a band of bruthas riding this wounded stallion straight into the hardpan. I try to dig for my keys and I can't get my fingers in, 'cause leather pants fall in love with you when they're drenched. There are lights coming over the rise now.

They ain't white and glowing.

They're circus red and neon blue, rotating in sick pulse up along the slow rise of the craggy rock-face and making the road signs flash like mirrors. Now I'm groping in my pockets a bit more desperate-like, and I'm looking in the trunk, shadows moving off and back like the gauzy wings of some dark beast.

I see the popcorn tin winking through the advancing streaks, the catcher's kneepad with a broken buckle and "McGregor" written across in white flaked cursive, some empty Deer Park bottles in the outer crevices, a stepladder, a pickle barrel, a length of frayed manila rope, a spade shovel with paint drops splattered up the shaft, a ripping saw, the crinkled edge of an oversized aluminum loaf pan, and an old blanket with mooses and elks on it, wet with more than the rain, only partially covering the parts underneath it now, the most noticeable—the dainty hand with the pale curling fingers sticking out from under the edge by the lock release.

I move the blanket back over her, thinking how much she'd looked like Mama, with those penetrating eyes and imperial shoulders.

They all looked like Mama.

I pull the trunk lid down, but it catches on something, the edge of Mama's blanket perhaps, and I hear the hiss of her laughter buried in the sounds of the recoiling hinge pistons.

I have been irresponsible.

The blue and red lights wash straight across my back now, making the landscape grin and laugh and revolve like some lunatic carousel. The engine cuts off, and I hear a door open in the rain. Then there's the distinct wet grit of boot soles finding purchase on the blacktop, approaching footsteps, the snap of his poncho in the wind, and I can imagine him pulling down the brim of his hat with one hand and the other unclipping the strap across the top of his firearm, The Lone Ranger, Superman.

A ripping saw makes for a poor attack weapon.

I never could find that tire iron.

My secrets are naked.

And I'm scared, asshole.

CHAPTER ONE

Jonathan Martin Delaware Deseronto swung back toward the open trunk, and one of the dead cop's heels struck the tail light, cracking it. The jolt in the rhythm of the pass botched the balance points, and the body started slipping between Deseronto's elbows, ass-first, arms and legs squeezing up like antennae. He tried to save it with a bear hug and a waddle, but the officer slid through his arms to the street.

There was a wet thump, and the cruiser's rotating lights washed over Deseronto's hulking figure and the fallen corpse beneath him, the guy's face hidden in the shadow of the fender, knees spooned down to the side, shirt pulled out, fishbelly showing. He'd been difficult, pure gristle, and he deserved better than to be left out on the asphalt under a rusted tailpipe.

Deseronto bent, took him by the collar and the belt, and dead-lifted him. The guy's head did a wonderful imitation of a trap-door on a hinge, and blood from the stringy vacancy his

Adam's apple had left after the ripping threaded off into the swell of rain drumming out toward the highway.

Deseronto threw him in the trunk and got up splash. The ponding had advanced faster than he would have expected, and there were pretty things floating and settling at the edges of the clumsy new baggage. It was Marissa Madison's collarbone area, her severed head with its long dark hair matted and swirled across the face, her ankle sporting a lovely tattoo etched in a long chained floral design with matching irises. Deseronto had cut that one off high up the calf to get the whole vine pattern.

The radio in the cruiser barked intermittently, farting static and bursts of mechanical orations that sounded as if they were delivered too close to a cheap microphone. Deseronto didn't have a feel for the coded language, and he had no intention of sticking around trying to interpret how long a non-response went unwarranted before they moved to a backup scenario.

He leaned down and pulled off the decal he'd stuck over the license plate that said "HAR $." Then he peeled back the Camry logo he'd plastered atop the Corolla insignia. He'd made both in the shop while pressing a sleeve of I.D. stickers for the fleet of rental arrow boards, and he had used a different custom plate configuration each time he had ventured out for a new "dig and bury." It was a bit too cute, a kid's trick, but it might have saved his ass here. He'd seen enough television to conclude that even a pullover to help a pedestrian with a flat was called in and logged. If they actually ran the plate they'd know it was a fake by now, but they couldn't link it to him through license and inspection. Yet. They'd actually have to catch him with the vehicle first, and if he could just make it to Exit 6 beyond the overpass there was a shot at finding an old barn for cover, or an abandoned warehouse, or even a thick stand of trees.

Deseronto snatched at the cop's legs splayed out over the edge of the trunk, trying to twist them beneath the rear lip, but the moment that he shoved them under, the head and an arm popped out over the front rim and started sliding. He saved the bundle with a knee and an awkward basket catch, the waxy face hanging there upside down in his arms, drops beading on it. And now the feet were sticking up free again in a tangle scraping the inner side of the trunk lid.

Deseronto went into a bit of a fury, thrusting and pressing, cramming and wedging, putting a shoulder into it at one point and then snapping one of the guy's legs backward at the knee in order to tuck it into the last available recess.

He shut the trunk with a thud and stood there for a second, catching his breath, rain hammering down all around him. Then he heard something join in with the rhythm of the storm, and he looked over his shoulder, eyes widening. The rocky border terrain rose fifty feet high just off the shoulder, stretching back toward town as far as he could make out before a slow curve in the road, but now the receding barrier of slate and shale was gleaming with more than the sweep of the cruiser's carnival colors. Someone was coming with their brights on, approaching the bend ready to light up the world out here.

Deseronto scrambled for the driver's side door and folded himself into the vehicle. Of course he hadn't gotten out his keys, so he had to do the push and stretch, feet pressed to the floorboards, head wedge-cocked against the ceiling. The leather pants were like Saran Wrap, so he had to grope and worm for a red-hot moment, thinking that time was one slippery bitch.

He fumbled out the keys, pawed up the one from the jangling mess, and shoved it into the ignition, calculating. The curve in the highway was a quarter-mile back at the most, and those advancing brights had looked pretty close to the vertex, fifteen seconds at best before the turn of the corner, and then the cushion got iffy depending on the clarity of the sightline.

The cruiser's flashers would be a focal point for a hundred feet or so, with the Corolla lost in the afterimage. How long did those streaks and flashes stay on your eyes, making shit look like a flickering film negative? How long would it be until the background gained enough perspective to show a cheap car with two flats doing its hiccup and waddle out of the breakdown lane?

Deseronto gunned it twice, next slamming shut the door and snapping off the external sound to a haunt. Then he threw it in drive, pedal to the floor, tires screeching in muted fury out there, back end swerving. He fought like hell to prevent a 180, knuckles white on the wheel, and then he got caught up in a rapid back-and-forth across the paint line dividing the shoulder from the lane. There was a stink of burning rubber, and the more momentum he gained, the harder the back end shook, scraping the undercarriage, dragging the fender.

Working it up to a rough forty or so, Deseronto got to the concrete bridge going perpendicular above him, shadowy age-stains watermarked up the pitted underbelly, the Exit 6 sign out front jerking in the flash of his headlights. There were still the remnants of flicker and glare in his rearview, but Deseronto didn't have the opportunity to determine how much was cop and how much was newcomer. He could only hope the motorist had made a careful approach on account of the storm, rounded the curve too late to have witnessed his exit, and then performed the function we all usually did when noticing old Johnny Law on the roadside.

Slowing down.

Deseronto made the turn at Exit 6, the Corolla cutting across the shoulder and bumping over a concrete drainage culvert with a shock and a bang. There was a bed of gravel that peppered underneath like shot, and the sudden rise of a grassy slope out front filling the windshield with high fern and cattails. Deseronto overcompensated right and almost tipped it, lurching back to the blacktop and hitting a sharp downhill. His stomach flipflopped as the nose scraped, and when the back end came down he lost power steering, stalled engine. At the bottom of the exit ramp fifty feet ahead there was a slow merge left toward a secondary road with a funeral home on the corner and a gas station up a short rise, farther than his momentum was going to bring him.

Dead right, there was a construction site, the dark skeletal ironworks and scaffolding rising from beyond the ridge of the hill that masked its ground area carved into the earth below. Deseronto cut it as hard as he could starboard, almost tipping it again but barely saving it, hurtling between two sections of plastic orange construction fencing that had been pushed flat by prior trespassers.

He was just thinking about how lucky he was that the pounding rain was already smoothing over the gouges his back end was cutting into the landscape, when he shot across the skirt of the slope and went airborne.

SURPRISE

I'm flying, asshole.

I was picturing a mild slope, a grassy hill with some bumps and knots of underbrush, not a straight cutaway and free fall into a pool of blackness. I feel the nose dipping and tilting and I can imagine the impact, the hard punch of the steering wheel, the column beneath it blasting through like a jealous bastard brother yanking the ruptured windshield behind for a burial veil. I'm coming, Mama.

Was dying hard?

I see all of us dressed in sulfur-colored gowns and gathered at your bedside last month, looking over the rims of our masks in smiling helplessness. I hear Cousin Suzie-Jean on her cell phone outside the sliding glass door in a muted argument with Uncle Joe, saying that none of us could have seen this coming, that you'd been ready for your chemo holiday for Christ's sake.

Go figure: all along you were allergic to the treatments, it was that last one that pushed you over the edge, and we lost three weeks chasing our tails deciding who was the most qualified for the updates that only came intermittently as you worsened, withering there on the mattress, going from that skinny complaining bitch trying to catch her breath with the help of a couple of nasal tubes, to the skeleton wearing the ventilator mask, trachea funnel pumping eighteen breaths per minute into you so hard that each blast made your whole body jump, and all you had left between burst and spasm was the ability to open one reddened eye from between the cross-hatch of the black headstraps, point your claw of a finger to the alphabet grid I drew for you on a pad, and spell out the word "H-O-S-P-I-C-E."

Overnight you went comatose, and we were all holding hands around the bed when the respiratory therapist finally took off that mask. It left purple bruises across the bridge of your nose, and your head lolled toward a shoulder.

Your face was stone on the pillow. A graven idol.

And you were frowning.

But don't even think it, asshole. Don't you pull your psychoanalytic bullshit with me, claiming that I'm killing women to go give my mama company in heaven or to get even or something. I was doing the deed long before she went and ate the dirt sandwich, and she fucked my timing, to tell you the truth. I'd seen her face in the faces of a dozen women after she got checked into the I.C.U., and I couldn't erase any of them. Marissa Madison was my comeback.

And now this.

I pitch into the sea of blackness for another bald moment, the flying Toyota, Chitty-Chitty fucking Bang-Bang, and I hit too soon, all shock and concussive whiplash. My knees fork out, my chin whacks the wheel, and my right middle finger jams into the dashboard.

The Corolla is sliding nose down, and by the chock 'n' gravel sounds it seems I'm on dirt, and it might go ass over teakettle, and I've lost a tooth. I'm trying my best not to swallow it, and my right hand is screaming bloody murder. When I whammed and jammed it I turned on the radio by accident, and it's classic rock, Phil Collins who can feel it coming in the air tonight, and this can't be my swansong because I always hated this soft motherfucker.

The back end bumps down and I swerve, passenger side first in a sweeping arc that sends a shuddering wave of reverberation straight through to my tailbone. My forearms are in front of my face now as I picture sideswiping straight into a perpendicular steel I-beam bursting through the window and pinning my head to the door rim . . . barrel-rolling hard and heavy into a bulldozer with its bucket-spikes up . . . sailing off the wide edge of what turns out to be the real recess and tumbling into a hundred-foot quarry.

I smash into something broadside, and the side of my head smacks the door glass hard enough to make it dimple and spiderweb.

Phil Collins hits the break where he sings,

"Well I remember."

The car rocks and settles. Through the crimped framework of the blown-out passenger window, I can see a dark curve of wet cement, and I know I've come to a stop on the long side of a massive section of concrete piping. For a second I try to recall whether the shape is concave or convex, and I wonder why on earth I give a fuck.

I hawk up and spit out my tooth, glance down at my bleeding hand, and see the knuckle has come straight through the skin. I cradle it to my chest and simultaneously reach across myself to turn off the headlights and the radio, and everything shuts down to a thick hush. The rain has backed down to a drizzle and the pitter-patters along the roof are like distant white noise. The wind comes up and quickly drifts off. I'm about to turn back the key and from behind I hear a click, a snap, and a distinct metallic squawk, like hinges moving sluggishly in poorly oiled recesses.

I look to the rearview and the trunk is coming open. I can see it moving upward, finally coming seated in the groove keeping it stationary in its raised position.

The back end of the car bobs down and then elevates to a level slightly higher than a second before.

And then, in the wet dirt back there, I hear a footstep.

CHAPTER TWO

Deseronto turned the car off and pushed up carefully, sliding the keys into his tight pocket, eyes glued to the rear-view. Was it possible the cop had actually survived the assault back there in the breakdown lane? Deseronto had torn the man's Adam's apple straight from his throat. He had eaten it too, swallowed it whole right there on the roadside. He had told himself that it was a haphazard sort of attempt at concealing evidence that the officer had in fact died out there in the harsh glare of his own headlights, but he really believed it had instead been some old buried Lenape tradition, preserving a piece of the soul you'd just stolen or some such ghost-dance skin-walker bullshit. Because he'd done it instinctively. Because he'd enjoyed it.

But was it in any way conceivable that the bastard could had lived through it? Deseronto had heard of people surviving all sorts of weird shit, gunshots to the head, vital organs crushed.

A few months back some nurse at Children's Hospital was on a late-night cable show describing how there was this ghetto kid who stabbed his seven-year-old cousin straight through the chest with a pair of sewing scissors, and when the blood-spattered victim was wheeled through the emergency room fully conscious and telling bad jokes no less, the handles were still pumping up and back with the beat of his heart. Deseronto even read in a construction newspaper last year about some guy fucking around on the jobsite, sticking what he thought was an empty nail gun up to his buddy's head and pulling the trigger so the piston would ding him. The victim had laughed about it, worked the rest of his shift, and only complained of a nagging headache when he couldn't fall asleep later that night. The eventual X-ray showed a two-inch finishing nail stuck straight through the middle of his brain. But could a man survive having his voice box torn out? He'd seemed dead as all shit back there on 476, that was for sure.

Deseronto looked at his mangled hand and noticed that the protruding knuckle bone had splintered. It could make for a weapon, one deadly punch to the forehead. Or maybe he could blind him. He made a fist and winced, the grimace turning to a tight grin. The fucker out there couldn't walk. He'd broken the guy's knee straight through, so who had it worse?

Something clunked back there and the car rocked slightly.

Enough. Deseronto opened the door. The hinges squawked. Broken chinks of glass from where his head had made contact with the driver's side window speckled along his thigh and tick-tacked into the groove between the seat and the rim. Rain feathered down, making sweeping dimples in the puddles, and Deseronto grabbed out onto the roof to pull himself up. The wind came on in a steely spray, and suddenly his dead mama in her ventilator mask spread across the breadth of his imagination, looking down at him with that one reddened, accusing eye as if to remind her son of how stupid he'd been leaving so many signposts and tokens exposed out in the great wide-open along the roadway above him, scuffs in the asphalt, the empty cruiser, the passing trucker.

Deseronto felt his jaw bunch up and set his feet in the mud. Time and place. What was going on here was immediate. Besides, Mama had no place in the world of his hunting, especially to remind him of the dark obligations she would otherwise condemn. And the fact that Deseronto was using her image against his own conscious will to punish himself for his blond moments in the first place was another battle for another day altogether.

His sneakers squelched as he walked slowly along the side of the car, the fingers of his left hand splayed out and running along the windows and frame almost in a subconscious attempt to keep himself grounded. At the periphery of his vision he saw piles of U Channel, most probably scrap, and the blur of a stationary wet saw. There was something covered with a tarp, an air compressor poking out from under a flap of canvas on a pile of block, the back side of a Bobcat utility vehicle, but nothing good and useful like a clawhammer or pipe wrench. Suddenly he pictured the new bag of El Sabroso Hot and Spicy Pork Rinds he'd left in the glove box, and he promised himself that he was going to wolf down the whole bag right here and now in celebration of finally wasting this fucker even though it had become ritual to gorge himself only after he had parked safely at the edge of the woods at the tail end of a kill-night, chilling there in the dark, thinking about digging the holes and scattering the body parts.

At the rear of the vehicle one of the officer's tactical boots suddenly kicked up and over the rim of the trunk. Then it froze there, toe pointed up. Deseronto jumped back a step as he came around the corner with his fists bunched and saw the dead officer draped across the short open space, trooper's hat down across most of his face on an angle, shirt pulled up bikini-like above that wide full-moon belly, poncho spread behind him like Batman.

The bastard started moving, rippling slightly as if bobbing in the ebb and flow of gentle ocean waves, and from beneath him came a watery scream.

It wasn't the cop who was still alive. It was the girl underneath him.

Deseronto's eyes widened. This was impossible. He had brought Marissa Madison's corpse to the tool place after hours and cut her into the usual seventeen pieces, careful of course to clean the mini cordless circular saw's shoe on both sides and squeegee the waste down the floor drain after pressure-washing the concrete with that special solvent they used in military labs and zoo animal cages. He'd been patient and meticulous in cleaning and rinsing all the hand tools he'd used for the trim and detailing in the industrial tubs over by the slab saws and rental compressors, and he'd worked extra hard getting the clumps out of the mouth of the Sawzall, as he'd had that careless moment when her hair caught, snapping her face down and skidding the blade up her cheek.

But "impossible" had just been redefined, and Deseronto was a bitter realist when it came to saving his own skin. Even though the idea of "ghosts" usually brought up silly images of hobgoblin anorexics with "scarecrow-face" doing nothing but clanking chains and rattling the rain gutters, Deseronto had never doubted the possibility that dark magic snaked its way through our world. He only wished there had been some sort of warning here so he'd had a chance to bone up on the "rules" or whatever.

He ran back toward a Porta-Potty and then veered off due west where they were preparing for the demolition of an old Motel 6, signage already stripped off the marquis billboard leaving a ghost pattern. The main building was covered by sections of canvas and dark tarpaulin with accordion-ribbed trash tubes coming down off the roof, wrecking ball hanging from the arm of a crane poised in the background like some dark praying mantis. Deeper in to the left at the back of the quarry there was a labyrinth of construction trailers, storage containers, dozers, and dump trucks, all interwoven by barbed-wire security fencing. Beyond that was the dark structure being erected down by the thoroughfare, its I-beams rising high into the night with the rain blowing through all the massive cross-sections. Deseronto was pretty sure he had read in the paper that it was to be a community medical center, and he made a beeline for it. So he'd have to jump a fence or two to get over there, rip his pants maybe, cut his fingers a bit. Once he had passed through the construction domain under the thick steel foundation posts he could make it to the by-street. He had seen that BP there on the far corner up the rise when he'd come down the exit ramp, and a gas station meant cars in the lot to be worked on, tools, spare tires, hope, no matter what was coming for him from the depths of his bloody, rain-flooded trunk.

He burst off toward the first section of gating down a mild slope and across what seemed a loading area surrounded by forklifts, pallet towers, and piles of wood scrap. There were long divots cut into the mud by heavy tires and twin dozer treads, and the running got tricky especially twenty feet or so from the chain link that barricaded off a row of equipment sheds. He almost had to tiptoe through it as the ground levels changed, and that took away the "run and pounce" he had planned for the fencing right next to the dented reflective sign that said "Hard

Hat Area." Not that it would have saved him all that much time and space as opposed to scaling it from the bottom, but he had a feeling that every millisecond and millimeter counted. Was she right behind him? He didn't look. He couldn't afford to let her get close while checking to see if she'd gotten too close, and he almost laughed at the irony of running away from such a pretty little young thing no matter what particular incarnation was pursuing him here.

He had originally spotted her from his Toyota making that crowded multi-lane turn into the King of Prussia Mall, and it was the hair and cheekbones that did it for him, as always. With the multitudes of store cameras internal and external, you couldn't go around "casing a joint," following one of your marks up an aisle or out to the lot. So Deseronto made quick study of all his victims on the open roadway, as they pulled up alongside him or drove past in their vehicles, portraits in the windows. The illusion of safety people took for granted in their cars was a modern, built-in cultural thing. It was impolite to look at your neighbors as you rushed by in the passing lane, as you rode neck and neck on the parkway, as you waited at a red light together, and so it was rare, very rare, that anyone caught Deseronto looking. And he only needed a glance for the hot ones.

Then he followed them home. Parked up the street. Moved the car when he had to and memorized their schedules. The toolhouse had him on part-time hours, and even though he stood to miss patches of his given target's routine, he was off enough days to get a good sampling. He learned their work hours, their favorite coffee stops and car washes and delicatessens, their preference for pets, and their physical conditioning routines, whether that meant jogging the neighborhood or lifting in the gym. By the time Deseronto went on a kill-night, he was more intimate with his given victims than most of their roommates or lovers, he supposed. He didn't know if she had morning breath, or if she took oatmeal bubble baths, or if she preferred to masturbate on her tummy or arched up on her shoulder blades, but he did know how often she took out her recyclables and whether or not she wore rubber gloves when she did it. He knew if she got a morning paper and if she had pizza or Chinese delivered once a week. And if he had a good angle and a bit of luck with the border foliage, he watched her grill out back in the summer and then drink wine while swinging gently in a hammock, he watched her sit on a lawn chair listening to Pandora with oil glistening on her stomach and then don a floppy hat and a sundress so she could be the quaint little picture reading a book under a tree. He knew when she woke up in the morning, what time at night she shut off the lights, and best of all, the places she went in her vehicle. Work, the Crate and Barrel, the spa, a weekly book club, her go-to gas station, the produce stand where she bought fresh corn and strawberries, her best friend's place, her second best friend's place, the domicile of a lover, the domicile of a secret female lover, and speaking of which, the places she frequented for the sake of satisfying some secret guilty pleasure.

That's when he had her.

For secret guilty pleasures were meant to go unseen, and there was nothing more gratifying for Deseronto than his hummingbirds designing the very borders of their own doom through personal patterns of stealth. They did the dirty work for him. He was just the finishing tool.

The fencing rose before him high into the night, and at the top was the V-section looped and threaded with razor coils. It was going to be messy. Deseronto reached up for a good grip and looked down to where he was going to press the sole of his right foot, knowing he couldn't stick in a toe like some kid, not with his big-ass shit-kickers. Maybe it would have been better to rush the barrier and try to bend and crimp it down like a fucking potato chip with his sheer body mass. But it was too late to be thinking outside the box now when he was committed here at the base.

He grabbed up for the fence, but his fingers closed on wet air.

The ground beneath his feet blurred, as if it were some ride at the county fair that had just kicked in its hydraulics. Deseronto almost windmilled in place there, the illusion so powerful, the simulated movement from right to left beneath him so violent he was tricked into thinking his balance point was fucked. Then it stopped, and there was actually a "gung" noise and recoil wobble as if some *Big Wheel* had been brought to a halt and it was quivering for a moment there on the loading springs.

Deseronto fell forward, as that was where his weight had been headed, and there was no fence, no hard hat sign, no pathway beyond that snaked between the storage sheds, only the dark haunt of a wrecking ball rising behind layered furls of tarpaulin, and a Motel 6 sign with faded imaging shadowed into the billboard marquis.

He belly-flopped hard into a long puddle and imagined that the gush and plume looked glorious, like a burst of fireworks. Of course it did. He was caught in some artsy independent filmmaker's dark symbolic nightmare about a "bad guy" trapped in a loop, caught between the Motel 6 and the monster in the trunk. He pushed to all fours, sucking wind, hair plastered to his neck on one side. Belly-flops hurt, especially when there was only about six inches of dive-cushion, and he wasn't about to run off to the left and down the short hill again. Fool me once . . .

There was a noise, and Deseronto looked back over his shoulder.

Marissa Madison was crawling out of the trunk.

She had already evicted the dead cop, a rumple and twist in the mud, and she was pulling up now, fingers curled around the edge of the lid, the other on the bottom lip, head bent with exertion, long hair hanging in front of her face like a sodden veil. There were hash marks where the body parts had been put back together, and some of them were affixed backward, insectile, sewn with what looked like the fishing line he'd kept in there on a wooden spool, the rough stitching cut off in stingers and barbs. The shoulders flexed and the joints angled in, the spider poised to emerge from the sack.

Deseronto pushed to his feet and turned toward the motel. Behind him there was wet suction and a distinct splat in the mud. He wasn't about to wait to see if she was going to scamper at him on all fours and mount him. Who knew what other goodies she'd found in the trunk that she could morph into the little Frankenstein skit she had going? Maybe she had ingested that old tube of tile caulking so she could eject it out of her newly formed spinneret lodged at the base of her bloated and spotted underside. Maybe she'd found that tire iron, jammed it up into her face, and made a snake's-fang sharp enough to bite through the straitjacket grave bag she wanted to wrap him in.

Derseronto sprinted toward the entrance rotary past the marquis. He kicked up dirty splashes and half expected the divine psycho-carnival intervention again, only this time instead of a gargantuan "Wheel of Fortune," it would be one of those moving George Jetson power walkways thrust into a sudden and violent reverse. The ground beneath him retained its form, however, and he slowed when he reached the carport plaza, its rectangular roof section removed from the two driveway pillars. The walkway beyond was blocked by two huge dumpsters, three massive skid steer loaders, and a series of Rubbermaid trash carts lined up under a wide corrugated roofing sheet nailed to a series of splintered framing supports.

From Deseronto's years in the trades he knew that what he was looking at was not just some haphazard placement of machines and disposal equipment, but a running dispute between two demolition companies, the first hired by the closers the Motel 6 brass had appointed to save every scrap that they could from inside, and the second hired by the larger corporation, most likely paid by the state, to tear down the bare walls and rip up the foundation. That crane and ball in the background was costing company B something like $50,000 a day to rent, thousands in union pay with men standing around, and the hoarders from company A had screwed the schedule, combing the joint and filling those Rubbermaids with every little piece and parcel they could salvage and recycle. One of the bins was filled with sections of mock granite countertop, another with squares of wood-effect flooring, another with laminate panel-board. There was even a dolly-bin filled with rolled-up black floor mats, and Deseronto wondered if they just turned 'em upside down for the next motel in the chain.

There was a wet hiss behind him, and he dodged around the first dumpster. Of course it blocked the path to the main building because company B had put it here, making a statement, slowing company A's progress to the point of a near-stall. The expression "biting off your nose to spite your face" came up in Deseronto's mind, but then it was joined by the image of what he did to Marissa Madison right after snapping her neck earlier.

Not now.

Time and place, right? He moved past the waste containers, shimmied between stacks of disassembled luggage rollers, and then stalked over to the entrance walkway. Instead of a set of revolving doors there was a black void with thick cables dangling down. For some reason it looked to Deseronto like those creepy long plastic strip shields they had at the supermarket, hanging from the top jamb dividing the warehouse from the meat room, and he didn't want to go in there, not as the visitor.

Normally, *he* was the one who lurked.

That reminded him of that show with the guy who had cancer and cooked meth, and for the life of him he couldn't remember the series name, but he remembered that line,

I am the one who knocks.

He liked that line, liked that series, liked the idea that a "nobody" could own something in this country as long as he had perspective and was willing to sacrifice.

I am the one who waits in the shadows.

And who wouldn't want that advantage? Who wouldn't want to have cased the joint first and gotten to know all the dark corners, hard angles, and "runaways"? So what if you had to go crawling through the maintenance portal to lurk in the pipe-nest behind the wall once in awhile, maybe reach up under some old moldy drop ceiling to fuck with the electrical, or shimmy in behind the water boiler where the dust webs would stick to the sweat on your face like gauze. Sacrifices, right?

I am the one who jumps from the shadows.

Not now, he didn't. And even though Batman was dead in the mud back there, whoever said Spider-Woman didn't have a sidekick? New rules, right? It was best to be ready for anything.

Deseronto stood there at the dark opening, running reaction scenarios through his mind, defensive strategies he could employ for those itchy antagonists who might try bursting out and nailing him just inside the entrance gate. Personally, he preferred for his own victims to enjoy a taste of the "walk and shiver" for the sake of atmospheric foreplay, but you could never count out those eager beavers, could you?

He bent forward hands to knees, squinted, and tilted his head around. Absolute black velvet in there, and from behind, the girl-thing knocked into the luggage racks. Deseronto reached for one of the cables, thick and black, and he prayed that there weren't any slits in the insulating sheathing. He pushed the tip of it up toward the frayed end of a red cable hanging an inch out of the steel channeling, and had to go up on his toes to connect them.

There was a thick pop and a shower of sparks, and Deseronto forced himself to keep his eyes open so he could focus on the foyer area lit up before him. A wavelet of rodents burst off toward the darker periphery of the space, which was ravaged and skeletal, seeming to grin hideously at the bright intrusion imposed upon it. The rough foundation was a cement base with machine-sized trowel curves raked across it and interrupted by a hopscotch of stubborn pieces of the remaining subflooring. The walls were a patchwork of corner posts and curls of fiberglass, the ceiling a nest of exposed pipes, steel strips, and dangling wires. More importantly, there were no holes to fall through and no equipment to trip over.

The flash only lasted a moment, but on the dying end of it Deseronto saw two important things. The first was a big flashlight lying on top of the counter-block twenty feet in to the left where customers would have gone for check-in. The second was the figure standing behind the counter, facing away, turning toward him ever so slowly.

Everything darkened, leaving spots on Deseronto's eyes.

From directly behind he heard the wet splat of feet on the brick pavers of the entrance walkway.

He ducked under the cables and stalked into the darkness.

BRUSHSTROKES

The pitch dark is like having a bag over your head, asshole. Everything gets close, the way a prisoner might feel right before the hemp circles his neck or the firing-squad sergeant presses the red reflective tape in an X on his chest. And at the same time it seems everything gets long, like infinity in a bottle, only you just got reduced to the size of a germ, floating in it, losing your starting point. Oh, and then there's the third dimension, the weird depth, 'cause it feels like there's a lot more space between my sneaker soles and the floor than there actually is, and I keep surprising myself, slapping down my feet before they're ready as if I'm tripping and staggering upwards or something.

I bark my knee against what has to be that check-in structure that they stripped of its laminate, and I fumble out my hands, palm-down, to cop a quick feel of the countertop. My search takes me over the rough grains and hardened bead-lines of wood epoxy covered with a film of what feels like WD-40 and tiny metal shavings that misted down when they were cutting the ceiling track with their abrasive wheels and their chop saws.

A hand comes over mine.

It is soft. A brushstroke.

I don't move. Then a whisper comes across the counter like dead-breeze.

"You're pure stone now, ain't you, Johnny? No quakes or quivers. Well, keep staying still. I'm gonna show you how you got that way."

The flashlight comes on.

And it takes all that I have inside not to scream.

CHAPTER THREE

There was a boy behind the light the Coleman funneled between them, and for a split second Deseronto thought the kid was wearing some strange hairy bathing cap shrinkwrapped around the back of the skull and covering his face down to the nostrils.

Then it moved.

It was just a fraction, and now it wasn't a bathing cap, but rather some furry black hand making a slight adjustment in its grip on the boy's head with delicate, knobby fingers bending at the joints and resettling.

It was a huge black tarantula.

Deseronto yanked his hand from under the boy's dry palm and backpedaled hard, eyes rolling in his head. He crashed into a forest of drywall studs, knocking them out of their tracks, crimping and kinking the ones at his elbows, and the hard landing made his teeth clack and his jaw sing. The figure before him came slowly from behind the rough counter-block and took a position in front of it, the spider pivoting with him in order to eye Deseronto spot-on, first and third legs maneuvering in simultaneous rhythm with the second and fourth. Now it wasn't a bathing cap, but rather a stubbly doo-rag, hanging down the back of his neck, exposing the boy's calm, emotionless face.

It was Jonathan Martin Delaware Deseronto at age twelve. He was in his clothes reflecting the short phase he'd gone through rebelling against the Grunge assholes and the preppy bastards, getting back to his roots with his dirty moccasins, carpenter pants, and long plains Indian war shirt covered with rosettes and sewn from the hides of wolves and coyotes that had roamed the Missouri river territory.

The kid let his arm come up ever so carefully, and his index finger was pointing toward the opening where the revolving doors had once stood. Deseronto looked over and saw Marissa Madison positioned there in the archway, hunched over and jagged, rough breath bursting against the hair hanging in front of her face.

"You picked the wrong little hottie this time," the kid said, "and maybe it wasn't fate that you found her, but rather that she found you. She had gifts in life you didn't know about, and you had certain skills she didn't expect." He gave a slight grin. "And now you're caught in transition, like a pothole in the road between now and beyond. But you can't just pop out of the abyss and head back the way you just came, Johnny-boy. Not yet, anyway. It's payback time. This place, this whole jobsite, is Marissa Madison's funhouse."

Deseronto felt his jaw tighten.

"So she's a killer-hunter setting traps?"

"Not all killers, Johnny, just you. She ain't God; be reasonable." The kid reached up and gently moved one of the spider's legs off his left eye. "And she's no hunter. That's your game. See, in life she could . . . read people. All sides of them, all the pathways, even the buried ones. Here, she makes picture shows. Your past is hidden somewhere in this motel. Hers is waiting for you there in the doorway. Choose."

"But you got it wrong," Deseronto said. "That thing on your head ain't right, it ain't accurate. This is a freakshow. It wasn't . . ."

His voice faltered as the kid was already moving off into the darkness of the hall leading to what looked in the receding spot-point of the Coleman like a stairway to a mezzanine, a stripped-down elevator shaft, and some emptied storage areas behind it.

The foyer was left in blackness. To the left in the dull slant of the moon Marissa Madison's crude silhouette loomed in the archway, rain dripping off all her points and hard edges.

Deseronto scrambled to his feet and followed the fading beam of the flashlight into the darkened bowels of the gutted motel.

BRUSHSTROKES: AN ENCORE

Only I ain't following the walking beam up ahead, because I'm the one holding the flashlight now, shaking it, whacking it, trying to coax up a wink for a reference point.

I'd been keeping up pretty good, gaining ground on the long straightaway that cut to the back side of the structure where they had a generator room and the laundry facility, the bobbing light up ahead leaving fading traces along the rows of stationary machinery and steel chutes coming down over the curved rail-track where they'd pushed their wheel carts filled with canvas bags of sheets and pillowcases.

But then he pulled a couple of quick rights, or what I thought were two rights . . . I couldn't be sure of the second one because I had a moment where I'd run into a nest of hanging conduit and I was elbowing and forearming through the loops and danglers like Tarzan caught in the vines.

After my duck and weave I made that quick second right on instinct, and I knew it was wrong the second I did it, the same way you feel when you hit that area the GPS can't read, and what's supposed to be a turn-off to the Interstate suddenly becomes a dirt road with grass growing between the tire marks and a wooden sign on an angle advertising a glass crafters or a winery.

I was in a restaurant, tables still bolted down probably because they used epoxy anchors instead of the removable sleeve type, and I only saw the checkerboard of tables in the first place because there was a beam of light that momentarily flashed across a low opening on the other side of the far wall where the bar had been. It was the hatch they brought their kegs through.

I scrambled for the floor-level cutout before I could forget where it was, thinking at the same time that this was all wrong, 'cause if he'd made a left where I'd taken a right he'd be behind me on the other side of the hallway, not deeper in where there hadn't been enough time for him to circle back in the first place, but I ignored my common sense and followed the last of the light.

I was lucky there in the dark, hitting my knees at the right moment, doggie-walking and finding the cutout, only off by an inch or two, and while I didn't hit my head or scrape my back going in, there was a moment where I caught a shoulder and had to adjust, pitching myself up in a kind of diagonal, pulling myself through from the other side.

It was cramped. I could tell because the sound of my breathing was heavy and close, and this didn't make sense because when I saw the beam cross the plane of the low opening from the restaurant side it had seemed like a walking beam, as if this would be a hallway and not just a crawlspace.

I felt back to where I'd come from, expecting my hand to pass through the void, but there was no cutout there anymore, just solid wall.

And I'm not lying on my side, soaked and sooty and desperate and pissed, but instead I'm sitting Indian-style, head bent because of the low ceiling.

I am the one with the flashlight now, and I'm whacking it because the batteries are half-dead and I'm having trouble with the buttons. My face is wet and it smells in here, smells like pickle preserves, and I'm ashamed because boys ain't supposed to cry, and I just turned six a week ago Tuesday.

I stop and I freeze because I think I hear a creak on the floorboards outside to my left. Then there's a clanking by my ear, and I jerk and moan because it sounds like the ghost captain I'm scared of, dropping anchor so he can limp across the splintered deck with his tattered pirate rags blowing back in the sea-wind.

It's Mama testing the padlock.

"Johnny," she says softly through the crack the trapdoor makes with the wall. It sounds like she's right next to me here in the dark, and I wipe my eyes with the heel of my hand. I drop the flashlight and it tumbles off my knees, hitting the floor.

"That's my Rayovac, isn't it, Johnny?"

"No."

"Really now? The darkness is the world's most ancient poison, and if you let it in your heart you have to be man enough to wear it on your back. Are you man enough, Johnny? You a big boy?"

I nod my head up and down, and she gives a whispery little laugh out there.

"God hates a liar."

"I ain't lying!"

"Aren't you? Where's my twelfth jar of apricot-pineapple marmalade?"

My bottom lip pushes out, and I feel a moan coming up like a siren. I stop it right there in my nose, but I know she heard it and, worse, I know for sure now that she knows that I climbed up on the stove yesterday while she was taking one of her migraine headache naps upstairs with the fan on and the window open that faces the Mackenzies'. But I'd been so careful! I reached up on my tippie-toes and got out the jar and didn't even eat any until I got back down to the floor, and I didn't use no utensils or nothing, I just popped the snap-ring cover and dug with my fingers, and then I buried the empty out back behind the shed and washed myself off with the hose!

There's the anchor chain sound again, and the hatch door to the low pantry opens, pouring light across my knees. I want to crawl out, but Mama's feet are right there, green beach sandals she bought at the dollar store, blue tribal ankle-band tattoo, and that thin white scar running up her left shin all the way to the knee.

"Come out of there, Johnny," she says, backing off half a step.

I crawl out slow and from above me I can tell she's got her hands on her hips and I stand up and while she taught me real good not to put my chin on my chest and cry into my shirt I can't look at her neither, so I fold my arms like a big boy and face away toward the kitchen where she's got all her batches going, windows covered with flypaper, jars on the stove dinging around in the boiling water, cheesecloth sack sagging down into the dented steel washtub and bleeding out pulp for the chokecherry jelly she's gonna sell to the farmer's market out in Devon or the trading post they got out on Route 3 with the totem pole at the front of the dirt parking lot and the big wooden Indian head on the roof smiling big and stupid like the baseball logo they use in Cleveland.

"Johnny."

I don't say nothing.

"Johnny, do you know how I know you took the marmalade?"

I shrug.

"You were careless, Johnny, look at me."

She reaches her smooth fingers under my chin and pulls my head back toward her, and I turn with it even though I don't want to, and I scrunch up my mouth like one of her dried prunes and squeeze shut my eyes. Her voice is close now and her breath makes a hot little oval on my forehead.

"It's bad enough that you don't figure I keep a running count of my own jars, Johnny. It's worse that you use one of the dishrags I always keep in the handle of the fridge to wipe up after yourself and then go packing it under the dirt out back thinking I'm not going to miss it. But the real sin is the sign you left in the great wide open, your trail of breadcrumbs."

She presses her dry lips to my eyebrow, and I do my best not to jump through the roof.

"That's a girl-kiss for you, Johnny. For the sneaker print you left on the back right burner."

Now she's leading me past the archway into the kitchen, holding my hand up high enough that she's half dragging me along, and when I get through I see there's something different in the near corner there by the sink, something out of place. It's the basement laundry hamper with its canvas bag and steel X-frame, and it don't look right so near to the clean squeaky china drying out on the bottom rack of the opened dishwasher, because it's the old sack we keep between the washer and the dryer down there and it's got worn-in grime stains leopard-spotted along the bottom and dust webs creeping up the sides with specs of dirt floating in them.

"I know," she says, yanking on my hand, making my shoulder feel like its gonna pop the socket. "It don't look right, does it, Johnny? Everything is supposed to be in its place, and when you turn the world inside out you'd better be ready to see what's been left in the dark, that's all I'm saying."

She lets go of my hand.

"Go ahead, Johnny. Look in the bag."

I don't move.

"Go on."

She gives a little push between my shoulders, and I feel my feet sliding along the bumpy linoleum like they ain't my own. I get up next to it and it smells like mold and I have to reach to hook my hands over because it's a bit taller than me and I need to get up on my tiptoes. I pull up nice and slow because I'm scared and because I don't want to use all my weight and skid out the bottom.

I clear the edge and strain my eyes downward. And when I see what's waiting there at the bottom of the bag, all black and furry and reaching out its front legs to tickle the low corner-folds, I want to holler and run, but then like hard-pinching pliers Mama's hands are under my armpits lifting me, and she's saying that if I buck 'n' kick she's gonna find one bigger than my hand, and that I only have to spend five minutes in there and it's more than fair 'cause it's only a fraction of the time she's gotta spend remaking the jar of marmalade that I stole from right under her nose.

And now I'm grown again and I'm not in the kitchen or the low pantry or the crawlspace the Motel 6 bartenders used to bring their kegs through. I'm in a laundry bag in the dark at the bottom of one of those roll carts they mount on the tracks under the steel chutes, and I can feel it inching back and forth along the rails as I struggle in here. When I was six my Mama put me in the basement hamper with a black tarantula, and I've been made to remember the drawstring being pulled closed across the top of my scalp in a shrinking circle, a bathing cap, a doo-rag, yeah, now I get the clumsy connection with the older boy behind the countertop, the elder version of the six-year-old who manned up and learned to wear his nightmares instead of letting them break him. I also realize that Mama's punishment made it so I ain't afraid to creep through the sewers or hide up in the ductwork nowadays, but that don't mean that I ever got to like spiders.

There must be twenty or thirty of them in here, all big as footballs, swarming, making hissing sounds, and covering me over like smoke and shadow.

I remember my bonesaw knuckle and use it to puncture the canvas. There's a "pop" and the sound of stale air escaping, and I dig two fingers in the hole and start ripping. Next thing I know I've tipped the cart off the track and when we hit I roll with it kicking and shredding and then I'm standing there giving myself a hard rubdown, the spiders dropping off and skittering into the blackness.

Their nails make sounds on the concrete like frying bacon, or rain on the window, or . . .

Love beads sliding off the string of a broken necklace, dancing and pinging along the hard Traxtile floor-section.

My right foot is asleep and I can't shake it out, can't go up one-legged and wiggle my toes, can't even take a baby-step in this cramped basement closet because it was the last make-up session for school pictures today marking the end of seventh grade and Mama made me wear the shoes with the clicky heels that haven't really fit for six months. There's the smell of stale cigars and cheap aftershave in here, and I'm hoping my eyes don't water and my nose don't start running. Mr. Nurve rents us the upstairs and Mama copied his key on the sly for emergencies, 'cause the fuse box is down here and we keep some of our stuff in storage in the white veneer cabinets by the pipe cubby and French drain in the back corner. Mr. Nurve owns a couple of the row houses here on Sunshine Road, and Mama calls him a "slum lord" 'cause these ramshackle rat-traps ain't fit for the niggers let alone the Indians who work in the Swell Bubble Gum factory or the ball-bearing manufacturer up in North Philly. She also calls him "Nurve the Purve," since she seen him hanging out at the high school in the parking lot by the dirt ball field, sitting up on the hood of the black sedan she calls his "mid-life crisis" and talking to the senior girls from the Vo-Tech beauty school, offering them cigarettes and looking at them with those "sideward eyes" after dropping off the cosmetics he sells to their teachers through his Amway account at "special bargain pricing the district can't ignore."

Earlier this week Mama was standing at the stove after a shift, still wearing the Harley Davidson bandana and the light brown jumpsuit that accordioned at her waist and wrists so that nothing got snagged when she fed the raw stock into the bending machine to make the fins for the transformer oil boxes out at the metal plant on Ridge Avenue. She had a hand on her hip and she was stirring up a pot of chili real hard like she was pissed, vapors threading around her head like bad dreams.

"He's lecherous," she was saying, "luring them into that dusty little hump-den down there. I seen him, parking in the back alley the other week with some ash-blond in a tanktop sliding out of the passenger seat, high heels, pants painted on her." She paused to turn on the hood fan. "He was probably ramming it in her before she had a chance to get her drawers down to her ankles, and now his latest project is that skinny one . . . spiky black hair, belly ring, black slinky boots."

"Julianna Conigliaro," I mumbled.

"What?"

"Julianna Conigliaro!"

Mama turned profile for a second, I could feel it as I stared at the table in front of me. I could sense her measuring whether

I was talking back, being smart, or raising my voice over the rattle and hum of the stove blower that didn't do much of anything anyway.

"Right," she said slowly, "Julianna Conigliaro. I remember her from back when she was in sixth grade at the alternative school, her and that weird girl with the Jew-fro and the wandering eye, both of them filling their book bags with the shavings from all the electric pencil sharpeners and dumping the stuff in the toilets, making them clog. Made it hell for me and the other three temps, having to answer to the head custodian like we was kids." She reached for the red pepper and shook it hard into the pot. "So I'm coming home today and I can't get parking out front because Trudy's oldest is out of lock-up and the whole clan's come out of the woodwork, barbecuing on the front porch, spilling out onto the sidewalk. I finally find a spot way up on Maple and while I'm passing the back alley, I see Julianna Conigliaro opening up the basement door for the both of them. Only Nurve the Purve ain't got no case of beer or nothing, like as if he threw her the keys to get everything open while he hauled out the booze, balancing it on his knee to shut the trunk and re-find the carry holes. Oh no, she's got her *own set,* like the two of them are a regular item, like a couple, and they're giggling about the whole thing, calling each other 'cannibals,' as if it ain't obvious what that stands for, and even though she might be willing, eighteen, and legal by now, she's still a *teenager* for Christ's sake, about to be lying there bare-ass naked with her knees pointed up at the ceiling."

I kept my eyes humble, staring down at the renegade Honey Nut Cheerios that were left sticking to the sides of the cereal bowl, and while I was thankful for the snack Mama always let me have before dinner when I was good (and a bit disgusted by the fact that I had to always cap it off by drinking the milk at the bottom and not wasting anything), it wasn't lukewarm sugared-up milk, humbled eyes, inconvenient parking spots, or rattling stove fans at the front of my mind at the moment.

It was Julianna Conigliaro, lying bare-ass naked with her knees pointed up at the ceiling. She was one of those older girls we knew about because her little brother played quarterback for the middle school football team and she went to all his games, backing in her dad's black pickup to the edge of that little hill you could get to overlooking the 30-yard line on the visitor's side, always whooping and carrying on alongside three or four of her girlfriends in the back bed with the hatch pulled down and the radio blasting.

They sure enough weren't gonna win any talent shows, but when they put their hands over their heads, moving their hips to the music like pythons in the mist, the cheerleaders looked more pissed than the opposing coaches. And Julianna herself wasn't about to win any beauty pageants talking about world peace and feeding the homeless or anything, but there was something about that wide mouth, those big teeth, and the beauty mark on the side of her chin that drove you a bit crazy, making you think that she was always pouting and ready to roll her eyes as if she was dying for you to go ahead and try to teach her a lesson or something. She had long neck and wore her jeans low, rose tattoo snaking up along the back of her left hip kind of butch, but if you were lucky enough to see her in the mall or making her way down an aisle at the ShopRite she had this real girly walk to her, swinging an arm with her hand cocked and knuckles up, clicking her heels, chewing her gum. Last summer she was all about tight jeans and heels, and this year she was into those shorts and black boots Mama was talking about, but I really wished she hadn't brought her up in the first place because at thirteen and a half I thought about sex all the time to begin with, and you weren't supposed to go around getting wood at the dinner table, especially when you were sort of getting a lecture.

Too late.

Even though Mama had already switched subjects, chopping up a purple onion and talking about the asshole shop steward who was basically telling everyone that it was time to tuck into their turtle shells because of the war and the recession, I was still stuck on Julianna Conigliaro and her long, toned, girly legs.

See, I was obsessed with Julianna Conigliaro, same as I was with Brianna Wackowitz, Mandy Fuller, Stephanie Triollo, and Rachel Witkoski, but the only difference was that Julianna Conigliaro was in *high school,* and last year when I happened to see her at the doctor's office, she put on a show I wasn't going to forget anytime soon.

I had bitten one of my thumbnails down to the quick, infecting it, and since I had been slow getting ready finding a "presentable shirt" we were five minutes late for the appointment, so Mama had to go out to move the car to a legal parking space after checking me in. It was flu season, and the waiting room was packed, mostly with little kids, a couple of them in diapers, the older ones playing at the roller-coaster bead-toy table squawking at their new play friends in the plastic mini-castle taking turns going down the bumpy slide. I sat across from Julianna Conigliaro and didn't even recognize her at first, because her hair was flattened on top, no fake eyelashes, and her nose was reddened up something fierce. She had on a black sleeveless T-shirt, a blue jean skirt with white frays at the edges, and faded pink Keds. Her knees were drawn up with her arms hugging them, feet on the chair, and she was leaning to the side, resting her head on her mother's shoulder, one of those big round fat ladies with a teeny-tiny black purse as if she was trying to be funny but you knew that she wasn't. Suddenly, she kissed her daughter's forehead and stood to go to tell the receptionist something or other, and as Julianna Conigliaro was straightening back up she caught me staring.

At her ankles.

Because they were the only things blocking a clear view up her skirt.

I felt her looking and I jerked up my glance, face burning. She widened her eyes at me, then looked off in disgust, lower lip hanging. Slowly she turned back as if she still "couldn't believe this" and she made an expression like, *"What!?"* I shrugged, a weak smile scribbled across my face, and then her expression iced down to, *"Oh, so that's how it is, huh?"* She lifted her chin as if she was challenging me to a game of tetherball or something, and then there was movement, sneaker soles rubbing along hard plastic. My glance fell.

Julianna Conigliaro was still holding her knees together but she was spreading apart her feet, and I saw a flash of the vertical band of her underwear, I saw the dark indentations where her thighs ended and the yellow cotton thinned down to a strip disappearing between the cheeks of her ass in a perfect double-sided fishing-hook shape, and then her feet were scraping back together blocking the view again.

When I looked up this time, she closed the deal by jerking her head forward, like a tough girl, fake-me-out, *"I'm gonna smack you."* The nurse called her and she got up to join her mother without so much as a word.

It was the sexiest thing that ever happened to me.

Well . . . maybe the second.

See, I was sitting there at the dinner table with my soggy Cheerios, my rock-hard boner, and a key to the basement dangling on the nail in the flour and sugar cabinet where Mama had stowed it in case of emergencies.

Oh, this was an emergency all right.

The next day when she made me wear the gay dressy clothes she kept in her bedroom so I wouldn't fuck up spilling Dr. Pepper on them or leaving them in a corner rumpled up with the dust mites, I didn't complain. When I had to struggle to button the pants and the shoes were too tight I didn't say a word, and when I stood at the sink and she licked her fingers, smoothing back the long lock of hair that always went renegade hanging over one eye, I didn't cringe or whine or voice my preference for shoving the tie in my pocket until I'd really need it fifth period when they were going to run the five or six of us that missed the original picture assemblies down to the auditorium to sit there like happy idiots looking at the birdie and saying "cheese" just so we wouldn't fuck up the yearbook with blank spots.

I didn't say one word.

Because I was going to be punctual for every class, I was going to fold my hands, I was going to get my picture taken like a good little seventh grader on the last day of school, and then I was going to rush home and raid that flour and sugar cabinet.

Open the forbidden basement door.

Hide down there somewhere and watch Nurve the Purve fucking the shit out of Julianna Conigliaro bare-ass naked with those knees pointing up. Because "cannibal" didn't necessarily stand for "eating each other" as Mama thought it did. A lot of the kids used it as a drug-code nowadays, taking it from that Robinson Crusoe story we'd all suffered through and aligning their calendars based on one of the characters. Nurve and Julianna weren't making a dirty joke, they were setting a date. Friday. Later today.

It was going to be a tight timeline, but a workable one. I got out of school at 2:25 and the high school let out at 3:00. The bus got me back home by 2:45 usually, that is unless Robbie Fraley or Chas Nalan or Skip Sullivan made the driver pull over to lecture them for throwing shit out the window or dousing people with the backwash of their energy drinks. And I figured that Mr. Nurve would be picking up Julianna and rolling her back here as quick as 3:10, 'cause first of all the high school was a half mile closer than the middle school, and second, both of them would be anxious for it all drooling and fidgety, hell, I didn't even think old Purve was gonna be able to do much more than slow down a little, beep, and make Julianna jump into the moving vehicle. It was last day of school, see? Celebration time! And if Nurve the Purve was doing Julianna Conigliaro as Mama was claiming, the fact that she was now out of high school not only confirmed her being legal, but made her *appropriate,* at least officially, and I was almost as proud of this rather sophisticated insight as I was anxious to see that old bastard cram his package into her and pump until she was holding on for dear life.

Or whatever.

I didn't really know what people looked like when they were doing it. Willie Nagle, this older kid from up the street, had a video, but when he was about to show it to me and Frank Garrison in his room last year his mother had come home unexpectedly, making him fall down to his knees and bury it deep into the shit he had piled up under his bed. She found it two days later and he got grounded. She also took away his Super Nintendo, and that was the last time he bothered talking to me, except that one time he called me a "cunt bubble" when I was walking home and he was drinking quarts of Miller with his friends on the corner, picking up big pieces of cinderblock and banging them against the light poles, trying to make the bulbs darken.

There had been other opportunities to see naked ladies, *Playboys* out in the garage, *Penthouses* up in the boy's bathroom at school, but they were always flash and dash so we wouldn't get in trouble and they usually only showed tits. There were butts too, but most of them were photographed sort of hazy or with silk lingerie hanging in front of them.

And I'd never seen a girl's kootchie.

Not without a strip of underwear covering it up, anyway.

I burst through the front door and shut it with a bang, breathing heavily from running all the way home from the bus stop, dress shirt clinging to me. The place was shadowed with stale sunlight coming in from the kitchen window facing the back alley, and I clapped across the floor. Mama's shift at the plant ended at 1:30 on Fridays, and she had recently picked up a small contract from the China House take-out restaurant on Bonsall Avenue to put menus in the screen doors of a delivery territory they were going to start advertising for in July. She'd covered Drexel Hill earlier this week, and today she was going to be caught up in Yeadon Heights, at least until around 3:30 or so. The drive back here was ten minutes with the lights, maybe more if she stopped off at McGregor's for a shot of Jose Cuervo or the outdoor fish stand at Birch and Dickerson where they had fresh bass on ice in big plastic coolers.

The kitchen clock said 3:10 and I looked through the back window breathlessly.

No black sedan, not yet. I opened up the flour and sugar cabinet, knowing Mama would kill me if she found out what I was doing, thinking that Mr. Nurve might actually kill me for real if he caught me, and I almost aborted. My plan sucked; in fact, there was no real plan here at all. I had about five minutes to play with before Nurve the Purve came back with Julianna (if I had guessed right about their intentions, that is), and once

I got down there I had absolutely no idea where to hide. Then on the back side, I had to hope my landlord did his business quick as a whip and for some reason had to drive the girl home right away, because I'd have to sneak back upstairs here, lock up the door, and replant the key before Mama came in, possibly loaded, looking me up and down the way she always did, hunting for weaknesses and trying to sniff out any indication that I had done something that she'd have to answer for.

Which I would have.

And chances were that Nurve the Purve was not going to be quick as a whip, that I'd be stranded down there, stone cold busted one way or the other. In fact, it was almost a certainty.

I snatched down the key and walked numbly toward the basement door. I stuck in the little steel tab. Turned the lock. I was a middle-school loser with the chance to see an older girl naked. The lack of an exit strategy didn't matter. I had to find a hiding place, and *that* was something I was pretty sure I'd be able to manage. The rest I'd leave up to chance.

I pushed the door open, and from above there was a light sprinkle of concrete dust that feathered across my shoulder, a tiny stone dancing along the top step and cascading down into the darkness. Dim light from our living room filtered in from between my feet, and the paint-flecked Lincoln green stairs were triangular, spiraling down into the dark. Above between the rafters there was a pull chain that actually had a metal coat hanger attached to the bottom, and I gave it a yank. Harsh bulb light flooded the area. To my left was a series of shelves crammed with dog-eared magazines and old cookbooks, soup cans, spices, a broken night light, a tarnished wok, blue wiper fluid, a tire pump, a red beer cup filled with plastic forks and knives—toss-away "forget me" shit. And to the right down over the curve of the banister was the flash-view of Nurve the Purve's little slumlord apartment, water boiler and heater mostly hidden behind one of those zigzag dividers, horizontal pipes partially masked off by this white vinyl material that looked more like connected shower curtains than something gauzy or flowing, two black wicker chairs, an entertainment center, a couple of low bureaus, double-level coffee table, iron floor-stand ashtray with an amber glass bowl, and a king-sized mattress on the area rug in the middle of it all.

Black satin comforter with a white throw-blanket folded at the bottom, fluffy pillows, scene of the crime. The question was whether I would get a better view from behind the zigzag divider or the pipe curtains at the outer edge of the "love den," but I didn't get the chance to make a good choice.

There was the sound of tires stopping short in the back alley driveway, now or never, and a smarter seventh grader going on eighth would have pulled the light off, backed up a step, yanked the door closed, and started planning his summer vacation.

I pulled the light off all right. I pushed shut the door too, but it was from behind me and I clapped down the spiral staircase as quick as I was able. When I reached the bottom I could hear the lock tumbling over, and as I took a step toward where I remembered the shower curtains were at the far side of the living space the back door came open with a scrape, light pouring in from the archway, figures standing in it.

There was no time for Z-shaped dividers or pipe shrouds. Mr. Nurve was in the foreground taking that moment to look at himself pulling out the key with the dark form waiting just past his shoulder, and I knew full well that my little grace period at the edge of the shadows here was about to end. Badly. I turned and opened a wooden door, temporary closet, large reach-in size that had been hidden from my view originally because it sat at the base of the stairs. I backed in, bumping up against the clothes hanging in there. And while I was lucky there was a handle on the inside so I could pull the door flush, I was unlucky in the sense that the double doors were set so close together you couldn't see through the crack.

The clothes were heavy behind me, maybe winter coats with that coarse kind of fur on the outside because it felt all prickly up my back and everything in here was dense and close and it smelled like cigars and the type of cologne that brought up pictures in my head of the old geezers who worked the newspaper stands down on 69th Street or the shoeshine booths in the subway concourse, the kind of stuff all us white trash kids were familiar with, living in the "burbs" a few blocks west of the city. The low ceiling had me cramped into a hunchback position, and I was leaning forward on the balls of my feet because of the pressure of the coats, feeling as if I was barely holding myself from tipping face-first into the door I was clinging to.

Outside, I couldn't really hear much. There was shuffling, Mr. Nurve's disconnected and muted voice, and a whisper here and there that I couldn't make words out of. My breath felt harsh up in my ears, and I tried to keep it steady and quiet as things progressed out there. I wanted to watch, but had the sense to know that they needed to be "occupied" before any kind of sneak-peek was gonna go down. The last thing I needed was to crack the door just to see Nurve the Purve looking right back at me because his eyes just happened to be resting on the closet while he was pulling his trousers down. I needed an indicator. But things sounded muffled and distant, a bump here, a murmur there, and I was too scared to chance it. The backs of my legs started to hurt and, to make matters worse, my right foot started to fall asleep. I swallowed dryly. Maybe if I could have walked around a bit or at least shook it out I could have halted it at the baby stage of those rolling waves that felt kind of cool if you were in the mood. But I couldn't do a thing about it as the feeling moved slowly but surely to the nest of hornets that hurt like hell and promised to overstay its welcome.

I was dying for sure, droplets of sweat starting to cut down my face.

I heard something clink. That was Nurve's watch. He'd just tossed it into the amber glass ashtray. They were undressing.

My eyes were starting to water and I had the awful feeling I was about to sneeze. I was also starting to get hard, as embarrassing as that was, and at the same time I was terrified about cracking the door, now thinking that I wasn't entirely sure whether or not there had been one of those latch mechanisms that set it in a groove when I'd pulled it shut, making it so there would be a soft "pop" sound when you pushed it back open.

I heard groaning, or I thought I did, and I undid my zipper. Took my thing out even though it was insane, couldn't help it, the whole thing had gone too far. This was it. I pulled my lips into a big ole skeleton's grin, held my breath, took the inner handle of the closet door I was holding, and pushed as gently as I was able.

There was a small sound when it came open actually, but from what I saw through the sliver, the two of them weren't in any sort of listening mode.

I had the perfect angle to see just enough, at least the region that mattered, a vertical slash-shot that started just below Julianna Conigliaro's belly button and ended mid-thigh or so. Nurve had her on her back lying across the bed, his face buried between her legs, I could see his palms pressed against the sides of her ass and the top of his head bobbing a bit from behind a long thigh, working it hard, salt 'n' pepper ponytail drawn together with a leather hair-band that had a jewel in it. I wanted to get a more complete view, but stood terrified that there would be a squeak or a squawk that they *would* notice, so I stuck with my thread and started touching myself, awkward brushstrokes because I was a righty, the dominant hand occupied with holding the closet door in its place.

Someone's breath exploded out there, and I could only assume it was Julianna, and I'd never heard a girl come before, and it was almost unbearable. Then it got even better. Nurve pulled his face away and there through the slot I saw Julianna Conigliaro's pussy.

It was sexy and alien, delicate and strange. She had manicured the hair down there into a thin brunette stripe and beneath it there were folds that layered and forked down to a sensitive opening, dull red and moist. Below that was the pucker of her dark anus, and I let my eyes dance between the two, the stroke of my left hand gaining its own kind of clumsy momentum.

Nurve the Purve hauled up, and a second later he was guiding his thing toward her with his left fist. It looked strained and corded up, the head of it bigger and the shaft thicker than I would have thought, and then he pushed it into her, slow at first, the rim of her opening widening with it.

I was really pulling on myself at that point, hot friction about to explode, and I was hoping I could be quiet about it, praying there would be some way to clean it up later, but I was so far gone, everything so bright and so hot that none of that mattered.

Nurve pushed his hips forward and settled in her, the muscles on the sides of his butt dimpling, and he drew back and then rocked his hips back in once again. And again. Then another a bit faster and the next a bit harder followed by another that determined a rhythm, hitting that stop-point against her with purpose, making her jerk back a bit each time on the black satin comforter cover with each thrust, and it started getting more rapid making a smacking sound, then so urgent and furious that she brought her legs around him in a cradle, and I saw she had a blue tribal ankle-band tattoo and a thin white scar running up her left shin all the way to the knee.

For a second it didn't compute.

Then it did.

That was Mama lying there underneath Nurve the Purve, not Julianna Conigliaro, and I had a choice to make.

Finish or bail.

I kept going. I had to. It felt too good to stop and when I exploded in jolts and spasms I realized there was nothing left for me in this world that anyone would ever forgive or begin to understand.

I also realized that I must have backed too hard against the coats, because something broke and gave behind me, and there was the sudden rat-tat-tat of them like marbles falling out of a bag, jumping all along the hard Traxtile floor section of the closet. There was a yelp and a shout out there, scrapes and scuffles, and it sounded like something knocked over.

The door in front of me was ripped open. I was still holding the inner handle, but I just let it pass through my fingers. I lowered my head and could feel the both of them in front of me, staring and broiling.

I kept my eyes down. All around my feet were tokens and stones, turquoise and onyx, spiny oyster pieces and coral and sterling silver drums, all of them loose and scattered, discarded and lost, all because I'd put my eyes where they didn't belong and then gone and broken so much more than the string of Mama's favorite necklace.

CHAPTER FOUR

Deseronto stood there in the stifling darkness, an upended Motel 6 laundry tub somewhere to his left, a rumple of shredded canvas at his feet. His palms were pressed to his face, his fingers clawed against the lids of his eyes. He wanted to rip at them for what they had seen, leaving jagged black craters and thick stains of crimson below them. The words *"Out vile jelly"* came up in his mind, but he had no idea where they came from. He had a vision of a guy in a toga wandering the land in blindness as a result of this sort of self-mutilation, but hadn't a clue where he'd heard the tale or the context through which it had been delivered. Probably school where he hadn't really been paying attention because he was looking across the aisle studying girls, a lifelong issue, a cruel full circle.

He had not remembered the closet incident the way he'd just been forced to relive it either. No way. In his mind, it had always been Julianna Conigliaro lying on that black comforter, naked as a jaybird for all but those long suede leggy boots. The necklace stowed in the closet was not strung with Indian love beads, but rather this gaudy set of colossal white pearls, Julianna's big fat mother's pearls that she thought she'd misplaced when they moved here from Jersey ten years ago. Julianna had actually found them at the bottom of one of those hidden zipper sleeves in a Samsonite in the attic. She took them for herself and never told her mother about the discovery, hanging them there in Nurve the Purve's closet because she was hoping someday to be more than his basement fling, to be taken out to dinner, or the theater, or maybe even to a fancy hall where they'd show off what they'd learned in their ballroom dancing class, because even though she'd been a wild child in high school she wanted the good things in life too, a touch of class, a bit of respect. And Deseronto's own Mama hadn't been the one on the other side of that basement closet door, all sexed up and sweaty with the white throw-blanket pulled across her shoulders and asking him what the fuck he thought he was doing, but rather, answering their front door on Sunshine Road, mouth dropping open when Nurve the Purve told her what her little Jonathan had been up to. He thought he distinctly remembered that the Purve was holding him in place there on the stoop by the back of his hair in a sweaty tangle and his mother was asking him what the fuck he thought he'd been doing.

Distinctly.

But if the necklace was made up of pearls, then why were the spiny oysters and coral and turquoise and onyx so God damned familiar just now? And how could he possibly have known anything about Julianna Conigliaro's dreams and aspirations to begin with, let alone the theft of the pearls or the circumstance that had made them available? He'd never actually spoken to her.

Deseronto stumbled in the dark, hands splayed out in front of him.

What was the name of that guy who came up with the idea that you didn't remember the bad shit that happened to you way back when? He thought it was Freud, but always got him mixed up with the dim recollection of a blown-up black and white poster/photograph by the board in 7th[th] grade literature class, portraying this ancient guy who looked like a skinny version of Santa Claus. George Bernard Shaw was his name, but who the hell knew what *he* wrote, and if he wasn't Freud, then who the hell was? This little roundabout to a roadblock usually halted his grainy memories of middle school pedagogy and historical figures in general, and he bumped into what felt like the hallway wall leading back the way he had come, struggling to remember this classroom shit he thought he'd never in a million years have a use for. He thought the words Id, Ego, and Super Ego had something to do with it, but he couldn't recall why. He was familiar with the concept of repression, but never really believed it when a defendant claimed it, at least not in principle.

Until now.

Maybe it wasn't just a bunch of slick criminals trying to get over. Maybe he *had* actually reinvented his own history because the truth was so fucking hideous it had acted as some sort of blinding element, forcing him to art up the blank slate with bits of charcoal, sidewalk chalk, crayons, and spray paint, anything he could get his hands on.

Blinding element. Right. Pull out the eyes. Ha. If only he could remember the story that came from!

A harsh flare of light came up and Deseronto brought his hands before his face, squinting into it as it slowly dialed back to a dim sort of wavering illumination. He blinked. He'd gone the wrong way again as layed out before him was what appeared to be an offshoot to the hallway he'd originally stumbled through, the aqua and bone-white wall tiles making a long curve around a bend with skeletal grid work patterned above him where the drop ceiling panels had been removed. He pressed forward and his feet made squelches and splashes, the "wavering sensation" caused by reflections dancing and flickering along the walls.

And it was thick and humid and smelled like chlorine.

And he was running, heart pounding with excitement, bare feet pounding along the damp tile floor and sending echoes up and along the corridor leading to the vacated pool area. Rudy St. Claire and Skinny Jimmy Whalen were still getting changed back in the locker room where all the old farts were hanging up their brown derby hats and bright colored pants, waddling around with their white hairy chests, skinny legs, and sagging dough marbled ass cheeks. Early hours on the hot days were open season for the elderly here at the Y, and they clogged up the shallow end of the pool just like they blocked your way in the mall, sucking down the free air conditioning and shuffling along in their walking groups.

Fucking bone heads.

About to meet up with pure genius. It was Rudy who started all this, with Jimmy for the access and Deseronto playing technical engineer, and it all really kicked off when Rudy said that they had to make the most they could out of these last days of summer vacation since there was someone awful waiting for them just around the corner in eighth grade, and it was this retarded old science teacher named Mrs. Levitz who still tried to discipline all old school and shit, keeping everyone in rows with their hands folded, chanting the ecosystems and biomes vocabulary words for pre-class every day, and then making everybody copy shit out of the textbook instead of being put into groups where you could goof like always and make the nerd or the ugly girl do all the writing. He'd heard she wouldn't let you sharpen a pencil because the grinding was distracting and she tracked how many times you took the pass for the bathroom, sometimes saying no even if you were gonna squirt yourself. When the three of them were over Jimmy's place earlier this morning chilling down the far edge of his back yard behind the wood pile, they decided to make a he-man teacher haters club the old crab wouldn't be able to touch. The Einstein shit came a bit later.

Like usual Rudy had a rumpled soft-pack of Marlboro Lights, and they sat in the damp crab grass not caring if it made the back of their pants wet 'cause they were "*dudes* yo," smoking and looking out into the thicket of trees and overgrowth doing that slow tumble and clutter down the short ravine that widened to a gully and eventually spread to the train yard SEPTA used for its hub between the Norristown line and the Market-Frankford El leading into downtown Philadelphia. Jimmy, with his long skinny face and patchwork sideburns, was cracking his knuckles and hawking and spitting back over his head, back over the mossy cord of wood his dad cut and gathered from the tangle of public forest last year then totally forgot about, and at first it was a good trick making them laugh, and then it got old and he stopped.

"First of all, we gotta come to class late," he said.

"Yeah, late," Rudy echoed, scratching his scalp through the black wool knit slouch beanie he hadn't taken off since last January. He had a wide dome and a beanpole neck making some people call him "Bobble-Head," but no one was about to give him that kind of shit here behind the woodpile. "How late though," he said, "and what's our excuse?"

"Something lame," Deseronto said. "Won't matter. She'll be into the lesson by then. When she says where were you, just mumble, or point to the other guy, or say you were stopped by security or an aide or a lunch lady or the vice principal in the hall and they didn't give you a note."

"Right," Rudy said. "And once we're in, take forever to get to your seat. Then take forever to take out your notebook from your backpack. Then ask someone for a pen or a piece of loose-leaf real loud and ignorant, or pretend to hurt yourself catching a finger while you're clipping your three-ring binder open and closed, or ask for some hand sanitizer or a tissue 'cause your nose is running. Then one of us, the second we've seemed to sit and settle, ask to go to the bathroom. When she says no she'll think she showed us, and then she'll go on with her boring-ass lecture."

"And that's when we derail the choo-choo," Jimmy said.

"Oh yeah," Rudy said.

"Absolute bombardment," Jimmy continued. "When she gets going one of us asks a question, as if it's serious business and all, like saying can I go see the counselor."

"Or the nurse," Deseronto said.

"Or the teacher of your last class where you left your homework, your pencil case, or your roster sheet," Rudy added.

"Check," Jimmy said. "And we have to interrupt on top of each other, like a machine gun, asking questions about stuff she just talked about so she'll repeat it like a dumb-ass, and then doing an overlap of stuff she thinks might be offensive, but whispering it so she thinks she might not have heard us right, like asking if monkeys really have nuts, or what a clit looks like, or whether bugs have sex and how do they do it. Then when she says, 'WHAT?' we cover by asking if monkeys live in huts, or what Brits dress like, or whether bugs have necks, and she'll know we're breaking her stones, but she won't do nothing about it 'cause she has to catch us clean for the documentation to be official."

"And she can't write up all of us, anyway," Rudy said.

"Nope, not every day."

"Makes her look bad."

"Sure does."

"Like she ain't got control."

"Damned straight."

Deseronto picked dirt out of his sneaker tread with a twig.

"Can we throw shit?"

"Oh yes," Jimmy said, and they laughed.

"But it's got to be subtle," Rudy said. He was fingering a zit on his cheek, but it wasn't ready for popping quite yet. "And her back has to be fully turned. Facing front she can still catch you at the periphery even if she's looking at her lesson plans or her roll book."

Jimmy blew out a drag like a hard laugh.

"Periphery!" he said. "What the fuck!"

"And if you do chuck a pencil or a balled of piece of paper and she spins around asking who done it, you don't have to worry, 'cause she'll get the wall of silence," Rudy said, "every time, you can bank on it."

"Yeah, it's a no-snitch zone for sure," Deseronto said, "even for the goodie-goods."

"It's a rule," Rudy said.

"A law."

"For sure," Jimmy agreed, and they all bowed their heads in reverence for a moment. It was all good, and Deseronto realized that he was kind of happy for once, well maybe a little, and the rest of the morning was promising at least until noon when he had to rush back home to walk all the dogs. But that was still a few hours away and for now they'd have fun throwing their Swiss army knives into the stump that used to be the tree that Jimmy's tire swing hung from when he was little. Then maybe they'd take turns shooting his dad's .22 at cans and squirrels and raid the liquor cabinet for quick sips of Southern Comfort or Jack Daniels or Christian Brothers, whatever would seem the most filled when they finished.

Whatever.

It was suck-ass at the house and it had been all summer, ever since Nurve the Purve told Mama up on the front stoop that he'd caught her little Johnny spying on him down the basement. At first Mama didn't believe it and then she wouldn't talk at all, turning her back cooking dinner then leaving the room so Deseronto was forced to eat by himself. A week later she quit her job at the factory and got hired as an assistant to a veterinarian named Dr. Goldstien who had her cleaning out cages, holding the animals still while they got their shots, handing him stuff during the minor surgeries, and making appointments for him, the whole nine yards, or at least that's what Deseronto had pieced together from the clipped little explanations she offered in passing or the snippets he heard from the other room when she was talking to her boss on the phone. And when people went on vacation and the kennel was filled she was boarding dogs in the house, shoving food in their cages, smacking them hard as shit, even the bulldogs and Rottweilers. Mostly though it was Johnny Deseronto who cared for the animals while she was out of the house running around God knows where. Goldstien paid for her to take a Summer II class at the community college and now when she was home she was always studying up in her room with her ear plugs in, only stopping outside her son's door for a second or two to holler at him to clean something up, or to leash up the pooches three at a time for a poop run, or to take the train in to 56th Street where there was that outdoor stand with the bootleg movies, the Muslim skin oils, and the gourmet pet food cash and carry dirt cheap, or to turn that ever loving

Grunge shit down before she threw the stereo out with the trash in the back alley where it belonged.

Deseronto sighed, looked out into the woods, and he wondered who owned them. It seemed they acted as a barrier of sorts between the outskirts of Upper Darby and the western tip of the city of Philadelphia, flanking the golf course on the suburban end, back-dropping the rail yard, and then following the elevated train all the way to the first stop at Milbourne. In the back of his mind Deseronto had always wondered why no one ever cut the trees down, why no one ever drained that choked and dirty little creek that was nothing but standing water with leaves floating in it at one point, why no one ever paved over that section between the first and second El stops that looked like the far edge of a forgotten highway in a sci fi disaster movie with overgrowth covering the asphalt, bearding the ancient light poles, and thickening behind into that dense jungle woodland that seemed to have been left for dead between borders.

Deseronto wondered about all kinds of weird shit like this lately, the weird pictures in the windows that we looked at but didn't really look at after awhile, the weigh stations, the landfills, construction sites, and maintenance areas. Like on a dog food run, he couldn't sit there during the rumble and screech into the switching yard between the high speed rail and the elevated train without wondering who it was that had originally set the black five-inch cables into the plated and bolted girder points, and who it was that did maintenance on the signal lamps, and if there was a steel storage container labeled "Production Box #1" where were 2 and 3, and who decided on the patterns of the merge and bend of the rust colored rails? Why were the sheds painted different colors as if a code for something focused and specific, and then right across the tracks there were areas left in decay and neglect, old steel poking out of the ground, dirt and gravel, balding wasteland, nothing but scars?

Where did the shit and piss and paper go when you flushed it? How many water mains were under the highway and who was the one keeping count? Where did the storm sewers lead to?

And why did Mama hate him so much?

She didn't seem to notice or care that he was getting sort of good with things, good with his hands, insane at figuring stuff out that most people didn't want to bother with, like the manual in the drawer that showed how the stove worked, or the tag on the air conditioner that explained the electric, or the parts breakdowns of the power tools in the middle school metal shop, or the operator's guide to the commercial heating system he'd found in the custodian's closet last year when he was roaming the halls cutting Spanish. No dumb metaphors or symbols or all that other Englishy bullshit that kept the answer hidden in a cloud. Just the facts, Jack. No bullshit. Duh.

But there was still no way to deny the fact that most other kids liked romance stories and video games and movies and sit coms, and Deseronto had to pretty much face the idea that he was into the stuff most people ignored. He was ignored. On all fronts. He was gliding through life like the bottom feeder no one was watching.

Except maybe Rudy St. Claire and Skinny Jimmy Whalen, because right after they formed their teacher haters club there behind the woodpile they came up with an awesome idea based on the fact that their pal Deseronto was so recently bent on geeking out over parts schematics.

Jimmy's old man worked security and maintenance at the Jewish Y out in Havertown, and it also just so happened that Rudy was brought in as a guest a few weeks ago by Ben Zatz, this kid whose Bar Mitzvah he went to last winter. It was there in the pool that he saw old Mrs. Levitz, paddling around with her yellow bathing cap and kickboard, in fact, that's why they were talking about her now in the first place.

Deseronto fingered out a dime-sized rock stuck half in the dirt and stared into the crater.

"Hey Rude," he said tonelessly. "Did Levitz go up on the diving board?"

"Yeah, it was gross."

"Why?" Jimmy said.

"Can you say dimpled cream cheese and flab?"

"I just barfed in my mouth, thanks."

"Told you."

Deseronto chucked the stone into the woods.

"We can jury rig the board, guys. Make it a time bomb."

"How?" Rudy said.

Deseronto shrugged.

"Easy. You just have to know how to get to the connection between the platform and the springs and coils. I mean, it's just a question of backing off the right bolts or set screws to their last threads. Won't know exactly what to do until I see it, but all I'll need is a Phillips or a flat head, maybe an Allen wrench and a set of sockets."

Jimmy's wide eyeballs spelled awe.

"Then the board whacks her in the ass the minute she gets near the edge."

"Or someone else," Deseronto added. "Doesn't matter. Either way it's a hoot."

"Done," Jimmy said, pushing up, wiping dirt off his butt and almost dragging his jeans down with it, they were hanging so low to begin with. "My dad keeps all that crap in a white pickle barrel in the equipment shed. He closes up Friday nights and he's always complaining that he has to police the grounds. He's always bitching that he ain't no trash man. We're gonna volunteer, hook the keys, open the equipment shed, and get Johnny the goods."

"And what if he gets caught dicking around under the diving board?" Rudy said.

Jimmy pushed one of his nostrils closed and blasted snot out through the other. It wasn't clean, and he had to wipe.

"No way," he said. "Dad don't like the pool. Says it's full of disease and germs. Says he gets foot fungus even through his hiking boots in there, and he made them sign a part of his contract that says he's only responsible for the dry areas like the weight room, the gym, and the aerobics classrooms upstairs. Shit, he'll vacuum the front foyer and the TV area like an old maid, but he won't count the pool noodles, right? Go figure."

"Safe enough for me," Deseronto said. "No risk, no fun anyway."

"It's a go, then," Rudy said.

"Tonight's the set-up, tomorrow we go in and watch," Jimmy agreed. They were both grinning like fools. Deseronto met their good cheer with his eyes, but he couldn't quite make his face join in like some happy little camper. No more cracking himself open like that, yes ma'am—no ma'am, sharing prayers with God, smiling for pictures.

Mama wouldn't look at him anymore. She used to wake him up in the morning with a gentle shake on the shoulder and a little "good-boy" scratch above the ear, but now she just pounded on his door a few times. She used to fold his clothes and put them on the chair for him, but now she just dumped a wrinkled pile in a basket out in the hall. She used to make his lunch, but now she just left him shit in the fridge.

Like he did so often of late when dwelling on his mother's neglect, he pictured Julianna Conigliaro's dark exotic pussy. It was his go to, his fail safe, and while he felt guilty as hell about spying it between the slats of the closet so to speak, in a way he knew it was better that way, forbidden, disconnected from anything but its own strange and delicate symmetry.

Pictures in the windows.

Flashes only revealing parts of the human body.

A mother's neglect.

Woods.

Tonight he was going to go into the Jewish Y up on City Line Avenue, sneak into the pool area, and rig a diving board to malfunction, but for the moment he couldn't get a strange thought out of his head. He didn't quite know why this particular idea had come to mind, but gazing out into the forest he suddenly realized how easy it would be to slip in there at night without being seen. You could even bring a flashlight and a duffel bag. Bury shit under the overgrowth.

You could live at the edge of the city and be the king of a forgotten woodland.

And they wouldn't find the body parts for three hundred years.

BRUSHSTROKES: PART 3

And I was running, asshole, I remember it like it was yesterday, running down the blue and white tile corridor, totally stoked, eyes wide, heart pounding. Rudy and Skinny Jimmy were still changing back in the locker room 'cause I had been quick about it, chucking my shirt and ditching my sneaks under a bench, no bathing suit, just the cut-off jean shorts I wore into the place. They probably had a rule about not wearing your undies in the pool, as if the mesh liner of a Hawaiian style bathing suit was a better filter for the microscopic shit-specs left in your asshole or something. They probably had a rule about running in the halls too, but I wanted to be the first in, to break the smooth plane of water with a humongous cannonball, anoint the space, soil the field. Then when the old heads came in, I'd be waiting there in the middle of the pool, treading water, chin buried just beneath the wavering surface, watching.

Coming through the archway they'd see me too, acting tough like they didn't, like they were streetwise or street-smart and *expected* this half grown Injun with his hair slicked down to be waiting for them all in the middle of the pool like a hunter in the brush. They'd know something was wrong, but they wouldn't bark about it, same as they didn't complain about the black guys Jimmy had told me about who'd bought memberships and taken over the basketball courts. That would make them *racists*, and the more that people let the prejudice build up inside about the poor folk who seemed to be spreading all around them like oil on the floor, the less they wanted to show it.

Of course, Jimmy and Rudy were gonna join me and while I would have rather watched it minus the hype at this point, they were in it with me like brothers.

I tore ass down the hallway of tile and banged through the thick wooden doors. The Halogens were still coming up and the place had a dim, dreamy feel to it, as if the edge of the horizon was about to pull the sun up over its shoulder and sing a hymn or something. There were shadows coming off the stacks of boogie boards, plastic rafts, and inner tubes to the left of the lifeguard tower, and the row of empty beach chairs looked like a pew. Even the shallow end seemed mysterious, with this neglected pair of black goggles laying there by the handrail at the edge of the slow waking fairytale.

The water was a glass treasure sitting in the middle of it all with the diving board sticking out over the far edge, so thin and flat and motionless in its own sort of dark geometry, suspended in time, the reflections beneath it angled and slanted through to the lane stripes.

It fucked with everything that made sense about balance, and I guess that was the point. See-saws had the base in the middle and bridges and stairways had supports at both ends. Diving boards probably came from some low-life's cure for boredom, drawn up on a napkin and first used as a dare.

Somehow though, we'd come to trust this lopsided piece of dipshit engineering like it was a natural blur in the landscape, and it was just the ultimate rude rush to think that a science teacher was possibly gonna be the one to cause the last step in the failure, now wasn't it...

Last night when Mr. Whalen brought us out to the equipment shed we couldn't stop laughing, snorting, joshing, fucking around. The floodlight over the shed door that worked on an auto-dimmer and fade up for night time was burnt out and because the glow of the streetlamp filtering through the trees from Haverford Avenue was sort of weak and spotty, Mr. Whalen had tripped in a divot crossing the baseball field. That just about killed us. I laughed so hard my eyes teared up. Rudy couldn't catch his breath, bent over, hands on his knees. Jimmy actually dropped to the ground and curled up into a fetal position, kicking into his high-pitched machine gun laugh like a mental patient. Mr. Whalen stalked away all cussing and spitty and by the time we caught up to him he was limping into the darkest part of the shack, looking for the litter sticks and mumbling that the points were sharp and us fucking kids better not get to poking each other with them, or worse, popping the tires of the mini-bus or the golf carts or the maintenance truck parked behind the trash dumpsters.

What. Did he think we were hoodlums or something?

It wasn't long before Mr. Whalen returned to the facility, and as he walked away I saw Jimmy in him, the skinny vision in his coveralls always limping back to sweep up somewhere. It bummed me out a little, but the pickle barrel with the carpenter's belt draped over the lip showed the sweet side of things, the fact that for every push broom there was a power drill, for each piece of lint you had to vacuum up there was a crafty little bit tip you could shove into a screw-gun.

I sat there in the dirt in front of the equipment shed pawing through the bucket, fingering the anchor packets, opening the drill bit cases, pulling the trigger on the Makita cordless mini circular saw, counting up the sockets in the dented yellow carry case. Jimmy and Rudy were in the outfield playing spear chucker with the litter pickers, and I don't really recall a lot of details as I dodged between my two pals, jogged over to the main building, peered around the corner of the back entrance, and snuck past the hydro message table. It was all in a haze, all mist and cotton candy.

The diving board was a breeze, my hands running over the surfaces and my fingers working the internal mechanisms like they knew their way blind. By the time I was finished the illusion was perfect, and now I was running full tilt through the fairytale dream room, with its old fashioned ceiling Halogens coming up in slow motion, its lazy morning shadows, its beach chairs in pretty little rows like church, and I was speeding toward the long rounded edge between the shallow and deep ends where I was gonna blast off for the cannonball of the century.

Four feet to go and I had to sneak over one last look at the booby trap I'd rigged up last night, in fact, I wanted to watch it while I was flying high through the air. I was a jet with screaming engines, a fighter pilot making his last sweep across the war zone that his massive nuke was about to absolutely flatten, a hard-ass general…

I slipped.

I fucking slipped right there at the last second where there was a puddle I hadn't noticed, and I didn't fly high but I sure as hell soared long, feet kicking up in front of me, rear end coming down fast and hard, crash landing straight into the protruding concrete border-fringe.

It was my tailbone.

Smashed.

I heard it, thought of eggshells.

There was that velvety, royal feeling all through my bottom side that you had when you were gritting down your teeth real hard or pressing your fingernails into Styrofoam packing material, and then my jaws clapped together making copper and everything was hands over feet over hands, all rumple and tumble, like dump-trash.

And I'm walking, asshole, slow and cautious as the adult this time, making my way down this dark corridor where the Motel 6 pool water around the bend is making wavery lines along the damp tile walls. Somewhere something is dripping and my breath is wet on the thickening air. I've been removed from the little re-run I just had to live through again as a teenager, and I'm left with the nothing but the scattered memories of what happened after my accident.

And I ain't stupid.

I pretty much know that there's something waiting around the corner here, something bad, something truthful. Like I said, I don't remember too much after breaking my ass bone, and I'll bet dollars to doughnuts that this dark twin of the Jewish Y has answers, reflections in the deep end, pictures in the ripples to fill in the blanks.

What I *do* remember after crushing my tailbone was being plunged into the chlorine and then soaked in sweat. There were sirens going off, but they sounded distant and mournful. Some time later I could see a tube coming from my arm and trailing up to a bag with clear liquid in it, but everything around me was all splinter and slash, dark and shadowed, grainy and disconnected. I had an incredible throbbing pain in my loin section, all up my back and down through my legs, and that gave way to throbbing and pulsing and sluggish waves that coursed through my stomach and up through my scalp. There was numbness, and someone kept putting sharp lights in my eyes, real close and piercing, and there must have been a kennel near the hospital because I always heard dogs baying and moaning, but when I think about it now I must have been dreaming.

When I got home I was bedridden for months. I missed a lot of school. I watched a lot of TV, read a lot of comic books.

Mama was all official about things, walking me around with an arm across my back, exercising my legs by pulling and pushing them like riding a bicycle, feeding me soup and beans and raw veggies out of Tupperware. She said that I had fractured my coccydynia or something like that, and that even though the surgeon had replaced the smashed bony structure, I might not be the same ever again. But she was gonna help me the best she could to live a normal, healthy life.

I walked with crutches for nine months, a cane for the next three. I missed half a year of school and there was a petition, this proposal thing Mama worked on in the kitchen for like three solid weeks. Then all the phone calls from the Department of Human Services stopped, and I was home-schooled by this old black guy named Mr. Goodwin who used to be a shop teacher at some inner city high school, and I hated him because he talked real low and proper and slow making me *listen,* and he had these big dark hanging body tag moles all around the edges of his eyes, but I liked him a little too because he didn't water stuff down with bullshit, especially English, where he just gave a lot of hand-outs and old state tests that we drilled as if he thought it was pretty much a throw-away too.

And no hospitals. Mama said they fucked me up real good in there once and we weren't gonna make the same mistake twice. She bought a shit-load of books on herbs and Holistic healing, real medicine man shit, hey, when an Injun-woman goes all spiritual, Shaman, and medicine cords its best to get out of her way unless you want a peace pipe shoved up your nose or something. First it was a bunch of talk about the mind, body, and spirit, and then came the non-fat diets and the incense and the New Age music. Sounds like a bunch of hocus-pocus, I know, but to this day I still sign off on my health insurance taking the payout. Doctors are thieves, fumbling in the dark, looking stuff up on Google, taking guesses, I mean, look how they botched her cancer diagnosis, fucking the chemo, running in circles. And in playing nursemaid to her boy, at least for awhile, my Mama was nice to me.

Well, not really. It wasn't *nice,* not quite, let's be real.

She used all of this to make me into some kind of crash test dummy, never really talking to me anymore, just talking at me with phrases. At first it was creepy in a way, but after awhile it was like shaking hands or saying "How ya doing?" when you didn't really care one way or the other.

I got my certificate in the middle of eleventh grade and left home at seventeen. It wasn't your typical send-off, but it wasn't all that new either. I didn't get a full ride to state college, growing up to be Dr. Biff Malibu, but I didn't drop out of high school and end up living on the streets either. I was lost in the landscape, a part of the blur.

But now, rounding the bend in this dark tile hallway with the little wavelets fluttering on the walls, I realize that something changed after the accident, something important, something I buried and never talked about even to myself in "real voice" or those little fucking mind numbing self-help catch phrases. It had to do with lust and ache and exotic dark pussy. It had to do with then and later, before and after, and the difference that I buried below the grains.

"You made yourself forget what it felt like, didn't you Johnny?"

I round the corner and the Motel 6 pool area is a bare womb, the walls stripped down, the doors to the locker rooms removed. There is light, but it is dim and I can't see what source is generating it. There are wavelets reflecting off the walls to the high ceiling, but the pool is bone dry, threads of sediment following the grout lines and forking down to the drain.

At the far edge of the deck by the kiddie steps at the shallow end there is a naked woman sitting on a bar stool, facing away and slowly brushing her long mane of black hair that goes almost all the way down to the tiny flower-petal creases above the narrow groove of her ass. She starts to come around then, her tan hour glass shape twisting at the waist, one arm positioned protectively across her chest, and I wanna look away, but I can't, and it's an old story, but that's the point, ain't it?

"Mama?"

It's a dead echo in here. She looks back at me with those stony black eyes, those tomahawk cheekbones, and I suddenly want her to swing her legs around to face me, knees together catching gleam going up the thigh, hair brush in her lap barely covering the pubic area, arm brought down to allow for the hanging turquoise, onyx, and spiny oyster pieces to hide one nipple and barely expose the other. That would make this the lowest low, right? A perfect piece of Englishy bullshit-congruity proving that in the end my signature in this blur of a world was never any more than a stain.

She turns away again and there are more brushstrokes, slowly, lovingly, shoulders set back high and regal.

"I'm a problem solver, Johnny," her voice says. "Thought I solved you."

"Solved me?

"Tamed is a better word. Funny how that backfired, huh?"

"What are you talking about?"

"Love beads, Johnny. It's all about the love beads."

She vanishes. And there by my left fingers on the bright white surface of the diving board there is a necklace. It seems to have been dipped in blood, all droplets and runners, its moist tokens the polar opposite of crafted pendants or mementos. They are marble sized globes, slightly oblong, each fastened to the choker by fragile corkscrewed threads. They look like sperm, and the ghostly whisper of my dead mother's thoughts hiss about the space like escaping steam:

"Close Johnny, but not quite. They ain't marbles. Technically, they are a packing material UPS was considering way back when, but wound up passing on in favor of the cheaper Styrofoam popcorn product. These were too expensive. They're filled with silicone. Took me forever to find."

"To pack boxes?"

"I only needed two, Johnny."

"Two necklaces?"

"Two of those small globes. Or should I say…implants…"

I gasp, and her voice whispers behind it.

"Why do you think I dated a veterinarian, Johnny? What procedure do you think I was learning to do all by myself all that time?"

I run.

Back down the hall, feet pounding into the darkness, and as the sweat starts to poke up on the back of my neck there is an eerie light coming up along the long tile hallway, the laundry room with its steel chutes, curved rails, and canvas tubs, the restaurant area with its checkerboard of thick wooden tables, and while I am thundering back the way I just came as fast as I am able I can feel the deep internal slipcover gliding off of my past, my real past and not the reinvented one. The thing that fucked me all this time is that I was always well aware of the way things really went down, but I stuffed all that shit back in with the old moldy invoices in the old dusty boxes in the back of the warehouse so to speak. The lies, on the other hand, were repeated in my mind like some favorite tune, built up with form and substance and sensory details like my life depended on it.

All my own Englishy bullshit.

I went to a party at Jimmy Whalen's house in sixth grade. I cut down his tire swing in the back yard with my Swiss army knife and his dad put me in a time out back behind the woodpile while everyone else got to eat pizza. And Mr. Whalen wasn't no maintenance man for the Jewish Y, but rather, a guard at the Graterford prison who organized the groups brought out for highway trash detail. After sitting by myself for five minutes, smoking a Marlboro Light from a rumpled soft pack and looking out into the public woods leading to the train yard, I snuck into the shed, found one of Mr. Whalen's litter pickers, and flattened all four tires of his Ford F150.

In seventh grade I got in real bad trouble in science class when I put a water-filled condom in Mrs. Levitz's desk drawer. Rudy St. Clair had stolen it from his older sister's backpack when she came home from college to do laundry and borrow money again, and even though he put me up to it, he broke the code of silence when I got caught planting it red handed, fucking me royal by coming forward with Jimmy Whalen and telling Principal Lally that I had been wrecking the class all year, coming in late, asking to go to the bathroom, wandering the halls, pretending to need to see the counselor, the librarian, and the nurse, and then calling out in class with dumb stuff, asking for a tissue, or hand sanitizer, or what page we were on when Mrs. Levitz had just announced it three times.

On the last day of school I got caught in the basement closet jerking off to the sight of my own Mama's privates.

The next week she started dating Dr. Goldstien, a veterinarian who took her under his wing, letting her assist him so she could learn all the procedures. He was nice. I saw him twice, once when he beeped for Mama outside in his gray Volvo, and the other when he looked after me one morning as a favor, taking me into the Jewish Y as a guest. In the locker room, after bitching a little in this smooth quiet voice about how I should have brought a bathing suit with me and there was some major problem with wearing your cut-off jeans and undies into the pool, he let me go play by myself outside on the vacant baseball field by the access road leading out to Haverford Avenue. One of the equipment sheds back there was open and in a pickle barrel with a carpenter's belt draped over it, I found a cordless mini circular saw. It was then that I connected the border woodlands with body parts, and it was a day or so later that I went under the knife.

For a crushed tailbone.

That never got crushed in the first place.

In a hospital.

That never had me registered as a patient.

I start to slow down, hand pressed to my side, breath heaving. Somehow I have made it upstairs, and even though the rug has been taken up leaving a hard cementous base, there are still old fashioned light fixtures left on the walls, spilling weak little glow spots along wallpaper striped down in green and maroon Applebee's colors. To my left is the elevator foyer, two open shafts, gritty cinderblock walls. To the right is a stripped area where they must have had an ice machine, squared casing lines on the floor, steel gooseneck cables pitch-forking out of a keyhole recess. Down the hall I hear a noise, like a whisper, like a mimic of my own hard breath.

I make my way down the green and maroon corridor, and this must be the floor with the honeymoon suites because it seems the rooms are miles apart from each other, and the farther in I go, the longer the hallway becomes.

The breathing mimic is louder now, and it's coming every seven intakes or so, a sound of hard air pushed through a CPAP ventilator machine, forced in because the fragile, damaged organs aren't strong enough to do it themselves. And it may be my eyes or the lighting, but it looks like the walls are bowing out a little with each of those forced breaths, then sagging back for a moment like limp tissue before they regain their original form. And it smells too, like death fingering down the corridor, from Mama's lungs straight into mine.

I am standing in front of room 457.

There is an electro key insert, but the door is cracked open a sliver, resting against the jamb. All I have to do is push it. I stand there, arms dangling.

After the operation and the recovery I only saw Dr. Goldstien once more, at his house, where he was sunning out by his back yard pool, there in his suburban lagoon setting with tea tables, lawn chairs, beach umbrellas, and a straw hut looking like a cheap tiki bar. Mama had broken off with him almost a year ago, and I found the address in the trash on a Post-it note stuck to the cover of a canine hygiene textbook she threw out with the Spring cleaning. He lived in Springfield. I rode my bike. Snuck up between yards. His fence was cheap looking compared to everything else, with those razor thin green and white slats going in criss-cross through the cyclone diamond wire, and there I was again, staring through the slivers, only this time it wasn't one appendage pressing deep inside another to the pelvis-to-pelvis stopping points. It was this old Jewish guy, with skinny bow legs, a pot belly, and curly gray chest hair.

How could she fuck him? How could she *do* it?

I hated thinking about that kind of thing about my own Mama, but I hated thinking about sex in general lately. Things were different somehow. I still loved looking at girls, at their pretty eyes, the backs of their knees, the curve of their backs, the swell of their breasts.

But I didn't feel it anymore…down *there.* The haunt of it still lingered, like a phantom effect, but there was some kind of weird disconnect. I still wanted to touch girls, hold them, feel their legs, kiss their throats, make them submit. But something was missing, something important.

I looked through the slats at Dr. Goldstien's diving board. It jutted out flat and hard and I wanted to dismantle it, rig it to fail, watch him go whoopsie in his own fucking pool, but I didn't know how to do it and I knew I wouldn't get away with it anyway. I was impotent.

I am standing in front of room 457 in the gutted Motel 6, and behind that door is my Mama's ghost, bedridden and cancer stricken like she was in her last moments of life, connected to a breathing machine that pumps air into her poisoned lungs every fifteen seconds or so, the three-inch mouth tube strapped to her face, one reddened eye looking out, one skeletal finger ready to spell out the word "HOSPICE" or some other horrific, undeniable truth.

On the last day of seventh grade I watched my Mama fuck someone and participated in the process by masturbating. She dated a veterinarian and learned how to perform a neutering procedure so she could drug her own son and neuter him, using silicone packing globes as replacements for his man-balls. Her son was a threat to her in a way that shook her to her core, and she was a problem solver.

I never lost my mental lust for women and I made damned sure I could continue as a participator. I never lost my hunger for the game, my need for the hunt, for the chase, the dominance, and that last gasp of breath, holding her close. Our big "O." I reinvented my past, blackened what was real with denial, and continued to fuck in the only way that was available to me. No hard diving boards for Johnny, no cigarette afterwards, no cuddling, kissing, and soft spoken whispers, just a Sawzall for the heavy work and a cordless mini circular saw for the finish. And a flood of public woods as a dumping ground.

Killing isn't sexy, asshole.

Killing is sex.

"Johnny..."

It is my Mama on other side of the door. She has crawled there, I can see the movement of her lips through the crack at knee level. She has clearly ditched the ventilator mask or at least pushed the funnel aside, and she is on her knees gasping.

"Johnny...one thing..."

No.

No more ghosts or buried secrets. I pull the door closed and I run, back down the endless hall that seems to hyperventilate all around me now, the walls like fragile elastic being drawn to the snapping point and then left to sag, and there on the approach to the foyer area with the elevator shaft I think about it for a second, about jumping the edge and doing a massive cannonball that will end it right here. But if the dead can just mosey on into a gutted Motel 6 smack in the middle of a real life timeline, it ain't too smart to trespass on their own home turf, not just yet, not without a roadmap. Besides. My survival instinct would probably make me grab at the cable on the way down, tearing back skin, slowing the descent just enough so the impact wouldn't kill me. Just break my tailpipe.

I bang through a fire exit, and instead of a dark stairwell I'm back on the first floor, pounding around the corner where the counter block is to my right and the drywall studs I fell into are bent and bowed to the left, and of course the logistics don't make sense in here, of course A plus B doesn't lead directly to C, because the horror, the real horror, is that nothing's a straight line for us, not ever, not really. We make that shit up so we don't get seasick, fearing ghost pirates, spiders, visions in the slats. But in the end, there's nothing but wasteland, warped and retooled, like memory, that fucked up mirror-shattered point of view we keep sweeping together and rebuilding.

There's a figure waiting in the doorway.

It's Marissa Madison, hunched over and bone pale with the fishing line stitching holding her together in seventeen places. There's a pale light from the moon outside and the rain's blowing in around her, ponding in the entranceway. Her hair is dripping, hanging in her face, bursting outward before her mouth area every second or so.

"My turn," she rasps. "So would you like to step outside?"

I put my hands forward, palms up.

"Why wait?"

"Thanks for the invite."

When she springs, I am amazed at the explosive speed.

And the teeth.

CHAPTER FIVE

Deseronto took it like a man. She was light as a feather, so he didn't even have to spread his feet on impact, he just stood there and absorbed the force of this barbed, spotted thing pouncing chest high and wrapping herself around him. His huge arms enveloped her in a sort of auto-response and she bent in, head slightly tilted.

It seemed she was to kiss him.

But their mouths were not parallel. Her damp veil of hair masked the sticking point, and just after a hot burst of her oily breath he got wet strands in his eyes, face first in the spongy jungle brush.

From beneath came the snake, as Marissa Madison jerked her head forward and clamped down her teeth.

It was awkward through the buffer, but what she lacked from direct contact she made up for with blunt force. Clumps of hair were pushed up Deseronto's nasal cavities followed by the gouging. His septum and bunching nostrils came up like old stubborn roots, and at the top end her front two incisors raked down between his eyes, curling back flesh until they found purchase just above that little Indian ridge that he had.

Hot blood burst down over Deseronto's lips and a thin stream jetted into his left eye. Everything felt greasy and while the pain was enormous in a way, it wasn't the type to cry and moan about, more the sensation that made you grit your teeth, firm up your backbone, and brag that you lived through it. You hoped.

The girl-thing went into a frenzy then, probably because she was swallowing a bunch of her own hair, so she started snapping her head like some mad dog, twisting and pulling at the last of the bone and cartilage that was stubborn and set in deep where the sinuses drained.

His nose came off, and it was not a relief. What had felt like lustful toss of hot spice suddenly became a galvanizing agony, air hitting the opened areas, blood pumping out in two massive cross streams that thumped along to the beat of his heart.

There were Indian war drums thumping in his head and mad dogs ripping at the soft spots.

Hard rain drumming on the picture window. It's Mischief Night and I am Marissa Madison sitting on the floor playing with Rusty, my little King Charles Cavalier spaniel puppy, my delicate little "British boy" who's trying to act tough, back haunches up, snapping his head back and forth trying to pull away the canvas toy shaped like a farm turkey that grew its legs too long for its own good.

I am Marissa Madison, and I am a freshman at Widener University. I'm a pretty girl, with high cheekbones and long jet black hair I like to toss over my shoulder because it's cute that way. I came home early this semester for some home cooking, but I'm here every Halloween because it is my favorite time of the year and I like giving candy to the kids, out of the plastic jack-o-lantern Mother bought for me when I was seven. I am boiling cinnamon sticks in the kitchen because it makes the house smell like heaven, and I'm disappointed in myself because I left the trigger-killer upstairs.

Without it, I might play here all night. Dr. Ruberstein was *very* specific about this *very* thing, and even though Professor Dixon keeps using that awful red pen to circle my overly expressive pop-up words like "very" and "so" and "really" and "uncontrollably," I am really so very uncontrollably enjoying being the perfect playmate for Rusty that I might lose my edge, miss a sign, deaden a superior piece of the patchwork by focusing too long on its subordinate. Of course, I could probably write a book on the subject of "premonition-overlay" and make millions of dollars, buy a mansion, become the most searched individual on Google, but I was never meant for fame and Mother dedicated a large portion of her life to teaching me this.

I was meant to assist, and I am darned good at it too, ridiculous, insane. Call it a gift, a calling, a curse.

I call it obsession. And I really should have had my device on my belt loop that night, because now that I am dead I am left to wonder if I missed a premonition of what seemed the first premonition I had of you the next day.

The dark virgin in the passing vehicle.

The one who must be forced now to see the shadow he has spread across the face of the sun.

MARISSA

Yeah, she's gifted asshole, I know it all too well now, and there ain't no I.E.P. or specialized resource program that could define or measure or channel her talents. Not unless you wanted her to rewrite the state mandate for you. I mean, I'm talking prodigy, asshole. Michael Jackson. Mozart. Sitting Bull.

Only better.

She is the one who assists. Like you wouldn't fucking believe.

And don't let the girly dog and the cinnamon sticks fool you. She's tough as nails, and sharing her consciousness is one rude fucked up ride, let me tell you. This girl is about cracking codes. Your codes.

Do you see what I'm saying, you numb piece of shit? Maybe not, so I'll spell it for you slow. I'm trapped inside a female first of all, so it's like sucking down a hard shot of vertigo. Guys are bad enough, trying to scratch their names into the world with all these hard rites of passage proving they're all worthy of each other or some such lame garbage, but this chick lets her "feelings" paint the pathways and guardrails. Everything is bright and happy chaos and if I could be sick in here I wouldn't wait for some quaint motherfucker to hold back my hair. Second of all, there's this unbelievable talent she has that makes others realize their dreams and potential.

It's psychic.

Not like she can read minds or nothing. It's patchwork. Pieces. Puzzle parts she's good at bringing to the surface so she can stick stuff into the blank spots.

She makes you a better you. She's good at it and now that I'm with her in the rewind, she's blanked me, left parts out, fucked me royal, her ghost still carrying on the tradition she maintained in the world of the living, making people understand their own genius. First hand.

See, I know I am going to waste her tonight just before midnight, that I am going to cut her up at the shop and avoid my usual path to the public woods behind Jimmy Whalen's old abandoned place because a cop is going to be parked at the border of the dark cul-de-sac and the golf course. I am going to improvise, going up on 476, looking for some area thick with foliage to bury the body parts and I'm going to end up with two flat tires for my trouble.

But I don't remember the stalking phase before all that, and I suddenly can't recall tonight's date in reference to the initial sighting I had of her back on Halloween day. See? I can't recollect the kill itself, the chase, the particulars leading up to tonight, nothing.

It's a blank spot.

Marissa Madison is going to let me experience what it is like to be hunted. By the dark virgin. The gargantuan shadow that she'd been fixated on since she felt him spot her making the multi-lane turn into the King of Prussia Mall.

I get to feel the pure and beautiful terror I create.

And understand why *I* am the one Marissa Madison calls "Prodigy."

CHAPTER SIX

After the drizzle and mist of the previous night, Halloween morning had crafted the world into some glorious illustration, with colors exploding into everything and the mischievous breeze making the leaves gossip. It was the brazen conceit of autumn pulling the sun on a kite string all along Montgomery Avenue where Marissa Madison drove her cherry-red Mustang with the Sirius Radio blasting through the door speakers.

She looked good in this car, and even though admitting that was sort of shallow, it was the type of exhibition out here that demanded participation. Marissa wasn't really hooked into the au-naturale, Whole Foods attitude anyway, and it didn't bother her to think of the world as a stage filled with pomp and circumstance. Girl, she was all about the accessories, Russian-red lipstick, baby-pink blush, and smoky purple eye-shadow framed off by her shiny black hair done long, straight, and sleek with full bangs and those gorgeous silver hooped earrings she found last week at Chico's. She was a shopaholic and she wasn't about to keep the bounty locked up in the closet, like her sizzling Louboutins with the devil-red soles and the heels so high she had to keep them on the seat while she was driving, or like her new Super Skinny low jeans and the black fitted Versace shrunken field jacket that made her waist and hips look like the curves on a wine glass. She always wanted to stand out on a spree, and it wasn't a vicious cycle, but rather a *delicious* one, and she had to make sure to write that down because there had to be someone with a business head who could use such a cute and sassy name like that for a shop or boutique or whatever.

She glanced in the rearview and smiled, simply because so many girls always forgot to. She liked her smile, at least now that she had maneuvered it into her package in a way that made it work for her. She had big teeth and a little mouth, so her grin curled up at the edges almost woefully. As a kid it made her all weird and "sad clown," but she had long retooled it into a sexy little "hello." By the time she was a sophomore in high school they were calling her "Half-Stick" because she was short dynamite, and two years later underneath her senior picture in the yearbook it said "Pretty Little Runway" because she walked as if she had a clue, and believe it honey, she would *never* tell a guy to "keep his eyes up here," even on a day when she was playing book-smart and subtle.

She came up over a rise and had to pull herself up by the top of the steering wheel to see over the hood. This car was *gorgeous,* but it rode "big," seeming to sprawl over the lane lines and fill up the parking spaces stripe to stripe. Often she had to back out and pull in a second time to get it just right—and parallel parking, forget it. She was always too far away from the curb or angled up on it, and the way the doors were built so heavy she had to use a shoulder to get out and two hands to push it back shut, getting behind it like a slave wheel and taking mini-steps that always made her giggle hysterically.

Marissa eased back in the seat and turned the dial to channel 66, Watercolors Jazz, perfect accent to the reddish-orangey burst of woodland rising up on the right and the stately entrance to Rosemont College on the left with its stone barriers and manicured border foliage. Outside Lawrence Hall there was a rickety scaffolding and a guy in coveralls and a back-turned painter's cap doing trim work on the windows. He bent to dip the brush, and the way he repositioned his feet and held his shoulders above his carriage instead of favoring the weaker side kicked up "the patchwork," mapped now across Marissa Madison's mind in vivid images, pieces and partials so explicit that the details were staggering, almost painful to behold. The music from the car radio faded to the distant background, and the landscape washed out to a listless black and white.

And suddenly Marissa Madison knew that the painter's name was Louis Gorsky, that he was twenty-six years old, that his mother died in 1994, and that he was a boxer, a good one, a club fighter who had been headed for his big break before the big fuck-up, story of his life, and even though everyone in the business knew he was no one's tomato can, he couldn't currently work his way out of the "back-yarders," so popular lately especially up in North Philly where the cops turned a blind eye and the purse could shoot up to five grand if you were willing to go gloveless. His manager had dumped him five years ago when he lost an exhibition match at the Blue Horizon to this ringer who was a stand-in for some Russian bum who had backed out on account of the flu, and that fight was Louis Gorsky's turning point for the worse, his dark defining moment, and it came to Marissa with a ferociousness that almost made her drive off the road.

The place was packed and the air was thick with the smell of cigars, the smoke like silk veils floating above some secret royal sanctuary. He was the first on a card of five, but when the fat guy with the headset gave him the nod to start up the aisle he felt like a frontrunner. The spotlight blazed him up, marking and documenting his casual strut to the ring like some crazy exclamation point, cheers echoing in his head and volleying behind the thump and wail of his entrance music, "New Divide" by Linkin Park, and when his cut man pulled up the ropes for him to duck through and his bucket man helped him off with his robe, he was a god.

He didn't even notice his opponent. The dude's music was hip-hop, some old-school Nelly crap that didn't sound all that manly. And when the guy stepped into the ring to a chorus of visitors' boos, all Gorsky registered was someone incredibly short and incredibly black, nondescript, a boy fireplug in a man's arena. Gorsky had this one and he knew it. He had heavy reach advantage, and his reputation as the clever taunter-counterpuncher, pride of Kensington, was about to be known all up and down the Eastern Seaboard.

But when the bell sounded he went apeshit, free swinging and brawling, toe-to-toe, looking for a knockout. What he didn't know was that the little black guy, built like a brick shithouse in the leopard-spotted trunks with the black trim, was a captain in the Marines, boxing ten years for the service, two hundred fights under his belt and only three losses. When you were first on a card you were usually an amateur getting a shot, not some experienced ring jockey with a reputation for pounding people into chop meat. The catch was that since this beast had been working under the umbrella of his rank for seven years this was technically his first professional fight, and that loophole was Gorsky's tragedy.

He got TKO'd in fifty-three seconds, knocked down twice, the referee stopping the bout after Gorsky climbed the ropes a second time and wobbled. He couldn't recall the ring doctor holding his face in both hands and asking through the catcalls who the president of the United States was, and he didn't remember not remembering. Back in the hallway by the dressing rooms a few minutes later, Gorsky was sitting on a clothes dryer with a towel around his neck. Rod (the bod) Rogers had ambled by with his trainer, wondering if Gorsky was OK, and he had asked Rogers in return when his fight was going to take place.

He kept working out in the gym after that, but no one ever backed him again.

And Marissa knew how to fix it. He had to break down his whole scheme and start over, learn to fight southpaw, adjust his plant foot and work on power-jabbing rather than dancing, the hard and crafty butterfly rather than the tricky little hummingbird. And he needed a haymaker. It would take a year and a half of rebuilding and two more years of promotion, but she could have him headlining Atlantic City and Vegas within a three-year window even though bantamweights didn't draw like the heavies and the UFC had made the sport almost obsolete . . .

She reached for her belt and pressed the button on her "trigger-killer," the small silver mechanism she had on her hip, clipped to a belt loop. It was the size of an iPod and looked like just another accessory. Daddy had constructed it for her years ago at Mortimer-Smith where he was an electrical engineer, and she hated using it the way diabetics despised pricking their fingers. Still, it was a necessary evil when she had to obliterate the patchwork and move on with her life.

The sound was inaudible, set on a designer frequency that only she and a rare breed of European feline were sensitive to, but it was about as delicate in her own head as an air-raid siren. The sound struck her like an electric shock and she was back in the bosom of autumn colors and roadway, the connections with Louis Gorsky fading, becoming slowly unimportant, the after-effect lingering but manageable as it blew off in whispers and threads.

Sports were bad. Dangerous. Definite no-fly zones, teeming with people who meant well but would inadvertently lead her to people who didn't. Marissa Madison had little interest in becoming some sleezeball's soothsayer even if the payday was grand, and organized crime was a bummer in general. She was put here to assist the individuals who were in search of their gifts, not those who would use her talents to circumvent the superstructure. That was just pathetic and lazy.

And art wasn't lazy. It was active and vibrant.

She rested her right wrist on the Mustang's cute little gearshift and dialed the radio down to the metal stations, not "Octane" or "Liquid" because the after-effect of the boxer had stunted her hunger for the hard stuff, but into the #39 and #38 zone, where Hair Nation and Ozzy's Boneyard would provide some nice syncopated throwback to the black asphalt winding its way through the thickening wood.

A tune piped through that she hadn't heard before, but she knew of the singer. It was Tommy Keifer of Cinderella, trying a solo thing after all these years. Poor, poor Tommy. So talented and damaged, stretching and straining those wounded vocal cords his whole career, working a little comeback. Bluesy, but nondescript. Good beat, but rather generic.

Marissa had one hand off the wheel now, conducting and accenting in sharp little right angles the bass drum and snare, seeing Keifer in her mind as if he were in his twenties, black spandex and flash, all that lovely sweaty hair sticking to his face on one side, that Gibson Les Paul slung low and kicking up gleam from the new offstage spot they installed behind the bar over the entranceway. It smelled like sweat and perfume, cheap beer and sex, and back by the girl's bathroom Jon Bon Jovi politely told a girl with big blond hair and a huge rack to move a bit to the left so he could see what he thought he was seeing, a rising star about to shine all over the place.

Keifer liked the Empire Rock Club as much as the Galaxy over in Jersey, and they were lucky to be headlining both most weekends on all ages metal nights. Eric and Jeff had agreed to tune down half a step tonight even though that meant they'd have to sacrifice the keys, and it was all good. They were kicking out "Somebody Save Me," and while Tommy knew how warm and full he looked in the spotlight, he could never get over how cold and alone you really were up here, trying to master the space with practiced moves that had to come off like casual improvisation, as if it were some brotherhood telepathy that made them all move the guitars back and forth across their crotches simultaneously.

Jeff took the lead tonight, and he was coming up on the finale. It was time for the new move, the choreography that they hoped would become their signature, the big waazoo, on three . . . flip the guitars around the back and catch them on the upbeat. No one had ever done it before, not three in a line like rifle girls in the color guard, and they'd actually placed a couple of friends like bodyguards outside their practice space at 1020 Studios the last three weeks (paying them with weed, of course), because lately everyone on Delaware Avenue wanted to watch them jam and this was a surprise meant for the stage and for the lawyers and the producers and the assistants, and assistants to the assistants who'd kept keeping them on hold because they sounded a bit too much like AC/DC. There was also a rumor going around that Motley's management had their eye on Tommy to temporarily replace Vince and . . .

On three.

Marissa was out of the flashback suddenly, and Tommy's current song "Solid Ground" droned on sounding thin, coming off vague, no salt, something missing, and Tommy's solo career was a no-go, a true blimp made of lead, and it was heartbreaking. He was the very definition of situational irony, from the early days singing in a way that made you think he was going to hurt himself doing so, screeching sweetly thus, and it had plagued and destroyed him pretty much right after the Moscow Music Festival he grew so famous for. First it was nodules, then dead vocal cords, and so on and so on. If only he would take a back seat the way Jeff did for him, rest his pipes and use his songwriting and rehearsal smarts to back up someone else, someone like, oh, I don't know, Punky Meadows.

She almost had to pull over, it hit her so hard. Glorious Technicolor, booms and explosions. She saw a small recording studio in Malibu, and sitting there with their instruments and headphones the boys from Angel were back together minus Gregg Giuffria. To fill in, they brought in Tommy Keifer to play rhythm, hardening their chops, supplying the edge they'd left in the background to play nursemaid to a litter of poorly disguised pop synth solos that had rendered them less than relevant by their third album back in the day. It would be a trick getting Dimino to back out of the Vinyl Tattoo project, and even more difficult to convince them that their first hit had to be a cover of "Walk in the Shadows" by Queensryche. They would run Volbeat, Halestorm, and Five Finger Death Punch straight off the hard-rock pop charts and have the biggest all-star combo project since Velvet Revolver.

Sadly, Marissa hit the button on her belt and drove on. The music industry was a rabbit hole, fickle and filled with egos and addictions, making any sort of business venture a minefield. By this day and age the whole record deal/stadium show concept should have been charted into a simplified roadmap with clear avenues up the hierarchy, but it wasn't. It was madness, and she'd learned her lesson with Jerome Anthony Franklin.

Suddenly her bottom lip started trembling, her breath hitched, and she shut off the tunes. Dialed home. The "patchwork" didn't do much for love, wrong skill in a foreign arena, and it was utterly snowblind in terms of self-healing.

"Where are you?" her mother's voice said after barely a ring. Her voice had a hearty echo to it, and Marissa usually had a good laugh at what she called the "Bluetooth Effect," especially since her mother was more about being witty than sounding all deep and godlike. Presently, however, it held no interest for her. She needed to reboot the computer and leave behind all the precious spotlights and power speakers she had promised Jerome, the ads for KFC and Budweiser flashing across the light panels up in the nosebleed sections, the hollow sound of the house PA droning on in its endless loop of hip-hop greats dating back even to the mid-nineties, the glow sticks doing their flip and boomeranging through the air and the occasional beach ball dancing across the upraised and outstretched fingers of the mob on the dance floor. It was all gone now, erased the moment she had tried to seduce him.

"Halfway to the mall," she said to her mother. Her eyes had moistened up and she was almost to the point that she was seeing prisms. "I miss him."

"You can't miss a ghost."

"He's not dead, Mother."

"You are to him."

Marissa reached inside her bag for a tissue.

"You made me spill," she muttered.

"Then pull into a gas station and fix your face, honey."

They both laughed, and in a moment of empathy that had more to do with common sense than telepathy, Marissa reminded herself of how difficult it must have been for her parents to raise a girl like her. Of course they must have been so proud when their eleven-year-old took over the fifth-grade tubular bell choir, and pleased as punch the very next year as she modernized the elementary school's roster and filing system. Heck, by the time their dear sweet Marissa was in eighth grade it was an adventure just taking her to the store! She couldn't roam around the bicycle shop without suggesting to the manager the specific purchasing maneuvers it would take to make the place into a boss Harley-Davidson franchise, and she had trouble walking the open-air market at Linvilla Orchards without describing to the lady with the weird braids and grandmother stockings the specific warehousing methods needed to up production and gain distribution contracts with the Giant and ShopRite chains for those yummy-looking cookies made for kids with odd food allergies. By the time Marissa Madison hit high school she had created so much area business expansion that Internet location finders like Mapquest had bolded up the town of Broomall to a font size twice its original thickness.

Then in ninth grade came the tutoring scandal.

It was innocent enough in theory. Marissa set up her volunteer after-school program in the cafeteria, helping students overcome test-taking anxiety by tapping into their natural gifts, like spatial prowess or interpersonal ability, and using those base talents to create more logical and advantageous thinking strategies. At first it was laughed off and ignored by administration, but when 98 percent of the students taking their PSSA tests that year scored in the 90th percentile including the special ed. kids, it was rumored that there was to be an investigation by the state.

It blew over. Publically, there wasn't anyone in the Pennsylvania Department of Education willing to lay their reputation on the line by actually acknowledging in writing that someone with a strange sort of telepathy had popped up on the grid, but Marissa Madison was never offered the opportunity to tutor anyone again, at least not on high school property. And Mother had no intentions of running some sort of side business through the house. It was already a full-time job keeping all this as low-key as possible, answering the constant barrage of phone calls, playing it down, and shutting out the media—Lord, she must have been tired! But no rest for the weary, ladies and gentlemen, at least not in the Madison household. For Marissa's hunger to connect with people grew exponentially with age, and by the first days of tenth grade she had already moved on to the next big obsession.

Love.

And it wasn't good. Not even a little bit.

It was Sunday morning, and even though she had had more than a few romantic fantasies by the age of fifteen, everything had always been in the abstract somehow. Perhaps this was a result of those liberal yet sterile explanations from her parents in the living room, or more probably some fail-safe built into her telepathic wavelength to protect her until she was old enough to understand the big picture. Regardless, the whole "love and intimacy" paradigm had kept itself pretty much at the edges like border design, playing on her imagination and tender idealism, suggestive and haunting, lovely yet indistinguishable.

And it was Sunday morning, and there were noises coming from her parents' bedroom down the hall, and it was an argument that had a strange ring to it, a lack of abandon. They lived in a split-level that offered a fair amount of privacy, as Marissa's room had its own bathroom and shower, positioned at the far west corner facing the back yard. On the weekends she kept to her space, rarely venturing out to more public areas, even downstairs, until eleven or so in the instinctive adjustment everyone naturally made to set boundaries and territory depending on available square footage. In return, her parents usually kept things to murmurs.

Usually.

It was Sunday and it was November, and she had woken with a start, sun streaming in through the window. For a second she lay there looking at the ceiling, eyes widened. She had dreamt that there was a fire out behind the house and the trees between properties were ablaze, flames licking across the gray branches, knots under the bark popping and sparking.

Popping.

Tones of frustration. Through her door it was indistinct in terms of specific wording, but a strange patchwork had come up in her mind, one that contained vivid illustrations of the mechanics of passion she hadn't been able to picture before, not really, not like this. It was animalistic role-play, ritualistic and savage even in its most gentle and loving form, more about dominance and entry than sentiment and myth. And it seemed to go against every social construct we trained ourselves for in every other human interaction on earth. It was all about tension and pressure-points, angles and friction, working itself to a psycho-emotive level that was almost religious.

She stumbled out of bed and walked clumsily across the carpeted floor, the Ladies of Elegance figurines on her bookshelves staring back blindly as she pushed through the door. Usually she wore her flannel robe out of the bedroom, but here in the cold hallway she had on nothing but her Sophie "Pink" short-shorts and a cut-off black T-shirt. Her palm was pressed to her flushed cheek and she had goosebumps coming up on her arms.

"I'm not doing it," her father was saying. "I'm sorry, I just can't."

"I'm not asking you to."

"Well, the fact that you bought them again says volumes."

"It's just a pill," her mother said.

"But they don't work. It's false advertising as bad as it can get, and I won't fall prey to the bogus psychology. They make me a cliché and I think about it too much."

"Then don't think."

"I don't want to discuss it."

"Well, I do."

"Well, that's the problem. I don't want to talk. I don't want to worry about a drop in blood pressure and an erection lasting four hours—"

"One could only hope . . ."

"Please don't make jokes."

"It isn't that serious."

"No?" her father said, then mumbling something under his breath.

"What?"

"I said it makes me feel like less of a man. Please, Katie, don't make me repeat it."

Marissa pushed the door open. It was messier than she was used to, with Daddy's dry-cleaning stuff strewn across the easy chair and the clothes in the hamper overflowing and piled against the wall where Mother had taped one of her comic notes with three lines stating the Olympic levels and the load an inch from silver-medal height. The jewelry box was open on the bureau, and there were necklaces strewn around because the two of them had rushed last night in order to make their weekly reservation at Fellini's. There was a bottle of Chloe with the top off, a gray bra hanging off the back of the chair in front of the dressing mirror where Mother brushed her short perky hair, and in the middle of it all was the massive king-sized bed with her parents drawing up the covers protectively.

"Baby? What's wrong?" Mother said, giving her head that little shake that was supposed to make her look together and nonchalant.

"I can help you with this," Marissa returned tonelessly.

"With what, honey?"

Marissa looked at her father.

"His issue. Your problem. I can advise. I can . . . assist."

Then she fainted.

That one put them in therapy, and all of it was detailed and rationalized with more of those long, clinical explanations. There were also crystal-clear borders now. Square footage. Her first no-fly zone.

But that didn't lessen her curiosity in terms of her own inner landscape, and she was the first to admit here and now that her attraction to Jerome Anthony Franklin always had less to do with his poetic ability than the way the very tone of his voice made her knees weak.

"I'm OK," she said to her mother. "Nothing a new skirt, a leather belt, or an anklet won't cure."

"Oh, stick to the sale items today, sweetie, materials only, no metal or stones."

Marissa frowned.

"All right," she said.

"And use the Discover card. We're a bit short in checking this week. Speaking of which . . ."

Marissa hit the gas too hard, and the rear-wheel drive almost swayed her fanny out across the double yellow. And on an uphill! *God,* this car had nice torque!

"I'm strapped at the moment, Mother," she said, adjusting the sun visor and shaking hair out of her face. "Dead broke."

"Honey!"

"It's not my fault! I had fifty for spending, and there was a booth in the student center where you could sponsor someone for the breast cancer walk. Then Professor Pratt added these nursing ethics manuals to the syllabus that cost a fortune and I have Comp 101 at eight a.m., which is absolute torture. And to make matters worse, there's this girl named Brittany Kirk with a big nose and heavy eyeliner that keeps interrupting the lecture with these rudimentary comprehension questions that I could help her with, but I can't because we agreed I should keep a low profile. And that takes energy, and there's the cutest little coffee shop on the first floor of Kapelski where I get these awesome caramel mocha lattes, but they're *expensive!*"

"And you've done no tutoring," her mother said.

"I haven't, I swear."

"No assisting the poor sweet football players writing their first real research papers? No telling the assistant professors the quickest path straight to department chair?"

"Mother!"

"I'm just saying . . . you could always move back home."

Marissa rolled her eyes.

"Really? Commuting? That's so high school."

"That apartment must get lonely."

Marissa swallowed hard. Her off-campus efficiency was quaint. Snug. Filled with stuff. And horribly empty. She fanned her face, blinked rapidly for a second, and then put both hands firm on the wheel.

"Mother, we both know the dorms would be a disaster, and I have to learn to live on my own. I'm a big girl now and I overspent my allowance. No big deal."

There was a pause, and Marissa could just picture her mother with the phone on speaker, sitting at the kitchen table in her plaid jammies with all her coupons and spiral notebooks, glasses at the edge of her nose because she wouldn't admit she needed bifocals, legs crossed almost double so the right arch was tucked behind the left calf. She was pretty once, but had gotten too skinny. She was trusting, but she worried so.

"Have you called him?" her mother said finally.

Marissa stuck out her chin defiantly.

"No."

"Not even a text filled with sweet little acronyms?"

"No Mother, *God!*"

"There's no need to swear, dear."

"I didn't!"

"Well, it felt like you did." Marissa sped up the hill and cock-blocked a white van trying to merge in from the Gulph Mills High Speed Station at Gypsy Road.

"I'm over him."

"Are you?"

"Not even a little bit."

They both laughed half-heartedly.

"I'm gonna go," Marissa said. "Love you."

"Same. And material only, no metal or stones."

"Oh, all right."

"And apply for a job, maybe Nordstrom's or Macy's or something like that."

"As if!"

"Hmm."

Yes, Mother knew better. Retail and middle management were things to steer clear of. Too much frustration. Too many opportunities to fill in the patchwork. Low profile, right?

She hung up and drove on, trying to focus on the scenery—the sprawling farmland to the left, the Kingswood Apartments buried in forest cover to the right, the Valley Forge Memorial Gardens with the humongous ducks plodding all over the access road, and oh my, she was thinking about *ducks* for God's sake, anything to keep her mind off the wounds left by Jerome Anthony Franklin and the nagging idea that there was no one in the end that could tolerate her "assistance" long term. And given that there wasn't anyone else like her to begin with, she was destined to be alone for all intents and purposes.

Marissa Madison passed Anderson, watching the trees back off to the rise and spread of the business district, and after a few lights she finally made the busy turn at Dekalb Pike, or 202, or whichever it really was, the signs always confused her. The traffic out here was thick, and she got all the way over after a tough merge to make the left turn onto Mall Boulevard. A car passed her going the opposite way, and she sensed the shadow in its window, something dark and malignant and perfectly cold. For a long moment she felt his eyes boring into the side of her face, studying every ridge and contour, and she was one with him as his breath thickened. Suddenly she exploded with the hardest orgasm she had even experienced in her nineteen years on this earth and almost crashed the car into a FedEx truck that stopped suddenly to allow for an old Buick that cut in front to make an illegal U-turn in between medians. Marissa's knuckles were white on the wheel, and she was gasping.

This was new.

This was special.

For she'd finally come in contact with her equal, and he'd imposed on her this delicious intricate patchwork, so dark and so rich that even she had difficulty making a read of it. Addiction? Oh, yes. Sexual compulsion? Not quite, but a close kissing cousin. Her need to complete someone had never been this strong, and she only hoped she could apply in practice what this particular burst of psychic insight had indicated to her just now, like a vision with footnotes, with guidelines, like fate. First, she couldn't tell anyone. Second, it was a game and she was going to win it. Period. She had to have faith.

Marissa made a right and headed for the cluttered parking area in front of the Court entrance. Faith was a tough sell, a stepchild we were tempted to toss away the first time it fell short of our expectations, and it still haunted her that she'd so recently failed playing gypsy girl, failed big-time and lost the love of her life in the process. But this was America, sweetheart, the land of opportunity, the place where the most revered were the ones who could handle adversity, pick themselves up and brush themselves off, start over, reinvent themselves.

She slowed at the pedestrian crosswalk, turning in left to look for a space.

"So bring it then, dark one," she thought. "I'll show you that we're not all victims with holes to hide in and the dumb obligation to get down and start digging them. Oh, no, honey. It takes two to tango. And I might just be more than you bargained for."

JEROME

All right, asshole. Enough. We'll go no further with this, because I know her now. Not like it would make any fucking difference to me that Marissa Madison regularly attended church or set up a program through her high school to feed the homeless up in the North Philadelphia ghetto. That ain't what I'm talking about, 'cause as far as I'm concerned that's all bullshit anyway, fancy smoke-shifting, face-paint and accessories. I've seen the real girl now, worn her skin, felt the pulse coming up behind her eyes, and I'm telling you, I want out. You want me to go admit to my mama's ghost that I'm lower than dirt, it's a deal. You want me to dig up the twelve girls I buried in the woods piece by piece, then just loan me a sliver of moonlight and a shovel, motherfucker. I ain't going back, not deep inside, not her, not again.

And it ain't all the crazy parallels going on, the carnival mirrors or whatever you might call them, so don't even go there thinking I'm too stupid to notice them poking up out of the dark or that I have some native fear of tokens and omens and mystical signs. I can't change the way the wind blows and I don't think dancing on the street corner is gonna make the clouds weep. I don't keep a rabbit's foot, I don't knock on wood, and I figured a long time ago that "theology" and all that other God-shit wasn't nothing more than a bunch of folktales meant to fill up all the collection baskets.

So look at us real close, asshole, look at the *real* religion, two virgins, the dark priest and the erotic nun, both of us shamed for pouring our souls through the channels of a parent's lust. We both walk the streets in warrior headdress, feathers and fur, war-paint and bone necklaces, the two of us making a foreground and background on both sides of the blur. My mask is "maintenance man," the shadow in the shop, the faceless shape working on the compressor in the back corner of the warehouse. Hers is "materialistic girly-girl" with the rosebud lips and porcelain jaw, the doll with no eyes, the gem without substance.

And beneath all that? Well, pull up any big rock and you'll either find a black hole crawling with vermin or a glowing treasure trove. Just don't be so sure that the gleam of the diamond won't blind you. Why the fuck do you think we're both loners? I mean, anyone with half a brain would choose a bright burst of insight over my kind of darkness, but there ain't anyone who wants to sit and play house with either deliverer, at least not long-term. Yeah. Best to keep behind you the bald naked sun and the shadow of the reaper, now ain't it?

We're both compulsive.

We both like to watch.

And in the end we wind up scaring the shit out of people, even the ones who might grow the brass balls to chuckle at the idea that I was a big guy in a little car and she was a small girl in a boat of a Mustang, that we both struggled to keep ourselves straight in the lane, that she had trouble parking and I couldn't manage to change a flat or two when the shit hit the fan.

I'm not laughing, asshole. I told you, spook house parallels don't mean shit unless you buy into shifty teachers, sweaty ministers, and the gossip of a bunch of withered old grandmammies cackling 'round a card table. I don't believe in that shit, never did and never will, but that don't change the fact that I can't take being inside this dead bitch.

It hurts too much. The love between a man and a woman, from a woman's point of view mind you, is like some dark persecution. I'm used to looking at life from deep in the pit, but at least from there you can see what the sky looks like. Love to Marissa Madison was like plummeting downward, hands over the head, wind whistling up her shirt, the rim of earth above her getting smaller and smaller until it became something she felt more than she saw, like a pinpoint of afterimage.

See, her pit is bottomless.

And the fucker who pushed her there was Jerome Anthony Franklin, branded on my brain now, a virus in the marrow. Hell ain't flames and pitchforks, asshole.

It's the scope and sweep of the fall.

CHAPTER SEVEN

It happened last winter when Marissa Madison was on her way to AP twelfth-grade English class, heels clicking busily as if she were some administrator or government official, no backpack, large designer Rioni Hobo Carrier slung low on a hip, a copy of *Macbeth* in her hand. She was ten minutes late, but Mrs. Wallace would forgive her. The roster was mostly comprised of seventeen-year-old juniors who cut the class mercilessly, especially Dean Figgs and Veronica Simmons who had been no-shows for more than a week now, forging notes from the law academy teacher claiming they were helping prepare for the mock trial coming up next Thursday against Conestoga.

Of course, Marissa was just dying to show Mrs. Wallace how to put those two in their chairs and keep them there with some of their own intimate backstory for ammunition. She wanted to help security find a better way to keep all the girls from overcrowding the third-floor bathroom, and she'd come up with a number of ways to finally stop everyone from pranking on one another's laptops by freezing the keyboards, but she couldn't go around solving every discipline problem poking up like crabgrass around her, or straightening out every dispute, or worrying that people were always talking shit about her. That would be madness and her best defense was this face, these Gucci aviator sunglasses with bamboo detail, a French manicure, and the sassy little stride she'd perfected. Hamburger with that shake? You know it, girl.

She clicked on up past the gym and pool area, aggravated nonetheless. It was a long, excruciating battle, always trigger-killing the patchwork, throwing a wet blanket over her constant urge just to throw down and show people how to fix things. At the moment, she wanted to turn on her heel and run straight back down the hall to tell Ms. Pennypack, the principal's administrative assistant with the wide hips and super-big tits (whom she had passed by the water fountain a few minutes before), to stop taking out student loans and going to night school for psychology. The woman just didn't have the capacity for it, and she needed to see that it was all an attempt to follow a stern parental ideal ingrained in her from the earliest moments of childhood. Damn it! The woman was headed for a lifetime of vague unhappiness and gnawing disorientation in terms of her place in the world. So frustrating! Girlfriend would be much better off in beauty school, cutting hair. By forty she would have her own salon, but this was a "blue-collar" aspiration, so named by Ms. Pennypack herself as the heavy influence of her stoic father from beyond the grave still had her translating her dreams in terms of a rather distasteful cultural snobbery. And was Ms. Pennypack conflicted about this personal prejudice on at least some subliminal level? Oh, yes, she was!

Marissa hadn't the time to fix this, of course. She also had no right to go interpreting what was or was not appropriate in terms of someone's position in the social matrix. Her own therapist was currently working with her on her strict responsibility to detour this very thing, and she had to focus!

Still, it would make a good book, or at least an interesting graph, wouldn't it? Marissa strutted past the shop, thinking about following the money in relation to the societal perception created by one's job over time. You would have to take into account the growth of cultural sensitivity, and the slow integration of neighborhoods, scholastics, and mass media, finally comparing all that with the level of tolerance for diversity morphed with an ever-shifting socioeconomic definition defined not only by wealth, but informational affluence in terms of the spread of data through electronic media with access growing at a certain rate as compared with the expertise of the techies. This could be calculated by figures and estimates, but the final tabulation had to be cross-referenced through the lens of new linguistic patterns running through the various media. What crazy math! Awesome ideas! More interesting than *Macbeth* anyway.

Marissa walked past the west stairwell and stopped cold.

Someone was in there rapping, barking out a bit of hip-hop, using the echo. It was an awful rhyme really, some AA scheme with weak similes, but that *voice!* There was something in the tone that was deep and resonant, edged with a rich sort of anger that pierced her between the shoulder blades and ran straight down her spine. She backed up against the wall and dropped her bag on the floor, toes pointing in at each other, the left heel coming up a bit. She was softly biting the nail of her index finger, and then this young man's past came up in her patchwork so hard she had to bite back a groan.

His name was Jerome Anthony Franklin, and he lived with his grandmother here in Broomall, in one of those shitty red-brick saltboxes they rented off West Chester Pike because the woman had saved enough money as a nurse's aide at the

Dunwoody retirement home over thirty years to actually live in the town where she worked. She'd bought a used car too, this Chevy Malibu from the stone ages, and even though they didn't have much furniture in the house they had carpeting. Jerome missed his friends, and playing b-ball on the lighted courts up at 17th and Mount Vernon, and meeting everyone at the Crab Shack and goofing and then going over Cameron's place with the guys playing *Assassins Creed 4* all night. He missed busting on Kamari for having a lisp, on Abdul for having a big head, and Quad for his nappy fro. He missed dragging them all to the car shows every year and hearing time and again that he was the only city-niggah they'd ever met who liked Nascar and the Indy 500 as much as any Southern redneck, keeping pictures of hotrods in his cell phone, posting more of them on his Facebook page, and dreaming all his life about having the bread to go to an auction and buy a vintage 1970 Buick GSX, Stage 1, yellow with black racing stripes, or a white 1969 Camero Z28, and oh-my-God, he didn't even have his license yet!

And now he was stuck trying his best to get used to the suburbs where you could hear crickets chirring even in the daytime. And while you lost the convenience of going to the store using your feet and a transpass (before you could afford your classy ride, of course), you got foliage. Lots of foliage. Lots of space, too much, and Jerome was lonely and too proud to say it, too closed off to make new acquaintances, too isolated with the minuscule demographic of African Americans here to feel he fit in even a little bit, and he was just going to walk tough, wear a face, keep to himself, do what he was supposed to.

But he'd never give up his dream of being a star, of being rich enough to buy ten hotrods, not for nobody, not even in the face of an absolute crushing failure like the cafeteria incident last year at the People First Charter School in downtown Philly.

Marissa sat down. Up until that moment the patchwork had been hard information, like reading some intricate personal journal, but the "cafeteria incident" at Jerome's old high school came up in full visual. It was his beautiful plague, the thing that haunted him, defined him, gave him that razor's edge and awesome personal storybook irony in that the baggage he dragged behind him would eventually become his chariot. He just couldn't see it now for the life of him.

"I see it," Marissa whispered, and she saw *him,* sitting in his classes in this strange institution where the boys wore blue pants, white shirts, and ties, and the girls had cross-ties and grandma skirts, where the hallways were too thin and the classrooms too small, where there were signs on the walls stating "Failure is not an option," and kids snuck in breakfast sandwiches from the trucks out on Broad Street. They played cards in the bathrooms and went to class most of the time, they often talked during pre-class exercises and played too much, but if the teacher was good the conversation always wrapped back in to the lesson. It was a back-to-basics school, no sports, no recess, no gym, just a crowded circus where there was a lot of pushing and shoving and laughing and being stupid, and there were fights for real sometimes, but not nearly as many as there were in the neighborhood high schools like Overbrook, Franklin, and Germantown. No one was blowing up toilets or pushing burning pianos out the windows, bringing in guns or hiding bags of weed up in the drop ceiling, but every once in awhile there'd be a banner pulled down or a yellow industrial trash bin upended.

Jerome never thought he would miss it. He was one of the tougher kids, sitting in class with his shirt out, looking right back at the teacher with half-lidded eyes, mouthing back what looked like the lecture and constantly jotting stuff down in a ratty old notebook.

Of course, he was mouthing his hip-hop, writing raps, collecting one-liners and playing on phrases. Marissa sighed right there on the floor. The boy was beautiful the way statues were beautiful, smooth dark skin, close-cut hair, and a military jaw. He was five foot nine and muscular, pure polished granite, more the model for Burberry or Saks Fifth Avenue than the street-hardened rapper making noise on the corner. Many misunderstood him, assuming that when he curled his lip he was forming an expression of superiority or something. But it was really just the way he smiled, as if he knew the inside line on you but would lose a limb before telling. He was older than his seventeen years, handsome in a neighborhood where tough and cunning really counted for more, and insightful in a poetic and sensual way that was going to change the game in a manner he could never even begin to imagine.

And on his day of beautiful failure he was a junior, and he was going to old-school rap battle Adonis Baxter in the lunchroom, and everyone was talking about it since it meant more than street cred. This was war, less about winning but more about not losing, and being ready to spit back the harshest when the dude standing across from you went for your manhood, your flaws, your hesitation, your mother. This was no popularity contest. It was a way to weed out the weak and re-establish the food chain in colors you'd wear till you graduated.

Most everyone was betting on Jerome, and it was rumored that by the time the smoke cleared at least a grand was going to pass hands. Jerome was bigger and blacker, quiet tension under a dress shirt, wire-tight and dedicated. No one really could name a time they saw Adonis rapping at all, not even lip-synching the rhyme of a fav with his ear buds in. He had transferred this year from Central, and no one really knew too much about him except that he was a bit weird, quiet, small, light-skinned black, and still wearing his hair in braids even though that style hadn't been cool since 2001. He was a bit knock-kneed too, shuffling through the halls like a shadow, always reading some kind of book instead of having his face buried in a cell phone like everybody else. He hadn't made many friends, and he always sat in the back row or off to the side, evidently oblivious to the lively conversations around him.

Jerome was known for busting on people, talking his way out of trouble like a snake-oil salesman, hanging with three different crowds, goofing, making girls feel salty, pranking, imitating administrators, taking pictures of classmates who were dumb enough to fall asleep in class and laughing so hard showing them around on his cell phone that he sometimes fell against the walls knocking papers off the corkboards. In return, he had to guard his own iPhone like a hawk, because if Eboni, Lisa, Khalliyah, or Shanice got a hold of it, they would literally fill it up with their own selfies all day.

And Adonis? He was known only for his note-taking and his penmanship, believe it or not. It was like artwork, calligraphy, and he did it with the paper turned three-quarters upside-down no less. And if that parlor trick wasn't clever enough, he also had some sort of deformity. His hands were curled in like crab claws, nasty! Many believed it was cerebral palsy or something like that, but he didn't seem to have accommodations and he never went to tutoring. He just sat there in class taking notes in perfect longhand, breathing steadily through his wide nose, looking up at the teacher with small, flat, unreadable eyes.

And all this bothered Jerome. What was he going to rap about? He didn't really have any dirt on this kid, and hadn't had time to go gathering it. This showdown had sparked up from nowhere, some kind of rumor from a group of tenth-grade girls who wore Hijab veils and who claimed kids from Adonis's old high school swore they knew a pocket of eleventh-graders here who had heard Adonis had called Jerome a simple-ass African retard with a black faggot face or something like that. By third period it had spread through the school like wildfire, and Jerome didn't have the right notebooks with him for prep.

He kept catalogues on all his friends and those who passed in and out of his circles for this very reason, this very thing. If you had big monkey ears or a gap in your teeth or something goofy in your past like getting caught snitching, chances were it was somewhere in his spiral-bounds colored green or red, buried in harsh rhymes with punch-lines meant to bury you. He had specific things about family members and friends of friends in his blue notebook, stuff about your fight game in the neon pink one, and rhymes in fluorescent purple if you were unlucky enough to be a guy who had ever been socked in the jaw by a female.

But all his stuff was at home. At first he had considered trying to get signed out to take the sub back to his crib in Olney, but there wasn't enough time. And it would have been difficult to splice the personal flaws of others into the little he knew about Adonis Baxter anyway. He needed to think! All he had in his backpack for reference was his black five-section job, filled with more scratch-outs than he'd ever had to do before and intricate political rhymes. He'd been moving away from the cut-throat personal stuff for months now, trying to come up with material that had more meaning and lasting power. He would not have admitted this aloud, but he never liked being an attack dog in the first place. It wasn't satisfying, and he was smart enough to realize how short-lived was the glory. Everyone had chinks in the armor, and payback sucked. Besides, it wasn't . . . nice, and even though he despised himself for being so lame, he couldn't help the fact that he was growing, becoming a man, leaving behind the petty stuff.

And now this.

He was going to have to scratch down something in math class, and whatever he couldn't hack out at the desk would have to be freestyled live. And Jerome Anthony Franklin didn't like freestyling, not his thing, and that was another issue that was difficult to admit, especially now when he'd sold himself so long as one who could rap on the spot, always making up for his lack of improvisational ability with secret anticipatory planning.

Did he go for the kid's handicap? That was the real question, and the issue wasn't only that it was a huge gamble in terms of what would be considered uncool and off-limits. Finally, he didn't want to go there because for reasons he couldn't quite articulate even to himself, it felt wrong. And while he wanted to avoid it, he was terrified that in the heat of the moment he'd slip back to the subject, turning the sway of the mob against him and at the very least, feeling like he'd fought dirty to get a cheap win.

The minute security gave the green light for lunch Jerome headed for the bathroom, knowing he would have at least a few minutes of peace and quiet in the third stall down that still had the door on it with a working lock. Math had been a huge distraction, with Isiah Thompson continually hitting the button on his Bart Simpson keychain so it whined, "Are we there yet?" and the ongoing argument Mr. Ratcliff kept having with Alysse Hicks, Kianna Drysedale, and Faith Bryson, in that he could see them texting even when they hid their cells in their laps or an open pocketbook up on the desk.

Jerome didn't have much. He'd put together one short stanza, talking about his adversary's height and the fact that he was a bookworm. Shaky. Kevin Hart had paved the way for the short guy even more than Allen Iverson did back in the day, and black nerds like Dave Chappelle and Kanye West had all but destroyed the idea that it was only the stone-hard thugs who had the right to interpret the hood. Of course, this nixed the idea of going gangsta with it as a fall back, and to tell the truth Jerome had always been bored with that old-school mess anyway, rhyming "glock" with "cock" and talking about the fifty million ways you could write yourself a one-way ticket to prison.

He was going to have to rap about his philosophies, his newer material that left his opponent out of it altogether, and this was riskier than attacking a handicap. It would give Adonis ammunition, food for his own freestyling if he was capable in the first place, and Jerome didn't like leaving himself open to potshots.

Someone banged on the stall door.

"Go to lunch!" It was Farell, the ninth-grade history teacher who had the room next door to the bathroom and therefore felt he had the right to police it. "Now," he said.

Jerome pushed out with his shoulders back and walked past into the hall. His face was set, black notebook in hand.

He had nothing.

He made his way slowly downstairs.

The cafeteria was a loud, numbing buzz. There were old withered ladies wearing rubber gloves and hairnets trying their best to rotate stock on the steam table, and the quiet woman with the humpback from the accounting office stood at the front messing with the state's ticker-counter that kept a record of who got a plate. The walls were dirty white with these big dog-eared posters of Sojourner Truth, Maya Angelou, Frederick Douglass, and Barack Obama staring down on the barely controlled pandemonium, with all those on the girls' side sitting in throngs, some up on their knees on the benches shouting in one another's faces. Others sat still trying to act sophisticated, looking off into space, chewing slowly as if unaware that right beside them there were girls putting on too much lipstick, practicing cheers, playing pattycake, and sometimes screaming for no reason at all.

The young bulls in the front of the boys' section had gathered in a mob. They were sitting fifteen guys per bench where they would normally fit ten. The pack was thirty rows deep, and there were mini-rapshows going on, where some dude would stand on the bench in the crowd and get animated, calling it out, showing his teeth, flicking his fingers. There would be a ripple effect of those laughing with him or at him, open mouths shouting "Ohh!" with fingers to the lips if the mini-rap was outstanding, then a cheer and more goofing with the guys slapping fives, wrestling around, and jumping out to the long aisle down the middle of the room, some of them bobbing in and out of the surging crowd, pretending to do crossovers and swim moves and running-back jukes around others moving in opposite directions through the slim arteries alongside the food lines.

Jerome slipped in and sat with Frankie and Desmond's crowd, chock full of the jokers he'd gone to school with for years, all of them pumped to the gills, but smart enough to save him a space so he could think. Leon cleared the place before him with his forearm, pushing the trash down and cursing when he got taco juice on his sleeve. None had gotten streaked on the table. Saved it. He nodded, and Jerome stuck his treasured notebook up there, flipping to the page where he thought there might be some ammo, some early stuff right after he'd transitioned that still had the right kind of venom in it.

He smiled. Old times. In his head he could hear the beat behind it, and he clearly remembered writing it on that school trip to the Franklin Institute late last year.

I ain't no actor when power is a factor,
My body be charged like a nuclear reactor,

And you're always working,
And jerking,
And calling out sick, just a niggah with a dick, and
Irking.
For certain.
Pastor in the church of Chick-fil-A
There's meat on the fire,
noise like a choir,
hymn on a napkin, that's your rap-game,
scripture in the fryer.

Maybe. But there was too much laughter in it, and you could tell he was moving on to a different kind of thing than rap battling in the lunchroom or the parking lot with this one. The rhythm of it was more about smiling and moving your head back and forth than shouting your throat raw for the thrill of the kill. Maybe if . . .

Wait.

Something had changed. There was a hush about the place and then a low roar, as heads turned and people stood, all of them jockeying for position, telling others to get the fuck out of the way, craning their necks for a view of the archway that led to the main corridor where Adonis Baxter had just made his grand entrance.

He stalked past the juice machine and people erupted in a primal rousing cheer. He was strutting in such an animated manner that it first seemed he was limping. His shirt was untucked. His tie was off. His hair was tied up on one side in a mini-pigtail, but the other had come loose in full frizz. He's lost one of his shoes and his eyes were crazy.

Somehow through all the mayhem, he found Jerome and tramped over, everyone trying to convince the ones in front of them to sit and chill, the place slowly settling into a tense crowded ring of anticipation, the two lunch monitors in the back looking around nervously, not knowing what exactly was happening and clueless as to how to put a stop to it.

Adonis came up to the row where Jerome sat five bodies in and kicked at one of the table legs.

"Fucking cheater," he snapped. "Y'all got your book!"

Jerome didn't flinch.

"I'm studying for a physics test. Ain't even thinking 'bout you."

Adonis folded his arms.

"Go ahead then. Spit. Y'all's first."

The place really quieted and you could have heard a pencil hit the floor. Jerome shut his black book and closed his eyes, reaching deep for it, a couple of the old rhymes forming in his head trying to connect. No problem. He'd outclass him, do his transition piece and tailor in the one he wrote a month later about niggahs disrespecting females. He'd slow it all down to make it real gangsta and aim his inflections as if it were about Adonis all along. He put up his hands, fingers spread.

"Yo, yo, bitch," he started, and Adonis cut him off to the quick.

"Bitch?" he said, and then his voice jumped up a notch. "Bitch?" He started climbing into the row through the thick knots of boys sitting there, tone rising like a siren, "You call me a bitch?" He pushed his way in directly behind Jerome Anthony Franklin, "A fucking bitch?" and by the time he leaned over him just above his right ear, he'd worked himself into an absolute fit.

"Who the fuck you think you're talking to?" he shouted. Saliva sprayed out of his mouth, and Jerome looked straight ahead. A rock. Adonis went almost hoarse with it then, hollering on one side of Jerome's head then the other, one ear then the next. "I'm a bitch? Just a dumb, fucking bitch? Then spit it to me, bitch! Spit it loud! Spit it hard! You big black dummy, you retarded jungle monkey, always playin' with your pisser, just to stick it in your sister!" He stopped suddenly and played the dynamics of the untimely pause. He pushed back straight and folded his arms, standing right behind, breathing heavily, a runner of snot gleaming under his left nostril.

"So spit," he whispered finally. "Spit to the bitch."

Jerome closed his eyes again and raised up his hands, focusing harder than he ever had in his life. The crowd was a wire, taut and ready to snap.

And nothing.

Dead battery.

His hands came down and his head followed, those sculpted shoulders making humbled points beneath the creases of his dress shirt.

Adonis didn't wait for the mass of students to voice an opinion. He jumped out into the aisle where everybody could hear him and started rapping so fast it was like a machine gun. The crowd stood and hooted along, echoing him. Adonis was marching back and forth, pants low, shirt filthy, face twisted. Then he turned from Jerome, turned to the girls' side, turned to the heart of the swaying mass.

"I'm more man than you, I'm more black than you,
I'm a fuck your ma, and I'm a smack your boo,
I'll say it slow so you'll understand,
I can even beat you with my fucked up hands!"

The cheers were deafening. Adonis fell into the swarm of boys, and they were congratulating him, giving high-fives, slapping him on the back. A lunchroom monitor named Mr. Ditno finally grew a set of balls and ambled on over to the row.

"Come here," he said.

Adonis ignored him. Next came the curling finger.

"Come out of there. Now."

Adonis ignored him still. Then Ditno became the airline technician waving in the craft, hand extended out flat and arm bending up at the elbow.

"Let's go."

Ignored a third time, Ditno pushed in and through and tried to grab Adonis by the shoulder.

"Keep your hands off me," the new hero cried, shaking him off, coming out by himself. He raised up his crab claws and said it again,

"Keep your *hands* off me."

And then it sunk in, and Adonis Baxter left that cafeteria to the most deafening applause Jerome Anthony Franklin had ever heard in his life.

And now he was in an all-white school in an all-white town where uncomfortable silences were louder than Broad Street subway trains and people looked at you funny even when you chilled. And he was rapping in the stairwell, rapping angry, cussing enough to get suspended but finally not caring.

Marissa walked toward the doors, one of them not quite flush with the other, the young man's beautiful classic figure hunched over and sitting on a high stair, distorted and blurred through the green marbled glass. She felt as if she were walking on air and her heart was a triphammer. She pulled open the door and it gave a loud creak, and he stopped rapping and looked at her with wide staring eyes. His mouth dropped open just for a moment, but long enough to make it more than obvious that he thought she was pretty. Then his face closed up, jaw tight, lip curled, his eyes working down to mere slits.

"What's up?" he said. He had a short crop-cut going straight across and thin tailored sideburns. His graphic fleece hoodie was black and silver with a dragon pattern, and it didn't hang loose like that of some weak little punk, but lay almost form-fitted along his cuts and toned edges, nice and tight especially in the arms. *"Gun show,"* Marissa thought crazily. He had core denim jeans and light brown Timberland hiking boots without even one scuff on the nubuck leather. His frame was iron and his skin was dark silk.

"Your rap game is weak," she said, "Pop Warner at best, and even if you came up with current and relevant rhymes, your breathing is all wrong. You're straining on every third sentence and losing your breath at the punch-line. It's a dead horse, so stop riding it. That rap battle with Adonis Baxter was the best thing to ever happen to you, because it gave you two valuable things."

His eyes flashed. If he was amazed that she knew these particular details about his past, he wasn't showing.

"And what do you think those two things are?" he said. Marissa folded her arms and shook her hair back over the shoulder.

"A broken heart, and the knowledge that you've outgrown what a lesser man used to hurt you. So now it's time to utilize that knowledge and admit who you are."

He got up off the step and walked over, head slightly tilted.

"And what's that, fortune teller?"

She raised her chin, eyes locked with his.

"A crooner. A heart-throb who writes and sings love songs, real sensitive stuff, with lots of background violins and keys accenting vocal climaxes in the high falsetto range you don't even know you have the ability to manipulate yet. And you'll bury that anger, that failure, that lunchroom, and you'll put velvet over it, letting it simmer and reforge down there into a razor's edge, barely perceptible as it hides there in the honey, and you'll cut your listeners right to the bone with it, breaking their hearts, wringing them dry."

He didn't respond, and her eyes then did lower.

"You don't believe me," she said.

"I didn't say that." She looked back up, and he moved a step closer.

"I never even sang in church or nothing."

"Well, that's gonna change."

"I write hip-hop."

"Not anymore."

He rubbed his thumb and index finger down along the corners of his lips, and Marissa had a feeling he was thinking about his breathing, about the credibility of her plea and the way one art form demanded a certain rapid-fire execution, where a soft sort of singing would let him do what he did best. Take his time. He nodded his head at her again, except this time it had a question in it and an indication that he was ready to start believing her answers, at least in a cautious, preliminary kind of way.

"Where am I gonna get my material?"

Marissa formed her lips into that sexy little smile she'd perfected.

"From the girl you can't have." She turned and started walking out of the stairwell, turning back for one last look over the shoulder.

And Jerome Anthony Franklin was smiling back openly, no slitted eyes, no curl of the lip. He finally knew the shape of his fortune. He'd finally met up with his muse.

THE RISE AND THE FALL

Yeah, he fucked her, but not in the biblical way. At first it was all peaches and cream because all the teasing and pleasing or whatever you'd call it was part of the game, asshole. It was business. They had a no-touch rule and they let it fester, building the tension and using it to write pop music meant to make the girls groan. Marissa Madison could play the piano just good enough to compose the grass-roots accompaniment to their shitty little love songs, and Jerome Anthony Franklin became a staple in that split-level on New Ardmore Avenue. Mother was cautious at first and Daddy secretly hated the idea, but Franklin won them over with good old-fashioned manners and a lot of "yes suh, no suh." And Marissa just melted for him. She even bought him an etiquette book off Amazon and gave him speech lessons. Turned him white.

The cocksucker.

I'm so filled up with Marissa Madison's visions of him that I'd like to punch her straight in the face (if she had a full one left). I don't know why she has to keep pouring this particular strain of poison into me, but I've been drenched with their short history, all those hours they leaned over the lyric pages and sheet music together, listening to each other's breathing, making themselves speechless.

But why the fuck would I care in the first place, Madison? If you're gonna torture me, why don't you pull my eyelids back and aim my face at the sun, stick bamboo splinters under my fingernails, chop off a toe, take a branding iron to a soft spot? Get to it! Enough of the gauze and the fluff and molasses. I already know what it's like to love him, so the bang for the buck ain't deafening no more, it's just long and drawn-out. I ain't gonna turn gay, so that can't be the plan.

Do you think I'm about to change in terms of my "humanity"? Is that it? You think I'm gonna "evolve" or some such shit, just because you drag me through the wet trenches of your broken heart?

Well, what if I don't evolve, or have some dawning realization about anything, or bother to say I'm sorry? What does that make you? Take a rat from a dark sewer to appreciate the sunrise and all you might get is a blinded rat, sweating, squirming, and yelping.

So you're making me sweat, taking me through the process of launching an overnight pop sensation, proving that it's not only talent and looks but packaging and timing, and that creating exposure creatively is as important as the material. You gathered all his precious notebooks and pored over every word together, finding the most important phrases especially from the black five-section job, and cutting them out like Scrabble pieces. You put them up on the glass-top coffee table and looked at the scatter together, the winter wind blowing through the pines outside and the glow of the fireplace reflecting off the polish of the baby grand sitting by the cherry wood mini-bar.

You almost held hands after tossing all the scraps into the fire along with the green and red notebook covers and the blue and neon pink, but for the sake of the project, you settled for leaning in toward each other and letting the shadows of the flames play off your faces as if the reflections were mystic cursive script of your private ritual or some such romanticized bullshit, and up on the glass of the coffee table there were two last scraps left, two of Jerome's phrases you'd put together in an unexpected way that said,

"You made me a memory."

That was it. That was your hook, simplified dumb-dumb stuff, and it doesn't matter that the verses looked too short on paper and the bridge seemed out of place. All of it was an excuse for those rainforest keys, the symphonic foreplay to the big chorus where Jerome Anthony Franklin could take the microphone, close his eyes, and hit those glorious notes of falsetto:

"Can't you see that you and me
Were never meant to be.
I'm holding on to what's long gone
Just sunset in the trees,
You made me a memory."

One song. One hook. Absolute simplicity, the project's attraction and eventual doomsday button, but you were falling in love, living in the moment, planning to put Jerome Anthony Franklin into the public arena through the back door so he could blindside the industry with a local send-off no one was expecting.

And now I'm squirming, asshole, as his big Philadelphia run that these two both secretly named "Project Launch" flickers inside me like snapshots run together movie-style with a loop of that fucking maple syrup song droning on in the background. They hooked up with this New York–based team called "In It to Win It," doing a tour of seminars to urban high schools during late day assemblies, with its two masters of ceremonies, the first a short black dude in a white blazer claiming that this wasn't a lecture, but more of a *show,* preaching the gospel of study, image-making, and money management, stalking back and forth, talking way too loud into the microphone, overplaying how "down" he was with what the students were going through in the hood, and intersplicing poorly produced video interviews he'd had with Spike Lee and Carmelo Anthony. Then there was his assistant, this hawk-faced witch with frizzy hair, tight jeans, and lime-green hightops who waited for the attention to fray at the edges and would then interrupt with this question-answer "Whoop-Whoop-are you feelin' it?" thing that would have been clever in the hands of someone like Jesse Jackson, but sad and pathetic here, and just too damned loud.

But even without Jerome Anthony Franklin closing the seminar, it would have been successful in its own clumsy, stupid way. Through the patchwork, Madison saw that these presentations were common in poor urban schools, where the message wasn't really so much about discovering the golden key out of the ghetto as that motivational speaking was a good fallback that proved the downtrodden loved getting stroked by the feel-good phrases, like "Keep on striving to be the best that you can be" and "If you work hard you can achieve anything," even though all that limp backwash had long fucking numbed them.

But then there was Jerome, their new secret weapon, and they hid the instruments under painter's rag covers for effect, making the keys, drums, and bass look like lumps of insignificant background until two muscle-bound roadies dressed in jet-black performed the unveiling of all the shine and gleam. Of course, Jerome had the good PA system with the soundboard, and even though the MCs complained a bit at first behind the scenes, they were smart enough to understand that the producers of "In It to Win It" weren't interested in a perfect, balanced show. They weren't even concerned with educating children, but were more about booking events, fulfilling obligations to their investors this first rocky year, and closing strong. They understood contrast, and the warm-up act, even the one with "the message," could never sound as good as the headliner.

And they made damned sure they closed strong.

Jerome Anthony Franklin would walk out with his low-cut crimson V-neck, dark blue straight jeans, red Prada kicks, and black Ray Ban sunglasses, and whether it was an auditorium stage or a gymnasium floor laid at the base of a packed set of bleachers, the crowds went insane.

Contrast.

Marissa Madison knew what she was doing. It was a sellout every show, an assured bull's-eye for age bracket, and a guaranteed positive response rate, as these kids had all been stuck under the buzzing fluorescents all day prior, cramped in their chairs, bored out of their skulls, then crammed into the silo.

Madison made sure to turn the heat up, and I ain't being "metaphorical," asshole. She literally asked the administrators running these things to crank up the heat past 78 degrees, said it was these new types of cellanoid triaxials in their computer link-ups that demanded a particular high temperature, and if they ever went below it there was a chance that they'd have a freeze-up, blank screens, dead space in the middle of the show. If there was anything administrators dreaded, it was dead space where student behavior deteriorated. They knew from their years in the classroom that you had to keep the kids occupied to keep order, that every moment had to have purpose, that long transitions were deadly, and they turned the heat up for Marissa without question (all except the principal at Goretti, who claimed it was all on a timer and he didn't have his head maintenance man there to change all the codes).

Uh-huh.

Cram a bunch of frustrated kids in the silo, make them hot on top of it, and what do you get when the god hits the stage, when the lights come up sharp, when the thump of the good sound system kicks in at full volume?

A near riot, and that's when Madison started filming on her iPhone, borrowing a strategy from the Justin Bieber playbook.

Jerome Anthony Franklin didn't only go viral. He had an entire *catalogue* of YouTube video clips, none with less than 300,000 views within his first month of touring (legally, Marple Newtown couldn't let him out more than twice a week during class time), and five with over 700,000 views by mid-March.

"You Made Me a Memory" was the first number one hit on the Billboard top 100 in history that was produced as a video on a cell phone, no label or backing, no radio play, no sales. And even though this was really an industry joke at first, all that changed when Geffen and Island made legitimate offers for legitimate backing. Jerome's one regret was that he never went back to People First to make things right, to finally conquer the lunchroom, but Marissa had advised against that move from the start. He was bigger than that and you never looked back. It was getting difficult not to believe her.

Jerome Anthony Franklin signed with Geffen Records for $200,000 up front and an obligation for a quick summer tour. The language of the contract was utterly incentive-based, cautious no doubt, but it gave a shot at fame, *real fame* to this kid from North Philly who only weeks before was staring dully into the lonely stretch of the suburbs and rapping to no one in the hollows of stairwells.

It was overwhelming actually, and two nights after the signing Jerome and Marissa tried to break a rule, make a new kind of memory that was just between them if you know what I'm talking about.

I'm the rat in the sun yelping now.

I know Marissa Madison is a stone beauty, or hot as all shit, or classically gorgeous, or whatever spin you want to put on it. That's why I chose her in the first place, asshole, and if you think I don't want to live the scene where she goes and gets pumped till she's breathless you're crazy; it don't matter whose consciousness lends me the side-saddle either, his or hers, fuck it.

But that's not what happened, just between the two of them. Anything but.

See, to begin with it didn't start out as any romantic get-together. It was an argument they were having in the car on the way to Jerome's granny's house after going out for specialty coffees at Starbucks (of course, both in hoodies and shades 'cause Jerome was getting recognized in public more and more lately).

Jerome was sort of wealthy and there were problems. He was almost a star, and there were pressures he hadn't expected, not this fast in the process. There had always been time. He was used to being ignored, barking in the woods to no one, making plans, dreaming.

Now he had accountants trying for his business, talking about investment portfolios he didn't understand. He had a temporary publicist telling him how to dress, and a lawyer working on papers that would give him a legitimate high school diploma a few months before graduation, playing the idea that he was a legal adult at eighteen along with the fact that there were some credits from People First they could use to "forward this process," as long as they had his grandmother's signature and a special exception drawn up by the superintendent in triplicate. His cell phone never stopped ringing, he was getting texts from New York to go on Letterman, and he didn't even have more than one song yet.

"It's a problem," he said.

"Why?"

"Really?"

"Exactly."

He laughed through his nose and looked out the window, leaning his forehead against it.

"Glad we had this conversation." With his finger he was making lines through his breath oval, and Marissa signaled to turn down Sproul Road. That was usually one of his grand openings for sarcasm, the sequential turn-signal lamps lighting one-two-three back there like a cheap neon. He busted on her constantly for her ride, for having an automatic, for buying a V6 instead of a V8 and driving a "girly hotrod" in general, but not tonight.

"You know there's nothing to be scared of," she said. "Part of the fun of it is jumping into the unknown." He shifted in the seat, and she caught the scent of his Polo cologne. It made her a bit dizzy.

"That's easy for you to say," he said. "I've got a record deal and only one song. I have concerts booked for this summer already and no choreography. I don't really know how to write the follow-up tunes. You said you were tapped out at 'You Made Me a Memory,' and I can't use my high school musicians anymore—"

"Says who?"

"Says Mr. Fienstein, my contact at Geffen! Also Ms. Finley at Marple. Gary Acchione's parents have never been excited about his missing school two days a week, besides the fact that he's suddenly being uncool about practicing his classical piano scales. And the band instructor's drawlin' about his drum core being all a mess."

"You mean," she corrected softly, *"the band instructor disagrees with allowing Fred Schuster out of band practice because it weakens the drum core."*

"Yeah, he trippin'," Jerome returned. Marissa looked over and tried to read how much of the spite in his voice had carried over to his face. They were coming up on that tricky curve where the road forked at the library, however, and he was looking away. She stared back out through the windshield.

"You're doing quite well, in fact, with your . . . speech," she said carefully. "You should be happy with your progress."

"But I don't want to change my speech. Shannon Sharpe don't change. Allen Iverson never changed."

"We've talked about this."

"Yeah . . . and I didn't git the right ansuh, Boo-Boo."

"Sure you did. You just didn't like it." She sped through a yellow light. "Those two are sports stars. You're primed to take over the world, cross new cultural barriers. It's different."

"And I gotta change how I talk, like a hundred percent?"

"Like ninety-five percent. It was in the patchwork."

"Did it say I had to give up my new white homeboys for studio musicians so fast?"

"I don't know."

"What you mean?"

There was a long pause.

"Jerome. I only get the flashes once per person. And they're partials. I never see the whole story and I can't get that initial part of the 'cloth' back. It's a one-time thing. Thrill of the unknown, right?"

"Why didn't you ever tell me this before?"

"I didn't want to scare you."

"You already scare me. You made me into this rich guy with a mirror that talks back to himself like a British prince or something."

He was staring intently; she could feel it.

"Jerome," she said slowly, "I want to talk about us. My feelings. Where we're going to go—"

"We're here."

She pulled into the gravel driveway of the corner plot, no car, his grandmother was working a double again. Marissa had met the woman once. She was beautiful and unsmiling, tall with silver hair in a tight bun and thick eyeliner pointing up at the edges like some ferocious tigress. She was polite and cold, soft-spoken and proud, making it clear she didn't want any of her grandson's money and that her house was off-limits for girls if she wasn't there to chaperone. But she never said anything about the driveway, now did she?

Marissa turned off the headlights and it was dark out there. The houses were spread relatively far apart from each other on this stretch of back road, and Jerome's neighbor to the left was on a late winter vacation or something, all the shutters latched, the boat in the driveway covered with a tarp. There was no lamppost or walkway lighting, and the only illumination filtered weakly through the trees from up on the hill in the back parking area of the vendor who sold gas logs and hearth accessories out on West Chester Pike. She shifted in her seat and reached across, putting her hand on Jerome's knee.

"Oh," he said.

"That's all you're going to say?" She was doing her best to steady her voice. This was big-time. Her hair was in her face, her breath was husky, and she didn't have a condom. "I want to come over there with you in the passenger seat."

"C'mon then," he said. She didn't move, and they both laughed. Short exhalations, then silence, smoothed over by the Mustang's idling engine, but not smoothed over all that much. The dashboard lights were making wavy lines across the side of Jerome's face. "Maybe not then," he said, and Marissa sat back. She carefully removed the sunglasses she wore 24/7.

"Well, which is it then?" she said. "I like you, Jerome. I think I might be in love with you, and I want to give you something, ya know?"

"Yeah. I know. But what about the no-touch policy? What about the credibility of the heartbreak music and all?"

"You've got studio musicians for that now," she said. "And I don't think I matter like that anymore."

"Oh, you matter, girl."

"Then show me."

He reached across and touched her hair. It was awkward and at the same time kind of heavenly, like a good movie script neither was qualified to act in quite yet. His finger ran along the edge of her forehead, and she shivered. She had the sudden wild vision that she was about to close her eyes, cradle her head in his palm, and purr. She didn't. She just stared at him staring back at her, and she felt it in the tips of her breasts, down the slope of her back, inside her vagina, but deep in the back of it, like hunger.

They reached for each other and her hip glanced the steering wheel. They were kissing, kneeling on the leather seat cushions on either side of the central storage compartment, sort of holding each other up because of the angle, and in the close space their lips made smacking sounds that almost sent Marissa into a gale of giggles she would have hated herself for, and then the patchwork hit her in waves.

Visions.

Of Jerome. Right now, what he was thinking, what he needed for completion, and she had lied to him when she had insisted that the patchwork only played out once per person, and she wanted to giggle madly again because her lie was that she hadn't told him the patchwork was limited so she wouldn't scare him, and all the while she had lied about that so she wouldn't scare him.

And she saw that Jerome Anthony Franklin was terrified inside, almost struck dumb with it, not only because he didn't feel worthy of any record deal, but in the sense that he thought she was amazingly beautiful, like goddess-beautiful, and he was afraid of holding her wrong, of being too rough, of coming off the virgin that he was and messing it up so bad that she'd find a way to send him back to the hood where he didn't think he'd ever again find a way to belong. Prince in the mirror, shadow in the alley, an invisible man without her to define him now, and he was vulnerable, wishing deep down that she would just relieve him by hand, give him release nice and hard so he didn't have to get involved with unfamiliar choreography, a theme that was becoming familiar, and he'd never thought in themes before, not like these, and he just wasn't ready for any of this.

She reached for his zipper. He adjusted for her and she still couldn't find the tab. It was stuck facing up, caught under the fold of denim just under the snap button, and the jeans were stiff and brand new and she wasn't going to get at this thing even if she broke a nail trying.

Stiff.

He urgently wanted her to take care of him, and they were kissing hard and it was sloppy because they were trying to do two things at once, and this wasn't easy and fluid, but clumsy and disconnected, and she wondered if she was supposed to be breathing through her mouth as much as she was, and through the patchwork she knew he was wondering if his nose was running.

His fingers explored up her thigh, and she moved her hand into a position where she could cup his bulge. She worked it, palmed all along it, and then found her way to the top where she knew he needed it the most, all fire and lightning even though she was technically just rubbing the outside of his jeans.

They were cheek to cheek now, together in this and in it like thieves, her elbow working up a rhythm that was careful at first but soon to build into furious circles, and she knew he was focused on nothing in this world but the motion of her hand, the smell of her hair, and a favored memory of her curvy little ass in those tight black yoga pants, and his breath exploded suddenly into her ear.

Afterward, they held each other up like castaways, and she wanted to kiss him. Her hands moved to his shoulders and she gently pushed off so they could be face to face. But he kept his head down, he wouldn't look at her, and when he finally did with eyes milky and strange, she knew that he knew that she had read his desires like an open book, that she had lied about the patchwork, and finally that he considered this whole episode to be a massive failure, like the cafeteria all over again.

"Thanks," he said.

He broke away and pushed out, letting in the cold for a moment before shutting the door too roughly. Then he bent into the wind, jogging up the walkway hunched over, a figure in the dark.

Marissa watched him with her mouth ajar, finally making herself put the car in reverse and back slowly out of the driveway. Before taking off, she made sure he got in as if anyone on earth would care about gestures right now, and he closed the door behind him like a statement, like an ending.

She drove off stunned.

She had made Jerome betray himself. By reading what he wanted in the moment, she had ignored the fact that he had to live with himself when the smoke cleared. At this point in time Jerome Anthony Franklin had desperately needed to see himself as a grown-up, a lover, a man. What he was left with, however, was the image of an embarrassed clumsy teen who worried about his runny nose, and he had done nothing but come in his pants.

It was over.

And Marissa never forgave herself.

CHAPTER EIGHT

Jerome Anthony Franklin recorded his debut record, titled *Signs of the Soul,* at Sigma Studios in three weeks and a day, and by the time the April rains tapered off, his grandma was just about ready to put him out for good on account of his pride and his moodiness. She claimed his emotional decline was a sin before God, but she didn't understand that the choreography for the upcoming shows was horribly sparse, more about being at this location in front of the drum kit and that position by the left riser at specific parts of particular songs so he could merely be picked up in the right spotlight or avoid getting a crotch-shot from the pyrotechnics. When he'd asked the stage manager what he was supposed to do *while standing* on the given "X," the guy laughed and said, "Show 'em your good side."

He was alone.

He wanted to call Marissa, but he didn't. For once, he was going to go into the unknown by himself and master something, as strange and tough as that seemed. His session keyboard player, Mickey Jennings, smiled in his face, but was rumored to have whispered back to his lawyer at Geffen that he was uncomfortable working in a supposedly professional environment with a "fellow musician" who couldn't read sheet music. The bass player, Jayden Clemson, was this old-school black guy who never spoke except to ask where the coffee was, and their drummer, Hans Gorbensagen, was trouble from the get-go. Even though he had cut his hair short for this gig, he was a hardcore metal veteran who had done studio work for Dio and then toured with Ozzy in the late nineties. He saw Jerome as the ultimate plebe and put him through the ringer the old-fashioned way, coaxing him out after recording all day to hit the dance clubs and the strip clubs and the parties and the bars, always making sure to let him know that it was tradition for the rookie to show off his "phat stacks" and buy dinner for the group, drinks for the house, and lap dances for the boys, and this was before they even played their first show.

Grandma was expressionless there on the step when Jerome finally threw his duffel bag and footlocker in the back of Gorbensagen's rental, mumbling about picking up threads on the road once they flew out of Philly tonight and something else that sounded vaguely like a "goodbye." For the past few weeks Jerome had been mumbling a lot, over his shoulder while shuffling through the living room when she asked him where he'd been, through the bathroom door when she asked where he might be going, from under the pillow he was hiding his head under when she tried to discuss the way he'd woken her up at all hours the night before, thumping through the foyer and banging stuff around in the kitchen.

They opened for Macklemore on the eastern leg of his spring tour, starting at the Wachovia Center in South Philly, and Jerome knew that very night that they weren't going to be optioned to accompany this superstar into the Midwest. They had no performance dynamics tune to tune, his show didn't tell a story, and in trying so hard to duplicate the magic of "You Made Me a Memory" due to a rather Hitleresque industry pressure, they had written a bunch of copycat tunes, all with that feathery tempo, all with the same kind of climaxes. The old-school veterans like Prince brought the house down with ballads like "Purple Rain," but that was after a collection of tunes that ran everyone through a wide spectrum of emotions, hitting all their release points: joy, dance, sex, philosophy. All Jerome had was his broken heart, and though he sold it with everything he had, by the time they got to his number one single at the end of the set the crowd had been sitting and chilling too long.

His hometown crowd gave him a mild ovation (half of them standing) when Mickey hit the first notes of "You Made Me a Memory," but New York applauded only sparsely from their chairs. Boston didn't call them back for an encore, and he actually got booed at the Georgia Dome.

There were a lot of excuses. Mickey complained endlessly about the tech, both in terms of the lighting and the stage sound, and Hans went nuclear over dumb shit like the dressing room mini-fridge having fucking Bud Light instead of a good amber. Old Jayden didn't bother reminding him that Bud Light was one of their sponsors. He just shook his head as if he'd seen this all before and went to find his Snark tuner.

Florida was a disaster. At the Cruzan Amphitheater Hans tripped over a set of cables snaking along the floor by his left crash cymbal during the entrance walk. The crowd responded with a rousing cheer as he played it off as though it were part of the show to fall into his stuff, but the moment didn't allow for much precision when he and the roadies shoved his equipment back into position. All the pedals and rubber tripod stops weren't on their drop points indicated with the soft-glow electrical tape, and half the microphones had been knocked out of place. His beat coming through the house PA was almost nonexistent, and you only heard him thunder on in when he did a run with his floor toms.

At the Citrus Bowl, Macklemore's sound engineer got food poisoning, and his understudy had them at such a loud stage volume that Jerome couldn't hear himself through the monitors. They adjusted manually, but since their opening was a medley, they didn't have a chance to do anything substantial until the third song portion had been completed. Jerome's hook wasn't about smash, pound, and thump, and there was nothing to hide behind. He'd been forced to over-sing and he missed almost every note, some so badly you couldn't even soften the blow by calling them "pitchy," and in response the audience became a sea of cell phones. It was the second time Jerome Anthony Franklin went viral, and this one wasn't pretty. By the time they hit the Seminole Hard Rock Hotel and Casino they were fighting about everything, and local papers were calling this tour the worst mismatch since Blondie tried opening for Rush back in the late seventies.

Coming back up the coast for a couple of those "up close and feel-goods" that Macklemore typically built into the tour for the purpose of fine-tuning, Budweiser dropped them right before they hit the Black Cat in Washington, D.C., and KFC followed suit just after their show at the Warsaw in Brooklyn. The call from Geffen came on the plane back to Philly. No renewals, and they were exercising severance and termination. If by some miracle a company here or a franchise there wanted to play scavenger on a piece of "You Made Me a Memory" for commercial purposes, Jerome was still entitled to royalties just as he was from the record no one was currently buying. They called him a "brief yet mostly extinguished local sensation, yielding little gain and impressive liability." They were drawing up all the forms and would have them in snail mail by Friday.

Hans dropped him off at his grandma's place, and Jerome dragged his duffel bag and his footlocker inside across the threshold, noticing immediately that the place smelled like medicine or cleaning solvent, something industrial. Grandma was working, and a lot of their stuff from upstairs was sitting in cardboard boxes by the flueless hearth. Of course, she'd had the exterminator come in. They had ants, and they had argued about his eating in his room, leaving the dishes lying around. He had promised to make it right, at least to help move everything so his grandmother wouldn't have to strain her back or take an extra painkiller for her arthritic ankles after being on her feet all day. Another missed opportunity. Another failure. Of course.

To Jerome's horror, he thought he was going to cry.

He was supposed to take over the world and had become nothing more than a parody of himself, a big public joke. Maybe he could join one of those kiddie concerts at this point, where you wore a smelly parade costume playing sing-along as Barney or a Muppet. He was supposed to have management solving all these problems before they occurred, but the brass had used this tour as an audition, leaving him out on his own, sink or swim. He was supposed to get the girl, but he wasn't worth her time now.

His shoulders sagged.

Look what he'd done with Marissa's vision. She'd been wrong about him. She'd backed the wrong horse. Read the tea leaves wrong. Moreover, Jerome was no longer a virgin, and that was another reason he'd never be able to see her again.

What if she got this one right and "read it" in him? At the very least he could spare her that kind of painful, hideous face-time.

He walked over the cardboard boxes, picked one at random, and sifted through the contents. There was the black-and-white picture of the grandfather he'd never met in military fatigues, a yarn spinner, and some *Good Housekeeping* magazines. Below that was the dull silver gleam of Grandma's .32 Beretta.

Another joke: she was no gunslinger. She had gotten it that summer when thugs were breaking in everywhere in the old neighborhood looking for copper, the year Jerome's mother had gotten shot. It was a knee-jerk thing. To this day, she had never even loaded it.

Things in boxes.

Stuff that you didn't need anymore, like Jerome Anthony Franklin the sob story, the stereotype. He'd blown most of his advance on parties he would have rather forgotten, piles of blow for people he didn't even know, and clothes he wasn't going to use, all of them currently warehoused in a POD by the airport that he wasn't going to be able to afford very much longer. He had enough left in the account for a security deposit on an apartment, and it was time to start looking. He sure as hell wasn't going to get that Buick GSX any time soon. If only all this hadn't been such a whirlwind . . . if only there had been just one small window of opportunity where he could have slowed things down and taken the time to think things through.

He wound up finding a place for rent in West Philly, on 46th Street above the check-cashing store. By June he had sold off everything including the Brioni Vanquish II suit he was partial to, but couldn't move the one that really had drained him—the Alexander Amosu. It hung alone in his closet like a dead man on a rope. By July he was wearing a red and green smock, and working the register at the 7-Eleven convenience store under the elevated train down 69th Street. In effect, he had died, and there was a smoldering anger inside him that never seemed to cool off. And it wasn't the cafeteria specifically, nor his inability to tell Marissa Madison how he really felt all along, or even his crushing miscarriage at the Citrus Bowl.

It was that Geffen contract. Jerome knew it was peppered with incentives as opposed to fail-safes and guarantees, but he hadn't had a clue they could ditch him so fast, leave him with nothing.

It was all about the words, and thinking that you could sit with a ratty notebook, pumping out street rhymes that could truly interpret the world. That was the bait, and it was a fool's game.

In the end it was all about the fancy words, the real words, the slippery words, the nests and tunnels and dead ends and quarries, all of them filled with volumes upon volumes that were riddled with amendments, hidden stipulations, and clever vocabulary. It was a mammoth labyrinth that had all the road maps written in code. It was a massive language maze that rich folks used to keep poor folks living under elevated train platforms and working at convenience stores.

Jerome had nothing left except a mattress, a blanket, a mini-fridge, a hot plate, and a designer suit he had no business wearing.

And his library card.

After work one Friday afternoon, he turned his collar to the rain and took the sub to the Free Library of Philadelphia. When he first walked in, he was more than intimidated. There were computers and thick wooden tables, balconies and columns, stained-glass murals and ritzy chandeliers. And books. Thousands of them staring down from the second and third floors, like stern old men with white bushy eyebrows.

Like the lawyers at Geffen.

Jerome took off his coat and slung it over a chair. He walked past the long curve of the circulation desk and made his way up the nearest stairway. It took him thirty-five minutes, but he found a meaningful set of racks on the east side by the bathrooms and a darkened storage area. It took another half hour, but he finally pulled down a book he felt he could start with.

No one told him he wasn't smart enough or experienced enough or worthy enough to take the book off the shelf, and he liked that. It had five hundred and ninety-three pages before you got to the bibliographic essays, but he had to start somewhere. He knew this wasn't the last book he would have to read, but he had time. Lots of time. And no one judging him.

He walked down the stairs, slightly conscious that his sneakers were squeaking because they were still damp. He sat at his table and opened the front cover of *The Cambridge History of American Law.*

By June he had read four such books.

By July, the librarians knew him by name.

SHORT CIRCUIT

Well, boo-fucking-hoo, asshole. Let's all feel sorry for the little blackie who found out he had to hole up in a shitbox, work for a living, put product on the shelves, and ring up lottery tickets. Am I supposed to feel bad that his "talent" got wasted or something? The son of a bitch couldn't write a song to save his life, and singing by itself just ain't that special, fuck you, it just ain't. There are fifty thousand chicks singing like Beyoncé in fifty thousand churches, but they ain't got the tits and those thighs, that face and them eyes. Look! I made a rhyme, Jerome! I'm a genius! Let's write it down in a notebook so some weird psychic can come along and make the scraps into something just as special as you are.

Go fetch me a pack of Marlboros, how's that?

Wipe up this spill.

Fill up the milk and creamers.

And go to the library and read all your books. See, we ain't too different when it comes to that part, you and me. I just have a better use for the diversion, so stop complaining. But before we even consider the extra-curriculars, understand right here and now that I work for a living too, I work like a dog in a warehouse, where you sweat through your jumpsuit in the summer and the ends of your fingers go raw in the winter. A day's work is a rack full of red plastic bins filled with grinders and screw guns and planers and roto-hammers, all of them needing brushes and armatures, switches and bearings, every nose cone or side handle accounted for with a manila tag and a twisty-tie, each tool matched with an invoice and a number. When I'm done with those, I can wipe my hands off with a dirty rag and walk over to the far side of the warehouse to tinker with the bigger machines that have gone down, over by the ancient shelving loaded with broken extension ladders, bent scaffolding, scrap metal, and rolls of old unused fiberglass insulation, all of it lurking in that darkened area I have to illuminate by bringing over one of those clip-on lanterns that brings up everything so bright the world becomes a relief map of dirt-hardened ridges, cracked paint, and grit. When that's done, I can clean off the rental machinery with a Brillo and a hose. When *that's* finished, I can go through the parts bin, counting bit tips and wire, o-rings and machine screws. Then I clock out. It's a tan card with green lines on it, but it's really an invoice with a number. See? I made a connection, or a parallel, or an analogy, or a metaphor, or whatever you smart bastards call it, and I didn't have to go to the library to do it either.

But that's your escape, ain't it? Makes you feel worth it, like you're not just keeping careful tabs on shit people don't notice in the end, all your life with your nose to the grindstone, scratching numbers into a log, hanging your clipboard in the dark receiver's shack at the west edge of the abandoned factory with the broken windows and crumbling smoke-stacks.

Reading keys you into something relevant.

Every page you swallow is a page someone else didn't. Every book you complete is a piece of precious scrap wood, a trophy that you can cling to, keeping your head an inch or two above the ebb and flow of the blur so it don't hypnotize you, dragging you under.

So I get it, *Jerome*. For me, each girl is a buoy. And they're all lined up, bobbing pretty in the waves for as long and far as the eye can see. Infinity is a beautiful thing, ain't it? You can have your dusty bookshelves, though. To each his own.

But hey, you pretty little nigger. Just 'cause you fucked up your shot at the big time, just 'cause you lost the girl and your momma got killed way back when, just 'cause you're bored as hell stocking shelves and ringing up Slim Jims and rolling papers don't mean you get to slack on the job. See, I grew up down by 69th Street and I know that 7-Eleven you work at. Since it's on the way from my place in Yeadon, I stop by every morning for my large coffee with that cardboard sleeve so you won't burn your fingers. Good coffee, too. You guys always have one of those pots that's been sitting awhile with about an inch or so at the bottom, pure sludge, strong as bull!

Never seen you there, pal. They probably have you on the graveyard shift, but don't worry. Someday you'll grow up and they'll make you assistant manager!

And you'd best be careful on that late shift. That place has been hit a lot lately, I seen it on the news. You'd better watch out for guys in twos or threes, guys in hoodies with gorilla masks, guys with agendas that would have made Zimmerman an American hero. Might as well follow his lead, find an ankle holster, and get something to fill it with. Tough old world, huh? Guys like us have to watch out for the thugs, don't we?

Poor niglet. Marissa Madison fell for you, but you ain't no Beyoncé. I'm no judge of guys even though I did have the fine opportunity to "experience you" through a particularly disgusting lens of lust, but you can't really be all that after all, now can you? Burberry? Saks Fifth? Hmm . . . didn't sell many records, now did you?

Hell, I don't even see you staying on at the 7-Eleven when all the smoke clears and you push into your thirties, wondering how everything went by so fast and wound up twisting straight down the toilet. I actually picture you in red and yellow with a paper hat, asking in that velvety tone,

"Want French fries with that?"

Go ahead. Greet me at the drive-thru window. Be good and careful that I get the right change, and make sure the receipt is tucked on one side of the small stack of coins for the perfect delivery from your fingers to my open palm. Fold the bag neatly at the top, and when you hand it out to me don't forget to smile, thank me, and wish me a good and safe evening.

Go ahead, nigger.

Make me a memory.

CHAPTER NINE

Marissa couldn't find parking up by the nearest mall entrance, so she had to drive down a level where the thick concrete ceiling came so close to the roof of the car she instinctively ducked. Shadows washed over the vehicle and a sudden dread came into her face; she could feel it. A moment before she had been the most confident girl on the planet, a superhero. But while it was one thing to connect with a demon on some psychic wavelength, to trust the patchwork, to have the faith to enter the web, it was quite another when you actually had to do it. Suddenly you realized that this wasn't a movie, that you were in this for real, that some grisly savage was working the periphery one step behind you and closing.

This guy was no joke: she had heard about him on the news like everyone else and had whispered about him with relative strangers in the hall after class, made speculations over coffee.

He was the talk of the Widener campus and the entire tri-state area mostly because there was so much mystery about him.

Since a year ago March there were twelve young women who had never come home. Since they were all extraordinarily pretty, the media had played it up by revealing the photographs on television like some sexual stable, all of them prize horses. It played on the same fascination we had with college cheerleaders and their lovely bare legs, the given school's insignia like an owner's brand placed just above the cheek and the colored ribbons fluttering in their manes.

So who was he? And more horrifying, what *type* of maniac was this? Was he the shadowy creep with the dingy basement prison or the soft-spoken bachelor with the side business that required night hours and a nondescript van? Was he a collector or a ripper, did he have an assortment of handcuffs, soldering irons, car batteries, and electrical cables, or was he more the meathook and freezer, smock and goggles kind of fella, slit and drain or bludgeon and spatter, breaking knife or meat cleaver, shotgun or axe, tarp or plastic, frayed rope or duct tape?

And if he *was* killing them, where were the bodies? And more so, if the poor girls were in fact corpses, the question was why.

Of course, one could draw the most obvious conclusions in terms of forced seductions, but there seemed to be so much more going on here. It was this fiend's absolute invisibility. He was faceless. A pristine enigma, a dark vacuum. Watching.

And girls kept on vanishing.

Marissa had no idea what he looked like. The patchwork had only sketched for her a pure evil, a black cloud that moved to the other back shoulder when you tried to pin your eyes on it. Of course, she'd thought of the police even though her psychic burst had indicated that she wasn't supposed to tell anyone about this, but she had no description to offer in the first place, certainly not one they would be able to use.

He drove a Toyota. Or a Kia or Hyundai, she couldn't be sure, something small or midsized. He'd passed her quickly, and she'd been occupied with the lust he'd brought up in her, another thing she wouldn't be able to relate very well to a badge trying to piece together some sort of sober documentation. And besides all that, she knew this monster would sense interference. He was attracted to her, she could tell, but he wasn't careless and she could tell that as well. The cops would put a protective tail on her and he'd sniff it out before they had even parked by her house and cracked open their first box of Krispy Kreme doughnuts. Then he'd fade into the woodwork. Move on to another prize racehorse.

Before turning left under the low ceiling, Marissa saw that out through the back of the lot, past a low barrier wall and a cyclone fence, there was a sign cluster for Route 202, 476, and the turnpike. In here it was nearly empty except for a spattering of cars parked way back in toward the mall entrance and two enclosed staircases, and she pulled into the nearest space available right here by the end of the ramp in front of a support column that said "2H."

She turned the car off, and her breath quickened. What was she doing? Why would she park in relative isolation here, when there were townsfolk, or at least their parked cars, over yonder by the stairwells?

Well, that one was a no-brainer. Clearly, she didn't trust fellow vehicles. Anyone could be hiding in them (as if he could have gotten down here first somehow). And stairwells were deathtraps (as if he'd not only defied the timeline and beaten her to the punch in terms of advancing and setting his physical positioning, but also predicted the stairwell, and the right stairwell mind you, that would have been her chosen exit artery).

Marissa's mouth went dry. She had instinctively parked by the ramp in a vast ocean of empty parking spaces so she could see him coming, so she was closer to the opening back here where you were in the same zip code as the street signs outside if you had to make a run for it. Marissa's heart was thudding now; she could feel it. Seeing him coming was a fallacy: she'd be nothing more than a deer in the headlights if he raced right at her, screeched his tires, jumped out, and manhandled her into the back seat. Moreover, any witnesses by the stairwells would be hard-pressed to make a description of him, let alone catch his license plate. And what was this nonsense about being in some nearer proximity to the highway signs? Did she really think she'd have an advantage making a run for it, jumping the half-wall, scaling the fence, and pushing through the decorator foliage?

She wasn't thinking straight, and she had to get her shit together. Boyfriend was playing for keeps here, and even with her advantage of the patchwork and the promise of a "win-win scenario" she couldn't just lay dormant, sit stupid, bank on cryptic prophecies. Jerome had not maintained her vision of him, poor thing, and if she had learned anything from his horrific public failure, it was that prophecies were tricky, sometimes offered in symbols and codes you never quite figured out.

She suddenly thought of the real victims here, the long string of abducted young women and just for a moment she wondered "why me?" wishing deep down that she was someone else entirely. If only she could become plain and invisible, free to untie and remove her own proverbial "cheerleader's ribbon" long enough at least to give her the time to think rationally!

Marissa laughed out loud, and it sounded harsh and forced in the car. To hell with this son of a bitch! She liked being a girly-girl, liked being pretty, liked being looked at, and hey, if she was aware that she was being stupid and hesitant, she was actually being self-observant and careful, wasn't she? It was called "metacognition," thinking about your own thinking, duh. Smart people did that, the strategizers. And she *was* going to win this thing, she just had to think positively! The patchwork had only failed her one time in a thousand—no, more like a million—and she had to have faith. She grabbed her shoes, got her purse, and made to open the door. She suddenly decided to walk back up the ramp in her stocking feet and felt herself ultimately practical for choosing not to hoof it in heels.

The hinges squawked. They never did that before! She pulled herself out, and after shutting and locking she thought she heard a pebble fall and tick along the concrete back by the stairwells. It halted her right there, making her do an impression of a Marissa statue that must have looked absolutely ludicrous.

But he couldn't be there, now could he? She'd been over this once already. If he was following her he'd have come in from behind, down the ramp, and she'd have seen him. Despite all this, Marissa leaned forward and squinted back into the gloomy expanse of the parking area. Nothing. No one, just a few empty cars.

Like tearing off a Band-Aid she pulled herself away, turned, and walked as fast as she could around the near corner and up the ramp, back out to the open, to safety. The air was different out here, and the wind in her face was refreshing, making her feel as if she were moving this forward, getting down to business, not letting herself get totally freaked.

Business. First things first, she had to throw out her underwear. As disgusting as it was to be aware of stuff like this from *Sex in the City* and *Californication,* some girls evidently were "squirters"—that is, if the writers had to keep that kind of stuff real. And though Marissa was most definitely *not* one, she might have spotted, and that wasn't acceptable even when you were being stalked by the evil faceless vicious black shadow. A girl had to do what a girl had to do, and she ran up the concrete ramp with her stuff clutched to her chest, her stocking feet pitter-patting in mini-steps she would have giggled insanely about in any other circumstance. By the time she got to the crosswalk she was breathless, and when she heard someone cough from behind, she spun too quickly and almost tripped off the curb.

It was an Asian man, thin, graying sideburns, and black turtleneck sweater, looking in a laptop he was carrying. His name was Frank Ho, and he was the third partner in a new medical practice that he had helped finance with a second mortgage on his house in Ridley, and he was looking at a patient's bloodwork, considering starting him on a combination of Uloric (40 milligrams) and Colcrys at 0.6 for gout. He was walking and computing as he usually did, but today he was simultaneously occupied with thoughts of his teenage son Stanley and the kid's ridiculous idea to come to malls like this and stand in front of the fountain area selling this new-fangled bouncy ball that turned to quivering slime-jelly when it settled on the floor, then forming back to its original spherical shape right there before your eyes. The kid had already invested his summer lawn-mowing money in seventy-five pounds of this crap that he had stowed in the second detached garage, and he wanted Frank to get him juggling lessons so he wasn't just some kid tossing balls in the air, but more of a performer, a professional, and no matter how many times they had argued about this and a hundred other little schemes Stanley had cooked up lately, the stubborn boy had no interest in burying his nose in a never-ending series of textbooks next year and wasting so much of his youth in "antiquated pedagogical institutions that were totally overpriced and far short on delivery when you considered the current global economical tendencies . . ."

Marissa hit the trigger-killer on her belt loop and paused there on the sidewalk to put on her heels. As a result of overhearing so many pre-college teens of late re-expressing the trendy idea that higher learning was more of an expensive, corroded ideal than a practical and useful avenue to success, she was tempted to tell Dr. Frank Ho to kick the kid out for a year so he could try supporting himself juggling magic slime-balls and quoting the fancy chatter he found on the Internet. Quick fixes wasted precious time. And some old dinosaurs, so called, still patterned themselves across the landscape for a reason. Shit, she didn't want to commit either, knuckle down, tread water in a sea of scholarly articles. She'd never been comfortable with the idea of becoming a nurse actually, but it was the most practical and positive way for her to utilize her psychic abilities, and even though she was falling into the same trap as the Internet mimics in that she felt she was draping her mother's words over her own, she had come to admit a long time ago that you couldn't run away from universal truths. We all had to work, and we all had to work hard learning the methods and traditions of something at least somewhat traditional, something we might not necessarily like . . . well, not in a shopping spree or run-up-to-your-bedroom-to hear-that-new-song-and-dance-in-front-of-the-mirror kind of a way.

That's why they called it work.

And just because the idea of forever reading the patchwork of the sick deeply saddened Marissa on certain emotional platforms, she knew on a more fundamental level that there would be long-term satisfaction in knowing she spent her time on this earth helping people understand and manage their pain as opposed to riding shotgun to a bunch of crazy dreams like slime-ball juggling, or pop music records that turned into one-hit failures at the Citrus Bowl.

She walked toward the Legal Seafood restaurant, heels clicking on the cement, and had that awful feeling that someone was going to stop her at the door and say, "Can I help you?" therefore forcing her to ask out loud for permission to use the restroom. That would be ultimately embarrassing, and even worse, it was always possible that she could get a real gatekeeper taking special pleasure in stating a patrons-only policy, and she was stressing over dumb stuff now, and she had to focus.

"Don't sweat the petty things . . . pet the sweaty things," she thought. It came from nowhere and she couldn't for the life of her recall its origin, but *God,* it was hysterical! She put her hand in front of her mouth to hide the mad grin that had plastered itself there and pulled open the door.

Smelled like fish, and that one almost made her double over. There was a hostess station across from a Plexiglas wall display with wine bottles stacked in it and strange bubble water rising up the facing. A family of four was waiting to be seated, partially blocking the path, and a there was a woman with a black skirt and loose paisley top bending to reach into the back of the podium for menus.

The guy was hooked on Internet porn and his wife was thinking of backstabbing a male co-worker who had spread it around the office that she was the one who misplaced the paperwork on the Garber account. Their boys looked like twins but were actually a year apart, the fifth-grader stuck on the idea that his high voice made other kids call him a faggot, and his sibling considering the idea of faking being sick so he could stay home from school again tomorrow and use the pump BB gun to shoot birds off the phone cables cutting through the back yard. They had all taken the day off together to get flu shots, and instead of the "sneak-away family day" both parents had envisioned, they'd all done nothing but fight in the car. The hostess straightened up and Marissa was struck with her perfume and her Daddy issues, and she hit her trigger-killer five times in a row. School was hard enough, but restaurants were torturous for some reason, as if people focused harder on their personal shit when they didn't have to worry about cooking, serving, and making sure they ate their lima beans for a hot minute. Marissa made her way past the oyster bar pressing the button at her belt loop again and again, chastising herself for choosing a bathroom in an eatery in the first place, and immediately forgiving herself because it was closer than the generic mall lavatories placed God knows where out there, and she was scared, damn it.

The bathroom was dressed up to look cutting-edge, but came off tired and worn. The black wall tiles had calcium build-up at floor level, and the steel sinks looked water-stained and dull despite the fake ferns in the vases between them. Marissa waved her hand in front of the towel dispenser, got two sheets, and moved to the handicapped stall. She slowly pulled the door open, more wary of the kind of deposit left in the bowl that would make you say, "Whoa!" than disturbing an occupant careless enough to leave the door unlatched.

Vacant. Clear in the toilet too, thank God for small favors. She pulled the door closed, turned, and took down the top lid. Feeling prissy and silly about it, she papered it with her two towels, careful to cover every square inch of the solid oval-shaped plastic, and no, she wasn't OCD or anything, but it was an expensive leather bag. She set it down on the makeshift tablecloth, kicked off her heels, and started to drop her drawers, thinking how silly that phrase was when she had to do such a wiggle-dance to get them down to her ankles.

She had just hung her jeans on the hook and pulled one foot out of her panties when the door out there to the hall crashed open. She jumped up on the toilet seat and gripped her knees tight to the chest. Her big bag contoured nicely to her bare bottom, but through it she felt the edge of what felt like her Kindle and it seemed that if she moved even a little bit the entire rank and file in there would make noise shifting positions and settling. There was an awful clattering out there, followed by a thud and metallic "toink" that sounded like a billy club making contact with the sink area.

"It's the Suitcase Murderer!" she thought crazily. *"He just hauled in an oversized luggage bag with one of those airplane carriers you pull behind you on wheels, and he yanked it so hard he banged the reinforced plastic handle rods against the sinks! Oh God, all the girls must have been small like me so they could fit and he could get the zipper around the lumpy parts!"*

She saw a pair of dirty black sneakers appear on the other side of the stall door, one foot then the other, slowly, deliberately.

If Marissa's eyes could have gone wider they might have fallen out of her head. She could hear his breathing and it was all through the nose, heavy as if he had a cold or more as if he were really amped for the roast that had just come out of the broiler and those hardened fatty parts by the bone he was going to carve off and eat right there at the cutting board.

There was a hard knock. Marissa squirmed and tried not to give out a squeal or an "eek" or some other lame giveaway. Next, the guy pounded on the door, this time shaking it on its hinges.

"Yo! Someone in there?"

Wait.

"Yo!" he said.

"Yes, God!" she exploded back, change of emotion, new flavor, are you kidding me? It was the guy's voice, too stupid and rude for the "Suitcase Killer" for sure. Of course, he was the janitor. Of course, the clatter came from the hardened rubber wheels of a mop bucket running across the grout lines of the floor tiles, and the metallic "boink" sound was the mop handle coming in contact with the sinks as he drew the affair across in an arc. Embarrassing!

"How come I can't see yer feet?" he said.

"Why are you looking?" *Asshole.*

"Didn't you see the sign?" he said.

"What sign?"

"The floor wet sign. I put it right on the matting outside."

"Missed it. Do you mind?"

"Naw . . ." he said, but now it was his tone that was doing a change in flavor. It sounded wistful or mystified or . . . gross! His feet had backed off and he was most certainly squatting, looking under the door. Marissa was pretty sure he still couldn't see her, but it was obvious what had caught his attention. It was her cotton panties, lying in a dainty rumple just inside the stall shadow.

She hopped off the toilet and snatched them up, and while she was putting her pants back on, riding bareback and absolutely furious that some snotty-faced high school dropout or whatever he was had the opportunity to picture her so, she formed a scenario in her mind where she sought out his manager and filed a formal complaint.

But then she would have to detail her actions in the stall, and even if she came up with a logical and acceptable excuse for having her underwear on the floor of a public bathroom, in an establishment where she was not even a paying customer mind you, there were worries here. How many assistant managers, bartenders, waitresses, and busboys would get a load of this one? Would it end up online? Would she have to give her name?

Marissa pushed out of the stall and saw that the bathroom was vacant again. Of course the punk was hiding, probably in the kitchen, or better in the back room with the food stock, somewhere he wouldn't have to confront her face to face. She threw her undies in the steel, waist-high receptacle bolted to the wall and passed her hand in front of the towel machine a few more times. She was going to put the paper product on top in there more as a perfunctory action than a practical one, because if the creep wanted her panties bad enough he'd just dig them out anyway, and this made her so mad she felt she was going to spit nails.

She exited the bathroom, and right there across the thin, dark hall area was a yellow wet floor cone. But it was nestled against the far wall as if stowed there for convenience instead of standing directly in front of the door for a purpose, and that piped Marissa to the moon. It was easy to miss and it was intentional, as if the guy were trying to *set up* these kinds of "walk-ins" as opposed to stumbling into a lone instance by chance, and she was actually reconsidering that complaint when suddenly the blood ran out of her face.

All thoughts of righteous wrath withered and died right there, her stomach turning to lead, one hand coming up to her cheek in hard shock. The problem wasn't the janitor here. He was irrelevant.

The problem was her, and it had nothing to do with some shifty kid who would say it was just "in her head" if he was finally called onto the red carpet this time for setting traps and peeking at the ankles under the stall doors. It was what had *not* been in her head, what still wasn't. Something was different, something off-kilter, and she would have recognized it immediately back in the bathroom if she hadn't been so filled with fear and adrenaline.

She'd had no read on that janitor whatsoever, no flood of pictures, no catalogue of his past. The "Suitcase Killer" idea had not only been wrong, but it lacked body, dimension, authenticity. It had been her imagination alone.

No patchwork.

Marissa was almost paralyzed where she stood. The entire restaurant before her seemed to have gone dull, at least in terms of what she could hear. There were forks and knives contacting plates, glasses clinking, and a low murmur of voices, all of it coming from the seating area just past the nearly vacant oyster bar, but she was apart from it all as if from another planet, standing on the edge of scraps upon scraps of meaningless, random surface conversations.

This was what it was like to be "normal."

And it was the epitome of being alone.

She stumbled forward toward the waiting area and the open frame exit behind it that would lead her into the mall. She passed a server with a blond ponytail and nerdy reading glasses, tables filled with customers, a guy in a dress coat carrying a briefcase with whom she got caught up for a second in that awkward dance where you both guessed wrong and almost bumped three times, a scattered few sitting at the bar watching ESPN, and the air was flat, no read of anything, no pictures, nothing. By the time she passed the hostess, who noticed her this time with thin eyes and a wide plastic smile, Marissa had gone from a state of near shutdown to an absolute terror, and when she stepped out to the wide hall she was hyperventilating, trying not to go prostrate, falling, going fetal on the floor, drawing the attention of the mall medics who drove golf carts around looking for the elderly who'd collapsed, had strokes, broken a hip, drank too many Bloody Marys.

This was unreal. Her patchwork had shorted out or something, and there by the information board Marissa reached to her belt loop and unhooked the trigger-killer, fingers shaking. Down at the bottom edge the tiny battery light, which had always been green, was a dull crimson. All the mall noises seemed to amplify around her now as if her ears had gained sudden recognition of what they had considered second fiddle for so long, and it was hard to concentrate. Had her battery ever gone dead? She couldn't remember. Daddy constructed this device for her back in middle school, and she didn't recall any time that it had been on the fritz. It was like the battery in your desk clock, or more like the one in those old-fashioned watches that seemed never to run out even as decades passed by.

Marissa looked up blankly at the mall map. There was no Radio Shack or Circuit City that could help her here. The device was custom-made, as was its power source, and she had to get her father into the lab and quick. She kneeled down and unzipped her bag, for a moment unable to find her phone in all the clutter. By the time she quick-dialed Daddy at the office and worked through Ms. Fehlinger asking her about school and all that, she was almost in tears.

"Hey, Rissa," he said. "What can I do you out of?" The sweet familiarity of his voice calmed her. Slightly.

"I need your help kind of quick, Daddy."

"What kind of help?"

"It's my trigger-killer. I think the battery died."

"Hmm. Is the light on?"

"Yes."

"Color?"

"Dull red."

"Hmm."

She crossed an arm across her stomach and looked up at the high ceiling. Daddy could be slow-moving at times, typical techie, caught in his world of gadgets and more interested in trying to let you see the brilliance of the equations behind the scenes than the final product in your hands. She heard him mute the telephone and ask an assistant or someone about a blueprint, and when he came back in full voice, his tone was in sing-song mode as if the conversation were ready for its signatures and sign-offs.

"OK, then, Rissa-bissa. Let me know if you need money or . . ."

"Daddy!"

"Hmm . . . no, the schematic of the south grid . . . yes? Oh, sorry. A little busy here with stuff, honey. Now what's wrong with your device?"

"Nixed battery! Daddy, is it possible that the thing went dead right after I cut off a particular flood of patchwork, and that it somehow kept me blank, like in a permanent state where it left me, sort of trigger-killed in the dark?"

"Neat-o!"

"What?" She rolled her eyes and couldn't help but forfeit a small grin. That was just so . . . *him.* She could picture her father sitting there at his drafting board, sleeves of his dress shirt rolled up, long thin face, silver sideburns and that friendly, trusting sort of elevated worldview as he was born the nerd, raised the nerd, and now paid so handsomely to be the nerd. He lived in his perfect world of formulas and contraptions, and he loved it with the pure joy of a child. It was cute in a way, and incredibly annoying in most others.

"It short-circuited you!" he said. "I'll have to jot down some notes on this, Riss, it's fascinating."

"Can you fix it?"

"Hmm."

"Stop mumbling, please! This is an emergency!"

"Oh, right. Well, in terms of your power source there's nothing to fix. The problem is that the battery itself is custom and minuscule and there's no charger, or recharger, at least not one I've invented quite yet."

"Can you make me one?"

"I'm kind of swamped here."

"Daddy!"

"Uh, yes, OK, sure." Whoever he had been mouthing stuff over his shoulder to there in the office must have left, because Marissa could hear in his voice that she had his full attention now. "I can do it," he continued, "but what happened here might not just be a dead battery, and there very well might be an issue with a repair, or at least what you might call minor surgery."

"What do you mean?"

"Why is it so noisy in the background there?" he said. "I can hardly hear you."

"I'm at the mall. So why not just a fried battery—short version please?"

"Right. If your patchwork is frozen or blacked out so to speak, it seems you have been the unfortunate victim of two issues, a worn battery and possibly a circumstance where the contacts have fused in the switch, in effect welding themselves shut, locking you in the dark. So in short, I need your device so I can file down the spotwell and smooth it. As for the battery, I have to start from scratch, cut down a unit and marinate the cloth in a complex brine solution. Then I can initiate the chemical process that will reconstitute the prototype."

"What's the timeframe, Daddy?"

"Two days, maybe three."

That wasn't good, considering that today was Thursday.

"Can you get into the office on the weekend?"

"No one here but the dust mites after 5:30 on Fridays, Riss. But I'll have you good to go by Tuesday, for sure." Marissa did her best to keep her voice sweet and ignore the fact that she was digging her nails into her left palm.

"Can't you bring some of the materials home, Daddy?"

"Aww," he said, sounding like the disappointed child now. "I was going to work on my calendar this weekend." It was his pet project, the process of creating a new way of sectioning off a "year" with thirteen months, all of them bearing new names combining the Catholic and Judaic hallmarks and somehow eliminating the need for daylight-saving time. Marissa had read this one in him many times, forcing herself not to tell him that some of the equations were numerical paradoxes that were no more than roundabouts. But he liked working the numbers, an illusion of forward movement and a harmless one.

"Please, Daddy?" she said, trying to keep her voice steady so she could play it this way believably. "Pack up a kit and bring it all back to the house. We'll set it up in the den, play oldies on the record player the way you like with all the crackles and pops. I'll be your helper."

"Hmm. Really?"

"I'll make chocolate chip cookies with macadamia nuts."

"Now you're talking! Wait."

"What?"

"Shouldn't you be in school? Don't you have reports? I thought you were going to be buried in the library this weekend."

She swallowed dryly. All of a sudden words like "buried" sounded prophetic. She smiled brightly.

"I'm home for a little while, Daddy. At least the weekend. It's Halloween, and the apartment is so . . . empty."

That gave him pause. He cleared his throat and said cautiously,

"Don't you have classes tomorrow?"

"It's the day after all of today's staff in-services, and considering it's sort of a holiday anyway they sent around a message on Campus Cruiser that we had off through Friday," she lied. Tomorrow was actually a bear of a day, with three of her professors collecting major assignments. She had a lab in Chem 105, three journal responses for Psych 105, and the rough draft of the analysis paper for Comp 101 that she'd never gotten around to bringing to the Writing Center for polish. But there was no way in hell that she was going to go back to Chester right now, to a college campus filled with unfamiliar streets and walkways, construction detours, empty classrooms, hallways. Too many people, too many places for a serial killer to blend in as a maintenance worker, a teacher, a student, or security. And her apartment? Forget it, there were just too many places for a killer to hide. There were parking areas with poor lighting at night, basement laundry and storage, a creepy spread of forest out back behind the Goodwill bins, no thank you!

"It's a deal," her father said. "I'll bring home a package, some tools for the close work, and a pair of goggles or two. We'll get silly with it."

Marissa let her breath out, and it was only then that she realized she had been holding it. Her father was just so out of touch with things that it was almost charming, and she nearly burst into tears thinking that if she turned up missing she might never again hear him doing his best to totally botch the concept of "cool," not only by messing up a phrase like "Let's get jiggy with it," but remaining absolutely unaware that it was long out of style.

"Deal," she said. She closed the connection, tossed the phone in her carry bag, and then took a real look around, trying for a level of intelligent, critical study and gaining little more than a series of glances that darted all over the place from behind her sunglasses. It was nice to have decided to stay at home for a short while where she was familiar with all the dark corners, but she still had to get there.

Everyone around her suddenly looked like a criminal.

Two guys in dirty blue jeans and reflective vests on break from some road crew, criminals. A guy with wavy hair and a goatee wearing a gray pea coat and carrying a guitar case, maniac. A thin bow-legged guy in black spandex pushing one of those baby strollers that you jogged behind, monster! Did that overweight dude with the grizzly sideburns just stare at her rack? Did the suit with the newspaper under his arm just glance back at her bum as he passed? Was the greasy-haired guy in the Eagles jersey giving her the north to south, the dirty old man with the jowls and brown derby hat looking at her sideways?

It was as if the lack of the ability to get a clear psychic read on a given male's libido magnified the possibilities, and her imagination was running wild especially since she had long decided that this was a killer with a sexual agenda. Marissa was also alarmed that in the sweep she'd just made, she had only noticed the men. It wasn't just that her patchwork was down, but her selective perception had heightened to the point that she was blocking and blanking the puzzle pieces that might distract her. She didn't like this. She had to be aware of everyone and everything, and who said the killer wasn't a woman? She had gotten a read that the black cloud was virginal, and she remembered sensing all-male-all-the-way, especially considering her orgasm, but when she thought about it her bodily reaction had been a result of the absolute purity of the passing evil, not its gender.

Wouldn't that be a kick? A female killer, playing on the camaraderie shared by most chicks almost like second nature, draping fabric across their chests in the clothing store, swaying and saying, *"Isn't this cute?"* to relative strangers, going to the bathroom together, exchanging bottles of lotion, talking about men. The "fiendette" would already be "in the club" so to speak, and the luring wouldn't seem so unnatural if a bait and trap was the play to begin with.

And that was the trouble. Marissa had become a token in a game filled with shadows and fog, where you didn't know the rules and you couldn't get a good read on the borders. Oh, and don't forget that there was also a clock. Ticking. She was next.

She walked over to the Victoria's Secret store, thinking that all this was eerily similar to that old classic movie she'd caught on TCN a month or so ago when she'd been channel-surfing late at night, bored, unable to sleep. There was a blind woman who didn't know that there were drugs hidden in a doll in her apartment, and criminals who came looking for the goods. Then she pulled the switch so all the lights would be off and they'd be even-Steven. *Wait Until Dark,* that was it. Only in that story it was the bad guys who got the lights shut off on them, just the way Marissa's patchwork had blacked out. And they were the unfortunate losers in the end.

That word made her think of poor Jerome, and she scolded herself for associating him with such a label. He was beautiful and she had somehow dressed him in the wrong robes, near miss, one wrong turn somewhere, that was all. She raised her chin and switched her bag to the other shoulder. What irony. She needed Jerome, needed him badly, and she couldn't call him especially to discuss the idea that the very patchwork that had failed him was now failing her. It was a guaranteed disaster, putting him in a corner and asking him to connect with the very thing he was not equipped to deal with. She tried to envision any possible conversation they could make of this, but came up with a big blank. Might as well send him a T-shirt with a big "L" on it.

She crossed through the arch of the popular lingerie store and marveled at the decor. It looked like a circus, all polka-dots and bright pastels on the walls and a similar theme piled in the bra and undie carousel bins. She was expecting all blacks, silvers, and frills; but, besides the larger-than-life wall decals of the famous models everyone knew from the television ads, this looked more like Chuck E. Cheese's or any of those places that decked everything out in bright colors to make you move on faster, fast food psychology, she'd read that somewhere.

She picked up the first item available on a sale rack that had a sign claiming "Very Sexy Lace-Trim Cheeky Panties." Wow. She usually bought underwear at Macy's or Kohl's almost as an afterthought. She turned the garment over in her hands. They were her size all right, with black and white tiger stripes and red edging. All she needed now was a Catwoman eye mask and a black studded whip and she'd have the perfect costume for answering the door on Halloween, bringing the dads up to the porch from the sidewalk for a better look-see and sending the kids running the other way screaming. Aesthetic as well as functional! She brought her forearm up to her mouth to choke back a run of the giggles, and her stomach was starting to hurt quivering with it, and she turned to go and pay for her precious booty, and oh God, not that pun, not now, and then she stopped laughing.

There by a bra display was a young woman squatting down like a baseball catcher to get to the sale items that were stored under the bottommost tier. Her gray stretch pants were pulled to a low arc, and her shirt had risen up exposing more than the curve of her waist and bare back. She had no underwear showing because like Marissa she wasn't wearing any, and you could see the tip of her crack just above the band of her pants, a full-on view of the skin darkening inside the sweet indentation, and you didn't have to be a lesbian to understand that the display was far sexier than the polka-dots and wall decals. Girlfriend had long black hair that caught the overhead lights in shimmers and boasted that manicured inward curl down at the bottom edge.

Marissa took a quick glance all around and was alarmed to see that there were three men looking at this girl, one with a backpack and a Yankees cap standing by the ankle sock rack, a forty-something in dress clothes staring at her sideways and pretending to read a tag with small print, and a curly-haired, unshaven dude who'd just stomped up right beside her. He was wearing a faded leather jacket with a turned-up collar, loose jeans, and black hiking boots, making no attempt at subtlety, studying her up close, staring hard at her skin, the contours, the tender ridges, her pores and dimples, her goosebumps and freckles, making a masturbation video in his head that he would probably be so caught up with that he'd have to take care of it the minute he got his car back on 476 where no one could see what he was doing from the waist down.

Marissa walked in to the right so she could pay and make an exit. Guys looked, she knew that. She usually thrived on it, thought it was cute and harmless. But why were these men in a women's underwear store to begin with? Were there no safe zones where a girl could get a freaking break? Oh, right. The girl's room, where they put up wet floor signs and peeked under the stall doors.

That settled it. No tanning booths ever again, no dressing rooms, no gym locker rooms or swim clubs or water parks. Trust no one. Guys were pigs.

She approached the register, and a young black woman with a hard, pretty face and blond tints in her hair fingered the underwear all brusque and professional and turned the tag up toward the light. Someone tall behind Marissa in line was casting a shadow across them both, and for a second she thought the cashier was going to tell her that she wasn't a good fit for this particular brand of cheeky panties, maybe try to sell her up to a different style or tell her that there was a minimum purchase rule for a Discover card.

The clerk was just looking for the barcode.

Behind Marissa, the shadow moved slightly and she got a sudden chill. The person behind her wasn't just tall; gigantic was a better word for it, and he was standing close to her now, too close, a total invasion of personal space almost like someone going nose to nose with you in the elevator when everyone knew you were supposed to look up at the floor numbers changing.

The store had to have cameras! He'd played his hand too early! She spun around and made to I.D. him, claim harassment, have him questioned. Then she could hint that he had been stalking her, giving the mall cops every reason to go directly to the local police or the staties, and then straight to the Special Victims Unit detectives for this jurisdiction, right up the pipeline. They'd get a warrant and find his basement torture chamber, or attic shrine with pictures he took on his cell phone of his victims, or the back yard vegetable garden masking the area behind it where the dirt had been so recently turned and mounded into a series of shallow graves.

It was a woman wearing jeans with holes in the knees, cowboy boots, and a motorcycle jacket. She was six feet at least and seemed even taller because she had her long curly hair put up in one of those cornhusks you did with a rubber band when you were in a hurry. She had long slanting cheeks and clever eyes. She was chewing gum and was holding a toddler on her hip, he who had his finger hooked in his mouth and one of the straps of his OshKosh overalls unsnapped and dangling.

"You've got a big piece of lint in your hair, sweetie," she said. "Spin around, I'll get it."

Marissa did so robotically, felt her hair move, turned back. The woman was holding it between her thumb and forefinger as if for proof.

"Thanks," Marissa said.

The woman flicked it away and laughed. Sounded hoarse and neighborly.

"I do it all the time, honey. Just ain't shy about the little things, that's all. Lucky you didn't have a piece of broccoli in your teeth or I'd have had my fingers in your mouth."

"Your card?" the cashier said.

"Oh," Marissa said. She pivoted on her heel and got it out, trying to complete this exchange and get out as quickly as possible. This wasn't her serial killer, and she didn't have to have patchwork to know this. She was drained suddenly, exhausted, and she just wanted to go home.

Back in the hall, she went to tunnel vision, moving straight ahead, no scrutiny, no looking at the people passing her and possibly looking back. A to B. One foot in front of the other. When she got out through the Court door she walked straight through the crosswalk without even looking both ways, just depending on her peripheral vision, and it took everything she had to avoid Bloomingdale's looming behind her left shoulder and the fact that she loved browsing through that place, checking out the new electronics, the latest styles in handbags and footwear, the sparkling jewelry counter where the assistants had an air about them as if they were ready to serve royalty.

Back to the parking area.

The low concrete overhang had a stop sign on the facing. She hadn't noticed that before. Another prophetic indicator and she ignored it, walked under it, and moved toward section 2H, ready to take off her heels and drive the hell out of this place.

There was a car in the space next to hers, facing away with the engine running. It was an economy car, and she couldn't tell the make or model because it had electrical tape pressed over the insignia. There was a dent knocked into the left corner of the bumper, water spots on the back windshield, and fluid dripping out of the tailpipe. Exhaust threaded up toward the ceiling, and she could see a dark form hunched at the wheel.

The tires screeched away, making her jump. The peeling rubber kicked up putrid white smoke, and the back end of the vehicle skidded back and forth fighting for a straight line in its rapid burst off through the otherwise barren section of the lot. It left ugly blackened tracks on the concrete, and Marissa instinctively screamed into the echo and stink with a good ole all-American,

"Fucking asshole!"

In response, he screeched his tires again, braking, swerving his car into a half-turn and a rapid halt. It settled next to one of the support pylons about two hundred feet away, facing Marissa three-quarters front. He hit on his brights, and now Marissa's all-American retort was the standard,

"What the fuck . . ."

He revved his engine like a race car driver showing off the horses he had straining against their bridles under the hood, and it made Marissa think of Jerome and whether or not he would miss her too much. She couldn't believe it was going down this way, for real, right here and right now, and she tried her best to do what she had to do with a rational adult's control.

She fumbled out her keys and hit the "unlock" button on the pad. Her tail lights flashed as she knew the headlights had up front, and as she approached her vehicle the guy on the other side of the lot jerked forward, then halted, forward again, then dead stop, taunting. Next he trumpeted a one-two-three-four on the gas, kicking up a belches of exhaust so thick the clouds actually crept up over the roof and feathered down past the headlights.

Marissa opened her door, but it was heavy and she had her keys in her hand, the other occupied with her bag and her purchase. With three fingers she pulled, thinking that she could have put the keys up on the black canvas ragtop or at least clamped them in her mouth, but when you were rushing you were stuck with what you did the moment before, and while she did manage to get it all open the handle snapped out of her grip at the last moment and she dropped her keys on the pavement.

She threw in her stuff, turned, and sat sidesaddle, reaching down to her feet to remove those high heels. The left one had a funky strap that always stuck, and she had to baby it. There was a screeching across the lot, fury on the pavement, and she took a second to look over the opened door and let out a whimper. He was coming, headlights bearing down, back end swaying with it, a hundred feet or so and closing.

Marissa got her shoes off and threw them over her shoulder into the car. Her keys were still on the pavement just out of reach, and she wasted a second trying to hold her position with her fanny on the side of the seat, stretching.

"Christ!" she said, pushing off, grabbing the small bundle, peeking one more time above the edge of the door. The approaching vehicle was almost upon her, and she hauled herself in. She barely had the wingspan to reach back out for the door, but with a painful stretch and dangerous lean she grabbed the void in the hard molded plastic and yanked it all shut.

The car screamed past her, inches from the closed door. Marissa brought up her hands and shook them by her face, screaming back to no one. In her sideview mirror, she saw him swerve and almost hit the side wall of the ramp. There was a stop, another screech of tires, more fishtailing, and he came back around her, across her bow then flat alongside her, driver's door to driver's door, inches away.

Marissa hadn't even put her key in the ignition. She'd been too shocked, too slow. His window was tinted, and she figured she had nowhere to run now because he'd blocked her ability to open her door. She was trapped, and while a small voice inside her was saying in a smooth and slow voice, *"Just turn on the car and drive forward,"* it seemed she was sunk down in tar, unable to move, breathe, blink: she just stared at the dark window to her immediate left.

It started to lower. Then all coy and gross he moved down along with it, making it so for a long moment he was just a pair of laughing eyes over the edge.

Finally the Plexiglas disappeared into the rubber rim and he was smiling at her, all chin-zits and crooked teeth, and she knew him, Harvey Glick, this weird guy she'd met in her classes at Widener who must have coincidentally been here at the right place and the right time and spotted her car. He almost always wore this maroon American Eagle hoodie and dirty silk gym shorts regardless of the season, and was the type that came from the suburbs and felt entitled, the type that had his hair mapped sideways across his forehead and made a living ranking on people, total douchebag. She breathed a sigh of relief, but it was tinged a bright angry red. He had been partnered with her back in the first week of classes when they had to do a think-pair-share concerning the film *Crash* and what it said to them as freshman about racism and cultural sensitivity. Since the paper had to be co-authored over a weekend she had had to forfeit her cell number, and he'd texted her back right there in room 118, saying, *"Send me a picture of your tits."* Now *this* was a loser!

Of course, she had long since read his patchwork that day and was therefore currently enlightened to the fact that he was no serial killer, wrong virgin, ha. She knew that he lived in the dorms above the ROTC building in Hanna Hall, that he drove his roommate insane by leaving soda cans all over the place and farting in his sleep all night, that he came from Freehold, New Jersey, and that he'd been in love with Caroline Jordan back in eighth grade when he was nicer. Eventually the girl had told him to pound sand, sending them off in different directions in terms of their life journeys.

He stopped laughing for a second, made a V with his index and middle fingers, and did that rapid flickering of his tongue in between. Marissa lowered her window.

"You are disgusting," she said.

"Made ya wet, huh?"

"Ted Wiess is the one who ruined you."

His face withered. Now it was Marissa turning the engine over and screeching her tires, though hers made a short, lady-like burst that was easy to control back out toward the ramp. She knew from past patchwork that as a young boy, Harvey had been into robotics and comics, the polite, quiet, and self-absorbed kid who lived in the corner house on Juniper and Vine. He'd met Caroline Jordan in science class and they hooked up, kissed, held hands, told each other everything. Then this kid Ted Wiess moved in next door, with his skateboards and his weed, and Harvey was over there constantly, making mischief, getting high.

Ted convinced him to call Caroline and play her, making it seem that he didn't care all that much. Her response had been, "Ted Wiess ruined you."

Of course, Caroline Jordan bloomed into a vibrant young woman, student council, yearbook, tennis team, and she was in the running for homecoming queen her senior year. Harvey wound up at Widener trying to sneak by with a liberal arts major they didn't really specialize in, and from the looks of things he wasn't aiming to commit to any kind of study that would allow him to stay very long.

Marissa drove up the ramp and back toward 476, stewing. It wasn't like her to use the patchwork against someone, even if he was an absolute tool. Cruising down the highway she looked in her rearview a number of times, but the scrutiny followed no logical cycle. Behind her were cars, lots of cars, and she had no idea whether one or the other had been in tow for more than a normal duration.

She wasn't good at this. In fact, she was horrible.

Enough. She was alive and well in the here and now, and she was going to stay that way.

When she got off at the Broomall exit she didn't make a left toward her house on New Ardmore Avenue. She made a right and cut back up Lawrence Road. He wanted to tail her? Fine.

She was going straight to the police station.

RUBBER MAN

Yeah, asshole. I'm guessing her little trip to the cops didn't help her much considering the endgame we're all so familiar with by now. Of course, I have no fucking idea where I was back at the point she pulled into the police parking area because she's making me relive it her way, but I can sure tell you what my "20" was just now at the mall considering it's "in the past" and all. I was the "pebble" ticking along the concrete by the stairwells. See, after first spotting her on Dekalb Pike I turned around double-quick and followed from a safe distance, parking two lots over when she went down to the lower level. That red Mustang stuck out like a junkyard rat on a wedding cake, and it wasn't difficult to find it after I made my way down one stairwell and walked the far edge of the lot to hide behind another. And it wasn't a pebble. It was a Pez candy. I love those fucking things, and they don't taste the same if you don't suck them out of the plastic dispenser. Problem is, I like to bite the whole thing, work it with my teeth like a cigar, and I'd damaged the orifice. I like that word. Orifice. So one of them fell out while I was gnawing at it, and I saw her look over. It spooked her and it was perfect. I've always been lucky with the timing all through the process, and this was no exception.

Oh, I know what you're thinking, asshole. Why is a clicking piece of Pez on the cement so special when I probably eat them all the time, dropping them out through the damaged orifices, making the girls look? Thing is, I don't eat Pez all the time. Like I told you before, the only ritual I have is munching on my El Sabroso Hot and Spicy Pork Rinds after the cutting and detail phase out on location right before the digging portion, so fuck you and your mother trying to peg me and my hunting style.

See, each girl is different, with her own special mannerisms and trepidations. You like that word? Not as good as "orifice," I admit, but I ain't particular when it comes to finding the terms I need to express myself. And I don't stalk each girl the same, because she has to be a part of the process. She has to suspect something but still expose that personal secret path for me to follow her down like a shadow. Every path is different, and when I jump it's as new for them as it is for me.

I got Becky Lockhart by the abandoned Copenhagen shack right down the street from her house. She went there to catch a smoke in secret every night at around 11:00 once her grandma fell asleep in front of the television with the Afghan blanket draped over her knees and her knitting in her lap. I hid under the rusted blade hood of an abandoned king-sized rotary rake for hay, down where she must have figured only the snakes and the rats kept company with each other. Sarah-Jean Kennedy took pre-dawn jogs, and really burned it up a steep dirt road that forked off Virginia Avenue and led to the park. Three-quarters up the hill they were doing tree surgery to make way for the power lines, and I waited for her in the funnel chute of their biggest Asplundh tree shredder. Veronica Kimbel was a secret purger with a lot of close friends and family, so she was extra careful to blow her cookies only in the Sunoco gas station, the one that was going out of business on the way home from the office on Maple Street, that ramshackle joint with the trash bags fluttering on the pump handles and the bathroom unlocked and isolated at the rear of the building. I hid in the dumpster behind the corroded water tank, walked in quiet as a churchmouse, and had a big surprise for her there in stall number two.

And don't try to time me. Sometimes the jump 'n' snatch takes a week, other times a day. Depends on her. Depends on the portrait she paints, the places she goes to do things in secret.

I like sharing secrets.

Fun, ain't it?

Asshole . . .

CHAPTER TEN

Marissa Madison did not alert the police. She couldn't. She just sat there in the parking lot weighing things, looking for an out, some loophole, any way to bend or twist this thing so she wouldn't be the target.

But there was nothing here but the doomsday option. She had no evidence, no description, and blowing the whistle at this point was a poor strategy on a number of fronts, more than she had originally considered in the mall parking area. If they put a tail on her, set up a van outside her house and then nothing happened, they'd pack it in after the weekend, telling her to call if anyone actually made contact. If the killer really wanted her and had patience, he'd make contact all right, and even if the Broomall police stood willing to offer protection past the weekend she had to go back to school sometime. She had classes and an apartment her parents were paying for, and even if they could be convinced she had changed her mind and stood in favor of commuting at this point, they would insist she stick it out the semester to get the deposit back. Be logical!

What's more, Marissa wasn't excited about her hypothetical protective surveillance passing hands from a small suburban precinct with officers who probably graduated from her high school and ordered from the same pizza shop to that of Chester, a wide urban area similar to Philadelphia where the only way to cut through the red tape and get a squad car into the vicinity was to report a murder or rape, and even then the response-time was a crapshoot.

Marissa stared out the windshield and shivered. She was parked next to a fleet of white police cruisers, proud steeds with their roof flashers and the slanted blue decals with the yellow bordering, all useless to her. And the evil wasn't just "out there," but he was somewhere close, right now, circling the block or parked across Springfield Road on one of the side streets, or maybe sitting right here in this lot pretending to read the newspaper, waiting for the splash of red from her Mustang to move in his rearview.

The phone rang, and Marissa jerked in her seat, her hand going up to her chest. She hit the button a bit too hard.

"Yes?"

"That's no way to talk to your mother."

Marissa rested her hands on the wheel and rolled her eyes.

"I had the volume up too loud again."

"Scare ya?"

"Hmm."

"You sound like your father now. Quit your mumbling and stop by the Giant on your way. We need candy for the kiddies."

"Whoppers?"

"I'm off them. The hard malt gives me heartburn. Get M & M's and Snickers."

"Mother, I hate peanuts!" She looked out the window and saw an officer exiting his vehicle and adjusting the brim of one of those black western-style Stetsons. John Law. The town sheriff. Mr. Man, so close and yet so far. "And I thought the candy was for the kiddies, anyway."

"Says who?"

They laughed together, and Marissa thought of all the mother-daughter relationships this monster was severing forever. The real issue here wasn't whether or not the Chester police would make lousy watchdogs, or even the idea that the Broomall cops might babysit her for longer than she was giving them credit for. The real point was, as she had hit on before in this awful mental roundabout, that if she alerted the brass to save her own skin the killer could simply move on. Then there would be another pretty young maid joining the row of corpses, and then another and another, each ripped from her mother, torn from her family and friends, immortalized in a creepy black-and-white news photo that shared the hollow, grainy quality of its replicas plastered on telephone poles and the back sides of milk cartons.

Every victim would stare back at her with those dead smiling eyes.

Monster victorious.

And Marissa would have been his accomplice. She put the car in drive and pulled out of the parking area, making a left across the double yellow line, wondering whether or not the cops policed their own lot and would give her a ticket. She didn't believe in omens, but if an officer pulled her over right now she knew she would give in to weakness, confess everything, put this nightmare in some other girl's hip pocket and live the rest of her life in a state of rationalization and unsuccessful dissociation. The sun was brilliant, and she pulled down the visor.

Of course, she wouldn't get pulled over. Of course, it seemed that every car around her had a killer in it.

Up past Latches Lane she signaled left at the light and saw something across the fork at West Chester Pike that made her breath catch in her throat.

It was an omen, whether you believed in them or not. There in front of the Pacifico Ford's service center was one of those inflatable monster dancing balloons that they pumped with bursts of intermittent air, making it pop and snap up and down, waving wildly at the sky. When did that go up? It was one of Marissa's phobias, one she'd had since she was in elementary school, one she couldn't explain in a million years, but the rubberized fly-guys freaked her out something fierce. She knew a girl named Gloria Minor who couldn't see a picture of Chucky from that old horror movie, *Child's Play,* without bursting into tears even in high school, and there were at least five kids she knew who couldn't handle clowns. For her, it was the wide smiling pencil geeks with the crazy streamer hair and empty white eyes, the flapping arms and spasmodic horror they threw at the sky.

And why here? These were usually city things, fodder for the flashy Northeast or down in Center City where even cheap advertising was good advertising, catcalling you as you drove by like, *"Made you look."* This one was brilliant yellow with a wide, toothy, apple-slice grin. It slowly did its crumple and bow toward the earth and then shot upright, making Marissa seasick and dizzy. Someone behind her beeped, not a polite tap-tap, but a long, harsh blare. She was nearly paralyzed, it seemed. Her arms felt like rubber, like those of the fly-guy, and she made her turn down the ramp without hitting the guardrail and parked without clipping anyone's bumper. Barely. The whole procedure was suddenly awkward and foreign, and her breath was hitching when she put it in park. She raised her knuckles to her mouth and hoped she wasn't developing the hiccups, because she was the type to retain them for what seemed like hours and they made her chest hurt like hell.

She looked all around and didn't see much. She loved her car, but the sightlines were horrendous with huge blind spots back left and right, and the teeny-tiny rear windshield. It was all slants and flashes unless you were looking straight ahead, like one of those vehicles that depended on its mirrors and those annoying warning beeps when it backed up. There was no panorama unless the top was down, and it was too breezy for that today, not as if she was worried about messing up her hair or even getting a stiff dose of freezer face, but it would look suspicious, as though she knew someone was on her tail.

She pushed out feeling exposed, but it had become important to her that she look natural. If this killer was as skilled as she thought he might be (still calling it a "he," she couldn't help this), even a slight giveaway in mannerism might make him disappear and start over with another girl. At the edges of the patchwork that she'd gotten from him when their cars passed back at the mall entrance, she thought there were hints that he was a gamer, wanting his victims to move forward with a dread they couldn't quite define even to themselves. But hearing a bump in the night or a creak in the dark was different from knowing you were being followed in broad daylight. And a guy like this wouldn't need something as obvious as a surveillance cruiser to know that you knew.

She closed the door and locked. Shit. What if her pulling into the police station just now stood as enough of a warning to him to keep driving? Had she blown this already, let him off the hook?

Marissa burst out laughing, and tears simultaneously squeezed out of the corners of her eyes. Of course she hadn't given herself away. Harvey Glick had just scared the shit out of her burning rubber by the Section 2H support column, and after considering it and stewing over it on the way home, she'd decided to report it to the hometown police where it felt familiar. She'd sat in the lot and reconsidered, as the killer would figure girls were famous for, and decided the sad sack wasn't worth her time.

She took a cart someone had left between two cars and walked it back to the canopy-station where it was meant to go. She wasn't laughing anymore. This had a more than ominous feel to it, like old dusty writings in sacred books hidden in buried vaults, like fate. Even when she made a mistake it was the "right move," bringing her closer and closer to this terrifying conflict she was supposedly destined to win. But no matter how much proof she had of the moment by moment, it was increasingly difficult to put trust in the big climax. Was she supposed to beat this guy, really? How on earth? She was no fighter and weapons frightened her, not as if she had any in the house to begin with, except for the kitchenware. She tried to picture herself holding the biggest carving knife out in front of her with both hands, or maybe the big curved meat fork, shaking hair out of her face, telling him, *"Come on with it!"*—and the image was pathetic, hysterical. She wasn't about to go stabbing anyone, so the patchwork promise itself seemed antiquated at this point, whispers and dreams that maybe she'd read wrong. And again, considering Jerome's failure she couldn't be sure of anything anymore. She'd been conditioned not to trust herself, and that was this scenario's most bitter symptom.

Inside, the Giant was packed and the candy aisle was basically trashed. Nothing much left but Tootsie Roll lollipops, Butterfingers, and those awful sugared fruit rings that looked as if they'd been lying around since the Great Depression. After two sweeps, Marissa settled for two bags of "fingers" and a jumbo pack of Nerds that had dents in three of the mini-boxes. So what if the kids frowned? So what if the Madison household ran out by 7:00 and had the living room lights out soon after? Marissa wasn't excited about answering the door after dark anyway, and she'd just fake cramps if Mother questioned her lack of enthusiasm.

She opted for the quick self-checkout line and was miffed when someone crept up behind while she was swiping. Marissa looked over her shoulder like, *"What?"* and an older woman wearing a bandana on her head met her glare with a look of sour impatience.

"Back up." Marissa said. "Now."

The woman's eyes widened and she backed up. A foot. Marissa finished and stuffed her receipt in her bag, trying not to shake. This wasn't like her and she was ashamed of herself. And it made her no more confident in her ability to use a carving knife on a serial killer jumping out at her from the darkness. It only proved that she was rude to elderly ladies at the supermarket. A proud moment, to be sure.

Marissa made it back to the beautiful home she'd grown up in without incident, without any trace of a stalker, but when she pulled into the driveway she noticed the mailbox and the "MADISON" in block lettering stamped across it. Might as well have been flared up in neon . . .

She parked up by the garage to leave room for her father and sat there for a second with her hands high on the wheel, getting her shit together. The exposed surname didn't mean anything. Information was exposed all over the Web nowadays anyway, and he wasn't stealing identities here. Keep it relevant.

She took a second to breathe and then adjusted her sunglasses delicately. OK. OK.

When she strode up the walk there was a loud, maniacal laugh, and she started, almost tripping on her high heels and turning an ankle. Then a wry smile. Mother had set up the first Halloween decorations and gimmicks, and one of them was the sensor that let out the ghost giggle. Soon the lawn would be laden with the spiderweb fluff along the grass and the border bushes, and at the corners of the garden would lie the feet, hands, and face of the "buried man." The small rubber skeleton they called "Pablo" would be dangling from the porch overhang, and by the door they'd finally set up the rocking chair with the bigger skeleton wearing the housedress, the one with the wig and the grinning skull face they had all nicknamed "Phyllis," because if you looked at it right it resembled their elderly neighbor who lived across the street.

"Mother, I'm home!" Marissa called out as she pushed through the door, her dog Rusty doing his Marissa-Welcome, the march up to her and the playful backtrack, feather-duster tail wagging so hard it moved his entire back end. She put her stuff on the sofa and picked him up. Love. That was what he was all about. Lousy watchdog, excellent bedwarmer.

"I'm in here!" her mother called from the laundry room behind the kitchen.

Marissa carried Rusty with her, whispering sweet nothings into his floppy ears, kissing him. She sat at the kitchen table, which was littered with an assortment of old photographs, three types of glue, scissors, tape, crepe and construction paper. Mother was getting into scrapbooking. Marissa waited there for her to finish switching over the clothes, and when she heard the dryer door shut, she worked up a smile.

Besides admitting that she'd lost her patchwork and that she'd only bought underwear, she told her mother absolutely nothing.

TRICK OR TREAT

That's right, asshole. That was me who beeped when she held up traffic there at the light by Latches Lane. I was right behind her bumper to bumper, and I risked everything, though it's doubtful she would have remembered me even if she had bothered glancing back. I had to play the role; she gave me no choice. And by the way, the sightlines were just fine, at least from my perspective looking in through that narrow back windshield. What I'm saying is, I saw what scared her.

And it changed things.

Strange, I had never thought of working it quite this way, putting things out of order of priority, doing stuff backwards.

Too much of a riddle for ya? Well, that's just an awful shame. I know who you're rooting for, and I also know that I'm breaking another sacred bullshit literary rule by telling you some things and masking others I'm aware of at this point. I'm playing smokeshifter like the drunk Injun telling the story poorly at the pow-wow, embarrassing the hell out of his relatives and lessening the credibility of the otherwise "wonderful and ornate Native

American oral tradition." Well, I got news for you, it's the same thing Marissa Madison is doing to me in that she's only letting me see the advance of the moment by moment with no memory of the outcome . . . so take it and like it, 'cause shit rolls downhill.

And whoever said I played fair? You made your choice and shaped your favor a long time ago, so I have no problem telling you to go and sit on Marissa Madison's shoulder and try to guess how and when I'm going to work my magic.

A hint? OK, fuck ya.

When I saw her looking at the dancing rubber dude, I knew I didn't need to study much of her coming routine anymore. It was a new game because I'd been shown her heart and soul, her demons and painted savages.

I knew right then and there how I was gonna kill her, or at least the exclamation point.

It was just a question of the timing, the tools, and some luck with the landscape.

CHAPTER ELEVEN

Daddy got home at 5:30, and he seemed more than disappointed about dinner. It was Halloween, so he'd expected Peking duck from the Thai place or at least some takeout calzone, not Mother's vegetable lasagna. In protest, he picked at his food like a child and Mother finally caved, heating up some onion rings and Friday's Sliders she had in the freezer.

Earlier, she and Marissa had set up the Halloween decorations out front, and the discussion had quickly gone from the usual surface banter to more current issues. And it wasn't difficult to notice that the mechanics of conversation had become difficult, the rhythm, the flow. Mother was so used to her daughter reading flashes in her mind that they often answered each other's questions before they surfaced. Now that Marissa's patchwork was on the fritz, it seemed they had to learn to talk to each other all over again, and of course Mother didn't tread in safe waters even when the airwaves above them were filled with pauses and static. She went for what she knew, and that usually meant college, the apartment, or Jerome.

"Why are you off again tomorrow?" she said. She was affixing the cotton ghost webbing to the porch roof over on the far right side by the big evergreen bushes they had planted last year to block the view of the Tuckers' property and the carport where they stowed any number of things that belonged in the junkyard: a cast-iron stove, some rusted bicycles, a toilet, old bookcases. Marissa went over to kneel down and hold Mother's stepstool in place.

"The holiday," she said.

"How generous! Did you call the Writing Center to see if there were any cancelations?"

When Marissa didn't respond, her mother looked down at her, almost startled.

"Uhh . . ." Marissa said. "I suppose I could have, but they said they were booked solid the first time I called. Here." She handed up a roll of spare tape, and her mother bent to receive it.

"You should call again," she said. "Squeaky wheel, right?"

"Right. I'll, uh, give them a try to see if they have Saturday hours."

"What's wrong, honey?" Her mother had stopped what she was doing and was looking down at her with concern. "I meant that you could call again for tomorrow, for Friday. I figured they wouldn't shut down the whole campus, and maybe you'd get lucky." She stepped down off the stool, Marissa taking her hand like a servant helping a lady from a coach; and in turn, her mother slipped her arm around her, bringing her in for a spontaneous embrace. She was tall like Daddy, and Marissa hadn't buried her cheek in the nook just above her mother's hip in years. She felt her hair being smoothed, and her mother's tone had gone soft.

"You told me last week they weren't open on the weekends, hon. Did you forget?"

"Yes," Marissa answered. *God,* lying was so much more difficult when she couldn't see the questions coming! She pushed gently away, walked a few steps, and folded her arms. "I'm just off-kilter because of my short-out, that's all. Seems like everything's covered in cotton and clouds." She pointed. "Like that fake spiderwebbing." Mother turned and looked at her handiwork. The fluffy see-through gauze stretched all the way across the east side of the porch, making the near area seem partially enclosed.

"I like it," Mother said. "Makes everything look dreamlike."

"Creepy," Marissa added.

"What's wrong, honey?"

"I told you—"

"I meant besides the hocus-pocus, which we all love you just fine without, by the way." She went over to the porch swing where she had stowed all the other paraphernalia and picked up a roll of black streamers so she could take a scissors and strip the edges into frays. They would go across most of the front overhang. She called them wind snakes. "It doesn't have anything to do with a certain handsome young man, does it? Black and beautiful?"

"Mother!"

"Just saying . . ."

"Well, don't. I'm over him and talking about him is like picking at the dead." She despised the image she'd just created, but it had its effect. Mother pursed her lips and got busy stripping streamers. Marissa moved the stool over to the position just to the right of where the steps came up from the walkway and stood ready with the Scotch tape. Across the street, old Phyllis was having a smoke, looking over. She was wearing brown paisley slacks and an apron. She had one arm flat across in order to hold the elbow of the cigarette hand, and her wrist was cocked at up her head, off-angle. She bent it back over for a drag, a deep one that drew her cheeks in. Behind Marissa was the skeleton in the housedress, and she wondered if Phyllis was standing there looking at it and having a dawning realization.

"I don't want to be a nurse," Marissa said. It came from nowhere, and she wished it had stayed buried. This was not porch conversation. This was a rebuilding proposal that required set-up and staging, scripted moments, planned rebuttals. And she had thought none of this through even in terms of her own wants and needs; in fact, she didn't know if she herself supported such an unyielding position in the end. It had just popped out. From the gut.

Mother stopped what she was doing and walked over to the porch swing. She cleared it of the construction paper and glue tubes and waved Marissa over. They sat, mother and daughter, the former with her arm around her baby. Even at age nineteen, Marissa's feet didn't reach the wooden slats of the porch floor, and her toes pigeoned in. Her hands were pressed together between her knees and she felt suddenly exhausted.

"It's just . . ."

"What, sweetie?"

"I'm tired of being sad all the time."

"Hmm."

Marissa glanced up and met her mother's eyes, which had gotten slanted and sharp. Battle guise. When Marissa was younger she secretly called this Mother's "hawk face." For comfort go to Daddy. The problem was that he was all fluff and rah-rah, falling short on answers and strategies. You wanted to fix things? Mother was the mechanic. It's just that she typically didn't use any sweet oil when she turned the screws.

"There are going to be sad moments, honey. That's life. But for every patient you lose, there will be two that you fill with hope. It's a good living and an honest one. You have a gift, and it wasn't given to you so you could waste it on something flashy or trendy."

"But I'm alone, like all the time."

Mother rubbed her shoulder, changing tactics.

"Sweetheart, you just so happen to be extraordinarily pretty."

"Ma . . ." Marissa singsonged. Mother squeezed her in.

"You feel this?" she said. "It's a big hug because you're an absolute doll. And that's not just 'Mommy-vision': you are universally attractive. It's like the old cliché where the girl who is drop-dead gorgeous is the one sitting at home on Friday nights."

"And throw in the weird psychic flashes."

"Exactly."

"Exactly."

They sat a moment nestled together. Marissa was fairly sure that Mother was going to transition somehow to Jerome, trying to roll him into her clever psychological paradigm that attributed all the negativity and blame to everyone else's insecurity, but she didn't. Too complex. Too many minefields. Instead, as advertised, she put the metaphorical warm and fuzzy touch-up paint back in her toolbox and got out the mallet that she was more used to wielding.

"You have a gift," she said, "and with that comes responsibility. I know you, Marissa, and you aren't one to sit around feeling sorry for yourself. We both know the gift separates you from others, and when people find out you can 'read' them, they run. The thing that's hard to fathom right now is that some won't. Give it time. Your circle of acquaintances is mostly made up of nineteen-year-olds. The maturity one needs to develop in order to 'get you' is going to take awhile. Four or five years, maybe double that until you finally see people coming around."

"So you're saying I should date a thirty-year-old?"

"Yes, when you're thirty." The joke was in her eyes but she was serious too.

Marissa sighed.

"The waiting's hard, Mother."

"But wait you will. And when it comes to your major I'm all ears, but you've got to move quickly. Your father and I have discussed this at length, and you will not, repeat, *not* go undeclared. It's a waste of time and money, and you'll need to commit to something substantial this year." She looked off. "I wish this were a Disney movie and we could tell you to just go exploring and find yourself. But that is not constructive nor realistic. It's a tough old world out there with a shaky economy, and we'll only support a solid scholastic focus."

Marissa was stretching her legs and looking at her toes.

"No philosophy," she said, softly mimicking. "No theater or communications or women's studies." Mother nodded.

"All good electives, for sure."

"Not good for making a living," Marissa finished. They sat for a moment together in silence, and even though the idea of forever sharing the pain of the bedridden seemed even more bleak now that she had voiced her reservations, it was far worse that it was possible she *wouldn't* ever have a chance to experience that particular drudgery, to put up decorations, to sit on this porch swing and get a hard dose of tough love. There were priorities here and she had to get Daddy on board, make him a loyal team player, working all night if that's what it took to get that darned patchwork flooding back into her head.

The problem was that Mother wouldn't want her husband staying up all night and possibly missing work the next day, for it was a sign of weakness and poor character to call out, at least in this household. And Marissa couldn't let on that this was an emergency. Urgent yes, life or death never. Mother would have this place crawling with cops, special investigators, township administrators. Marissa hopped off the porch swing, folded her arms, and looked left down the street toward the rotary cut into New Ardmore Avenue like the ones in New Jersey you always had to fight through on your way down the shore. She had grown so used to driving around this particular one and checking for those soft merges at the perimeter that she didn't really notice anymore the huge border stones at the near edge of the circle, the butterfly bushes and midsized trees that could have been cover for the demon at this very moment.

She turned casually, and next to Phyllis's house was the cyclone fencing and the generators and converters of the Broomall substation, a mini piece of industrialism that stuck out like a sore thumb and had made their property here across New Ardmore a steal. Then far right up the hill on West Chester Pike there was the area where the storefronts had burned down years ago, never repaired or rebuilt, an eyesore the family was long done talking about. There was nothing left up there on the other side of the bluff except a flattened lot now, bordered at the near edge by craggy trees and wild grass. Could he be lurking up there right now, the wolf in the brush all subtle and still? Could he be waiting on the back side of those substation machines in the shadows of Rhonda Avenue? Absolutely, and she had to be subtle herself, make it look as if she wasn't looking. Beg Daddy without begging. Persuade Mother that the father-daughter weekend with an early start-up was a necessity without making it seem like such a dire one. But considering how much in tune Mother was through her own scary sort of intuition and interpersonal sensitivity, convincing the woman to break a personal family ethic for some lukewarm substitute of an excuse would be harder than changing majors.

"I want my Daddy!" Marissa said suddenly. She felt her mother coming from behind, and she countered by walking back toward the house. She put her hands to her face and she was crying for real. The emotions had just welled up for reasons her mother never would have guessed, but that didn't lessen their effectiveness. Marissa knew this and felt horrible about it and played it to the hilt anyway. She spun around, fists to the side, face moist. Mother stopped in her tracks and put her hand to her chest.

"Baby?" she said.

"I want my father!" Marissa spat. "I need for him to work on my trigger-killer and I want to sit with him while he does it. I need for him to stay home with me tomorrow, because I'm lonely and confused and depressed. And you're no help. Positively none!"

That one rang between the rafters for a second or two.

And the dagger left a wound, she could see it in her mother's face. Again, Marissa felt awful about it, but this was war, desperate measures. And Mother was not the only one in this family who knew how to turn a screw.

"I'm shocked," Mother managed.

"You're not built for this," Marissa said. "I want my—"

"Father. Got it." She walked past her daughter, arm swinging in that frail womanly way reserved for retreat. And surrender—at least that was what Marissa was hoping for.

But she *would* surrender. She had to. The patchwork promised (didn't it?) that Marissa would win (she thought), and she wasn't planning to do this without a loaded arsenal.

Suddenly alarmed, she looked back across the street, wondering if the old crow had witnessed the spat she'd just had with her mother. Phyllis was no longer standing there having a smoke, but Marissa saw the living room curtain fall back into place. Nothing was sacred. And worse, it just proved how easy it was to watch, to steal moments, potentially to learn about a mark. We were all conditioned by social design to depend on common trust in neighbors and strangers. We walked around utterly exposed and protected only by the promise of good will, so easy to break if you wanted to fight dirty, play the system, take your chances.

Marissa struggled over a big footlocker stored with extra extension cords and outdoor seating cushions. She wasn't tall enough for Mother's stool to do any good, and she stepped up on the black trunk with scissors in her hands and a roll of black streamers under her arm. She had to strip the ends and put up the rest of the wind snakes. Mother would recover. And it was supposed to look like Halloween around here.

Marissa and her mother were avoiding direct conversation except for the formalities like "excuse me" and "pass the salt," but Daddy's gift (and flaw) was that he remained blissfully ignorant of the drama most of the time. In this case, he was thrilled that he'd been given the sudden opportunity to play hooky with his daughter, and now that Mother had silently cleared away the vegetable lasagna he ate his Friday's burgers with a fresh gusto, talking about some of the nifty machinery he'd seen on a recent tour of the DuPont plant in Grays Ferry where he had a job up and running. Next he was all gung-ho over a philosophical exchange he'd heard on talk radio on the way in this morning making the claim that computer entries and text messages did not chronicle the American family, but it was more the kitchen refrigerator that functioned as the true household heart, boasting the memories, the triumphs, the reminders, and bonding agents.

"And the shopping list," Mother said, pointing her fork. "The most important part that I seem to be the only one keeping current around here."

"Oh, I don't know," Daddy said. "I'm rather partial to the frog-clip." He looked at his plate. "And I forgot to put up there that I need shaving cream."

"Put it on the list," both Marissa and her mother murmured simultaneously. They smiled at each other, and Marissa slipped her fingers over her mother's knuckles for a gentle makeup squeeze. Since they were both so awkward at closing off the tender moments, however, she removed her hand quickly and gazed at the fridge, really looking at it. Indeed, the front of it was a kaleidoscope of busywork, magnets galore holding up the most current pack of stamps, an old birthday card yellowed at the edges, a paper coaster from the Hotel Monteleone, a bunch of coupons. The side of the unit had the all but forgotten and discarded paraphernalia, the US Healthcare magnet, a food-stained digital timer, some phone numbers on Post-its, an ad for the eye doctor, old recipes. Littered between were a bunch of Marissa's little girl projects, a square of popsicle sticks with her handprint, a crab missing the claws on one side, and there by the mesh basket with all the takeout menus was the frog Daddy mentioned, a Father's Day present from pre-school. Marissa actually remembered gluing it, sitting at the table with the attached bench seat at the Play and Learn, tongue poking out one side of her mouth, setting the paperweight on the clothespin and affixing the circular black magnet underneath. Maybe there was something to that radio talk show, and maybe Daddy wasn't so oblivious after all.

He was reaching down offering Rusty a piece of hamburger roll.

"Don't feed the dog," Mother scolded, winking at Marissa as a clear confirmation that they were friends again. She rose to clear and the doorbell rang, making Marissa jump out of her seat, almost knocking it over. She played it as if she were just so excited to greet the first trick-or-treater that she couldn't contain herself, and she moved off to the living room for the Butterfingers.

She opened the door to a fairy princess wearing a pointed hat with a light purple veil.

"Trick or treat!" the little girl said, smiling the way kids always did, showing the whole rack of teeth in a near grimace. She had a wand, a pillow case, and a hole in one knee of her white stockings.

"Aren't you cute!" Marissa said, taking a candy bar out of the jack-o'-lantern and handing it over.

"Can I have two?" Now the smile was more genuine, eyes twinkling. Marissa laughed and gave over another, fighting the temptation to pat the kid on the head. Didn't want to mess up the sparkles in her hair. Behind her, Dad was waiting patiently on the sidewalk, no jacket, black T-shirt, tattoos up both forearms and one side of his neck. Looked like the type that worked in shipping and receiving somewhere and thought it would be appropriate to have one of those moonshine flasks stuck in his back pocket as long as it remained out of plain sight, but without the patchwork this was conjecture, and Marissa was not one to judge. The only thing she cared about was whether or not this was her serial killer, rapist, or kidnapper. When the girl ran back to him and nearly jumped into his arms in excitement over her double dose of candy, Marissa was convinced this wasn't her man. Of course the fiend could have been anyone, playing a role and playing it well, but she had to make command decisions and move forward. There was no room for false accusation. This was a monster looking for miscues, ready to shrug and move on at a moment's notice to some other poor girl out in Exton or West Chester or Radnor or Blue Bell, working his craft, pressing ghosts into the fabric.

And Marissa would hear them weeping.

The temperature had dropped and the street was starting to get populated. There were women in small clusters walking the little ones in groups, all capes and masks and makeup and accessories, and a few other dutiful dads who had taken the reins, one of them trying to seem nurturing and patient, calling out to his kid in the fluttering black cloak and Scream mask that it wasn't a positive idea to run across properties. Behind her, Marissa heard Daddy starting up the dishes, and she went to the piano stool by the fireplace to play sentry. The heaviest volume would come through the neighborhood in the next hour or so, and she would use every opportunity when drawn to the door to look for something suspicious out there. Mother walked past carrying Rusty with one hand and holding a glass of red wine in the other. She was retreating upstairs, and she paused to look over her reading glasses.

"We will continue our discussion at a more opportune juncture," she said.

"Aye-aye, Captain," Marissa answered. She'd gotten what she wanted, and after Daddy fixed her device she would be more than willing to listen to the series of lectures to come, most probably not so fixed on the content of her argument out there on the porch as on the way she'd expressed it. And she'd give Mother that. An easy win on both sides. "Going to bed so soon?" she said.

"Reading. I'm in the middle of *Fifty*."

"*Shades of Gray?* Mother!"

"Girls will be girls." She moved off toward the stairs and Rusty looked back with those soupy eyes that never seemed to stop leaking pigment. He was a good boy, usually keeping quiet unless another dog was being walked outside. As far as the kiddies went, he would have hung in the background wagging his tail, most probably too shy to approach. There was a small chance he would try to run out with the door being opened and shut so much, but the few times he'd "escaped" in the past he'd done nothing but sit on the lawn waiting for someone to direct him further. He'd never been a barker. There could have been a Bible salesman pounding on the door then trying to get a foot in, and Rusty would probably just hide behind the sectional. Marissa figured that Mother was just getting him out of the way more than anything (he yelped if you stepped on his paw), and the dog loved her best anyway. He slept with her and Daddy, and maybe Mother was making her daughter feel guilty, having her notice that she'd driven the hawk lady upstairs for snuggles even though it was hours before the time she'd shut off the light up there, pull up the covers, and have the doggie crawl under to curl against her middle.

The doorbell rang again, and Marissa didn't start or jump or have some other kind of industrial accident. It was a group of what seemed middle schoolers, including a short, roly-poly Batman, a fabulous Sponge Bob that must have taken hours to craft, a Dracula with big ears and too much makeup, and a kid in his thermal jammies simply wearing an Eagles helmet. Dracula complained about the candy bars and Batman asked for Marissa's phone number. His voice cracked, and they all had a good laugh about that one. She closed the door and turned. Daddy was wiping his hands with a dishtowel, smiling at the joke.

"I'm going to get started," he said. "I'll be in the den. When you shut it down out here, come keep me company and I'll show you how everything works."

"Can't wait."

The doorbell rang again, and Daddy moved to the room with his turntable and album collection. Marissa opened the door to a lanky kid dressed like Freddy Krueger, looking at something going on down the street and snickering. She frowned. It was Gregory Gibbs, a guy two years behind her from high school. This annoyed her to no end. It was one thing to hold on to your childhood, and another to push it. The night was for kids, and he was walking around probably teasing the smaller ones, ripping off their candy if they were old enough to be doing their rounds without an escort but too young to defend themselves. He was probably drunk or high or both.

"Trick or treat," he said through the side of his mouth.

"I don't think so."

He turned and squinted. He had applied makeup to his face to look like burns, but it was just a bunch of black marks. Both the hat and the striped shirt looked dusty and motheaten, as if he'd found them in the attic as an afterthought and then thought himself clever for figuring out how to be slovenly and still have it work for the outdated character. Marissa wanted to delouse just looking at him.

"You're the hot girl," he said. "From school."

She closed the main door just slowly enough to make it seem she wasn't the rude one here. She was thirsty and thought of hunting the fridge for a Diet Coke, but walked past the piano and down the carpeted step to the den. Dad had his sleeves rolled up and his thick black glasses at the end of his nose. The stereo was playing old Fleetwood Mac at such low volume it was almost indistinguishable, and he'd laid tools out on the folding table they usually kept under the couch. He had her device apart already, and there were little pieces of it placed in complicated patterns that seemed to make sense, at least to him. She sighed. He was a good man, a real worker-bee, and he knew how important this was to her. Well, he thought he did anyway.

"Go on and tend to the children," he said without looking up. "I've got this. By the time it peters off out there I'll be deep into the process. Further than you would think."

"Thanks, Daddy."

He waved a hand. There was a knock at the door, and Marissa went to it, feeling the love for her mother and father so deeply it was draining. She opened the door, and there on the porch were some tween girls wearing costumes far too revealing for their relative age bracket. There was a devil in spandex with knock-knees, an Indian squaw wearing a shitload of rouge, and a cat in black tights showing midriff. In the shadow behind them was their "ugly duckling" friend in a white pants suit and matching smock with her hair tucked behind her ears. It took a second, but Marissa finally concluded it was the Progressive Insurance lady from the television commercials, and she thought, *"You go girl. Best costume of the slutty bunch."* The parents were waiting out on the sidewalk, laughing at some joke, one of them braying loud enough to hint she'd dipped too deep into the spiked apple cider before running the kids around. Marissa was actually thinking about approaching them and suggesting the girls drape coats over their shoulders, if not for the sake of decency then because the breeze had picked up. She'd just dropped candy into the devil girl's bag and straightened when she noticed something. There, through the rippling wind snakes hanging from the porch roof, across the street at the back corner of the cyclone fencing of the mini-substation, there was something odd.

It was a dark shape. A man. Looking. Marissa couldn't make out his face because of the distance and the mask, brown and squared off at the top, giving him Frankenstein-head. He was big;

in fact, he was humongous. The signs that said "Keep Out" and "Maintenance Only" were six and a half feet off the ground or so; she knew this from when she was little and Daddy took her over there so she could try sounding out letters. Her father was five foot eleven and had had to reach up to point out the characters. This dude was at eye level with them and he was crouching. She folded her arms and glanced down the street to see if anyone else was seeing this guy, and when she looked back he had vanished.

"Hah," she said out loud to no one, voice drifting off. It was a Michael Myers moment, on Halloween no less, wind snakes making gentle waves in the wind.

Marissa closed the door carefully, leaning and resting her head on it. She was going crazy. She really was. Now she was just dying for a cup of hot chocolate and a hug, but she didn't think there was any in the cupboard and Daddy was not to be interrupted. She thought of her mother saying to her, "Man up," and she laughed out loud at that one.

Right at her forehead there was a knock at the door, and she jumped back as if struck in the face. It wasn't a pleasant triple tap, or even a more commanding "one-two." It was one hard bang, meat of a fist, and now she was Liv Tyler in *The Strangers.* My *God,* was every old-school horror movie cliché making to gather on her porch to say hello? She grabbed the knob and pulled open the door, half expecting to see Jason Voorhees, Pinhead, the Boogeyman, Leatherface, and the girl from *The Ring*, all arranged like a chorus ready to sing her the opening number to *Slaughter on New Ardmore Avenue: The Musical.*

It was a group celebrating the movies, but a different flavor altogether. There was a wizard with close-set eyes and crud in his nose, a Harry Potter with the lightning-bolt scar done on his temple with mascara, and a Lone Ranger holding the hand of his younger sibling wearing a green pillowcase over his or her head with one eye painted on it and cutouts for the arms like the *Monsters Inc.* Mike Wazowski character.

"Aren't you sweet!" Marissa said to the little one, and something caught her eye in the background. Through the black flowing streamers she saw that the big dude had advanced his position and was standing behind the light pole across the street, one palm resting on it, staring through the eyehole that was unobstructed as if the pole gave him some kind of camouflage.

"Hey!" It was the wizard. "Pay attention!" He snapped his fingers and Marissa's eyes widened.

"Calm the 'tude," she said. "And your robe is too long. It's filthy because you're dragging."

She shut the door in their faces, thought about it for a moment, and opened it back up again, mostly because the cute kid in the pillowcase deserved better. She also wanted to kick herself because she hadn't kept her eye on the big dude, and she knew he wasn't going to be standing behind the light pole anymore.

He wasn't.

The wizard kid muttered something about her being a dumbshit and she hardly heard, handing out the candy and looking up and down the street in flickers and starts.

Her phone rang. She'd just changed her ringtone to that Warner Bros. whistle, and it sounded creepy as hell. She drew it out of her back pocket. Same area code, but she didn't recognize the number.

"Hello?"

"There's a man in your bushes."

"What?"

"There's a man—"

She looked across the street, and it was Phyllis the busybody standing on her steps with her phone to her ear. She pointed toward the evergreens, and Marissa turned.

There through the ghost webbing she saw a blurred form, hulking and staring.

"Hey!" she said. She ran at him as if to jump through the webbing like a superhero, and he moved off down the side of the house and most probably through the back yard; she couldn't see because the angle was cut off. She stopped right there by the porch swing. There was a section of decorator fence back there in the dark and then the ravine, the back yards of adjoining properties blending into the small piece of common woodland forming a short valley, and then the gradual incline up to the houses on Dartmouth. He was gone, and she'd blown it. She couldn't fake not knowing at this point, and it was done. Just like that. She strode back across the porch and stepped inside, closing the door behind her and dialing 911. She hit the wrong buttons twice and had to dial again.

"Three times the charm," she said, and put the phone up to her ear.

There was a soft knock and Marissa disconnected the call. It couldn't be. Not this obvious, not right here on her own porch with so many potential witnesses.

She opened the door and there he was, towering above her. He was wearing a potato sack on his head, and through one of the dark holes that wasn't quite lined up she could see an eye staring down at her. The mask tilted slightly then, as if in curious study.

"Yes?" she said, trying to sound brave yet coming off nasal and brittle.

He just stared.

"Can I help you?"

Nothing. And she noticed he didn't have a trick-or-treat bag.

"You can't just stand there," she tried. "Do I know you?"

He slowly cocked his head the other way.

"Use your bathroom?" he said. The voice was muffled through the mask.

"What?"

"I gotta pee."

"Of course," Daddy said. Marissa hadn't heard him come up from behind her, and she looked up at him trying to catch his glance and say with her eyes, *"No, Daddy, please! This isn't the time to be trusting and neighborly! Don't let the wolf into the fold!"*

Daddy amazed her by saying to the giant,

"Take off the mask."

"Aww, it's Halloween."

Daddy moved forward, reached up, and removed the crinkled Idaho Russet Potato bag. Beneath it was Larry Green, face full of tater-dust, the big mentally challenged guy who had worked for the Pathmark doing maintenance until it closed down a few years ago leaving him jobless. He had been a staple of that place, the only supermarket in the area with underground parking and an elevator, and for years he was the one gathering the carts and lining them back up in front of the pharmacy, pushing around a U-frame with the deli, seafood, and bakery trash and taking it to the back room, filling up the mobile freezer boxes, and gathering up the handbaskets by the registers to restack them out by the front entrance. Everyone knew and loved big Larry. He talked in that low monotone about the weather and the latest sale items that he "tried himself, just ask anyone." He was weird if you didn't know him, especially since he sometimes smiled and laughed at his reflection in the metal stand by aisle four if there wasn't a sign in it, but he was harmless. When the store closed down he never got hired at the SuperFresh in the Manoa Shopping Center or the Giant in Lawrence Park. Lately you often saw him wandering the streets talking to himself, and Marissa felt terrible about it now.

"Straight back," Daddy said. "Through the kitchen to the rear of the utility room."

The big guy shuffled to where he was told, and Daddy wiped his glasses with a soft white cloth.

"I'm set pretty well in there, honey. I used one of your old nail files to smooth the contacts, and I've got the cloth soaking." He moved behind the mini-bar and got out some white wine. "It'll only be an hour or so before I have a reconstituted battery charging."

"How long then?"

He held up the glass and studied the contents as if it were some fascinating potion he'd conjured.

"A day or two. Earliest tomorrow night some time. I'd explain the flow of electrons, but..."

"Yeah."

He smiled. "Want to watch a movie?"

She backed to the door, and jerked her thumb toward it. "More candy to give away. Favorite holiday, you know?"

"Yes, of course." He took in a mouthful, savoring it as if it weren't just house wine.

"Good stuff."

Larry came back through from the kitchen area. He was smiling, but his eyes were dulled at trying so hard for so long to figure things out.

"I flushed, you can check," he said.

"I'm sure," Daddy answered. "You be on your way now."

The big man nodded, and looked at Marissa.

"You're sure pretty. Sorry I scared you."

She let him out, and right on cue there was a group coming up the steps. It was a kid in jeans wearing a werewolf mask, a zombie in a hoodie, a ghost wearing a sheet with a hank of rope around the neck, and an incredibly realistic Voldemort who had the slitted nose done up with some kind of putty and then blended it in at the edges with face paint. He was either bald or wearing a skullcap, and Marissa complimented his effort by giving him a triple portion of Butterfingers.

She ran out of candy at 7:20 and turned off the porch light. Her father had already gone upstairs to join Mother and Rusty, and things were quiet. She looked in the den and saw Daddy's work table covered with tins of solution, a soldering iron, three different kinds of tweezers, cotton balls, parts, screws, springs, and neat rows and groupings of other items she couldn't even begin to identify.

Tomorrow night if she was lucky. She folded her arms as if chasing a chill and felt suddenly as if someone were watching her. She spun, and there was nothing out of the ordinary—just the house she grew up in, all its shadows and nooks and crannies familiar like an old chair or that special place on the couch where you watched TV all through your childhood, laughing, eating microwave popcorn, dreaming.

Suddenly she was filled with such an overwhelming loneliness that she almost cried out. She put her hand to her mouth. She made a spot decision then and moved off to the keypad by the front door, tabbing the alarm code that was her parents' anniversary, "0727." It started beeping down from sixty seconds, and she made her way through the kitchen. There were motion detectors covering every square foot of the first floor, and all the upstairs windows were on permanent "stay," making it so that no one could break in without kicking up a hell of a fuss. Made it so that she felt safe in the basement at least, and Mother wouldn't hear her down there.

She was going to call Jerome.

Oh yes she was, girl, because it felt like now or never. Marissa Madison was being stalked by a man clever enough not to have tipped his hand the first night, and she felt things closing in on her, as if she might not live to see another sunset. Promises in the patchwork had been broken before, and she wasn't going down without a final testament to the only man she'd ever loved.

If Mother found out she'd kill her, ha, ha.

Marissa opened the basement door by the upstairs clothes dryer, flicked on the light, and shut the door behind her. Her parents would not think it strange that she'd hit the alarm and retreated downstairs to watch some TV as opposed to hanging out on the first floor or heading up to bed. Even though they had a fifty-inch flat-screen in the living room, Marissa often wanted to be by herself in the "sweet dungeon," and the smaller Sony was nice down here with the black cushy sofa, beanbag chairs, and the two Kashmar Persian area rugs.

She treaded carefully down the stairs, as the unfinished wall to the left was built "close" and if you weren't careful you'd scrape an elbow. Mother had put beautiful Asian lamp covers over the bulbs down here, and the soft glow took away all the sharp corners and cracks common to most cellar areas. Just off the stairs there was Marissa's television space set up in a semicircle by the near catty-corner, and beside it to the right was the second area rug, a soft legend navy rust twelve-footer lying bare across the space all the way to the corner of the basement meeting with the front wall. It was the area they had cleared for the poker table and wet bar Daddy had been talking about arranging down here but had never quite gotten around to. To the right off the landing, of course, the illusion of decor and careful arrangement slowly deteriorated.

Daddy had put in a false ceiling and PVC covering for the pipes, along with the two keyless padlocks and specialty security bars on the egress window, but the balance of the space had become a stowaway barn, a pleasant eyesore with a clutter of family history. Beneath the stairs were the plastic tubs of Christmas decorations and old books including all the spiral-bounds and research papers accumulated by both parents when they'd earned their respective master's degrees. Farther back in the darker portion of the basement area was a collection of end tables and small cabinets Mother had bought at a number of flea markets during her antique refurbishing phase, cans of paint, lacquer, and varnish on old groundcloths, a treadmill they rarely used, and a bench-press on a red wrestling mat next to three milk cartons filled with free weights. At the rear against the wall was a wooden cabinet with the winter clothes and a smaller one where they stowed the toolbox, flashlights, duct tape, replacement bulbs, batteries, and coffee cans filled with renegade screws and fasteners, all of it across from the water boiler and the old heater with the chutes and draft hoods that reminded Marissa of steam engines and folktales. The thing still knocked and made noise intermittently, but they'd all gotten so used to it that it didn't even startle Marissa anymore when she was hanging out down here and it kicked in.

She walked past her TV area and stood on the bare rug where Daddy's poker table was going to go. She checked to make sure she was out of the sightline from the entrance at the top of the stairs, and waited for the muffled beeping in the living room to go into quick-mode, the last ten seconds before the alarm was set. She moved a bit more left. Even though her mother or father would kick off the motion detectors long before getting to that basement door, a girl couldn't be too careful.

From upstairs, she heard the alarm go to its rapid final ten seconds, then silence.

She got out her cell and dialed Jerome, still on her speed-dial—heck, she was a silly, sappy, hopeless romantic. It rang four times and dumped her to voicemail. She smiled brightly and looked at the ceiling, knowing she should have prepared for this circumstance.

"Jerome, it's me, Marissa," she said. "I'm . . . umm . . . sorry that I failed you so terribly and I wanted you to know that I never stopped loving you."

She hung up. He wasn't going to call back, and she didn't need patchwork to know this. It was over.

Now it was just a question of the lingering silence.

NIGHT SOUNDS

You're kidding me, right, asshole? You think I'd be that stupid, snooping around with all those eyes everywhere, especially when they'd be paying such attention to what people *looked* like?

Well, hell with ya, it worked out to my advantage without anyone second-guessing me anyway, but like I said I've always been lucky with the draw, the set-up, the circumstance. Halloween, right? Everyone's attention was out front, or if you're Marissa Madison, you were focused on the side of the house and the retard in the bushes.

She never even came close to figuring my angle, because she created her own misdirection.

See, I did a drive-by when she was first parking coming back from the Giant, and I noticed the ravine at the edge of her back yard. Hopeful, I pulled a 360 around that first rotary, tailed back passing her place going the other way and made the next right on Vasser, the street next to hers. Then I banged another quick right on Dartmouth. There was no outlet there, but one of the houses was vacant and under renovation, with its front all covered with Tyvek House Wrap and a dumpster smack in the middle of the yard. And the job had been abandoned or stalled: you could see by the fluttering caution tape they never refastened and the safety cones meant to zone off the entrance and exit pathways that hadn't been repositioned after getting knocked over.

To be honest, I thought it was all too pristine to be real when I made my quick survey through the windshield, but when I got back to Madison's street I passed her house to confirm what I thought I'd seen out in front. Then I went through the rotary again, continuing up the hill to go down the far side of it, and my heart started clapping like a monkey with toy cymbals, I shit you not. There on the left I could see it coming into view as the trees thinned, a set of basketball courts, a playground, a sign that said "New Ardmore Ave Park," and the treasure behind it.

A creek.

I came back long after dark and parked there at the house being renovated on Dartmouth. I had a hard hat, sunglasses, and a reflective vest, but it was all overkill because no one was going to notice me anyway. Just in case there were trick-or-treaters still working the streets, or more likely some sneaky bunch of older kids getting high, I was careful when I slipped in back of the residence across from the place under construction.

I'd brought five rolls of two-hundred-foot measuring line, and I slipped down into the common ravine located at the back side of all these neighboring properties. By the time I shut down that phase it was past 11:00 in the evening.

And I was far from finished.

Oh, sleep could wait.

Because this wasn't about sex anymore, or its substitute, or whatever the forensic psychologists would most likely run up the flagpole so they could jerk each other off in the situation room and call each other sensitive geniuses. It wasn't even about Marissa Madison. It was about pulling off the big one that no one would want to believe, it was about taking new risks, upping the ante, and waving it in everyone's face.

It was nothing but pride now.

And committing to the perfect kill they'd write stories about.

CHAPTER TWELVE

Marissa's eyes flew open, and for a moment she was disoriented. It was too dark, and she was lying the wrong way. Her right hand was asleep and she flexed it, sitting up, looking at the clock on the cable box under the television.

11:43 p.m.

She was home, that's right, home sweet home in her upstairs bedroom where she was safe. She lay back down, pulling the covers up to her chin. The quilt smelled like cedar, like love, but she could sense how barren the place was without all her stuff. Growing up, her living space always had a comfy disorganization to it, with her jewelry and knickknacks strewn all over the place, teddy bears and collector figurines, the mega-piles of clothes on the chairs and the bed (if she wasn't in it, of course). When she'd moved into the apartment in Chester it had all seemed too spread and thinned even though the place was technically an efficiency. Everything there was neat and clean and sterile, and she realized just how very much she'd grown to hate it, lying to herself all along that it wasn't so bad and trying to make it work.

She turned on her side and decided that if she survived this (*when* she survived this, girlfriend!) she was coming back here for good. She would fill up this room again and start over. Rethink things. Make everything make sense.

There was a noise outside. Out back, something weird and metallic. She sat up and cocked her head, tucking her hair behind her ear. Nothing now. Thick darkness. Goosebumps on her arms and cold silence. She was about to lie back down when there was the noise outside again, something clunking, muffled, displaced in a way she couldn't identify.

Marissa put aside the covers and drew across her legs. She did this with great care, knee to knee as if the dark itself were measuring her subtlety, and she stepped down onto the carpet. She had on her royal blue Widener T-shirt that she'd bought big on purpose, and of course her plain cotton underwear—can you say vulnerable?

She walked to the window. For a moment she thought about turning on the light, but that giveaway would make even the rookies scatter. And this was no greenhorn. Besides, with a glare she'd have to go right up to the glass, pulling one of those jobs where you cupped your hands at your temples making a view-tunnel, and what if there was someone pressing up against the window on the other side of it, say a serial killer on a ladder with his own hands cupped around his eyes looking back in at her? Better to sneak up, move the curtain ever so slightly, and glance from the side.

She approached. One side of her mind was soothing her, telling her in a low steady voice that he'd never be stupid enough to put an extension ladder against the house where everyone in the world could see him like a bug on the wall. There were ADT alarm stickers all over the windows. They even had a lawn sign, so at the very least he would be aware that a break-in would kick off some kind of siren. And if he was familiar with this particular system he would know that after busting through he'd have sixty seconds of countdown to catch her in the dark and fight through her parents whom she'd certainly have woken with her screams. The alarm would be raising the dead at that point, and even if he managed to struggle her out through the front or back door there would be witnesses.

She'd reached the window. What if he was so fast he could do a smash 'n' grab, yanking her right here off the carpet and back into the night before she could move or utter a sound? She reached toward the shade, her hand making faint outlines in the darkness. Even if he was inhumanly swift, it was doubtful he would be able to muscle her down the ladder without killing them both . . . and by the way, why would he leave such a big piece of evidence behind? This killer was invisible. For a moment she pictured a faceless man trying to hold her under one arm kicking and scratching and biting and thrashing, and dragging the extension ladder with his other hand, bumping over roots and dragging up crabgrass. She almost smiled and moved the shade aside just a tad.

No face pressed close to the glass on the other side, but she was so jacked up with the spooks she half expected some large bird to come smashing into the window, bouncing off and leaving a web of splinters and cracks to distort her vision while the shadow stalker snuck off through the Tuckers' back yard, or behind the Molinaros' shed, or over to the other side of the Winstons' wrought-iron garden trellis with the overgrown vines. The wind was kicking up, moving the branches and cutting the moonlight into wavy beacons that gradually faded and surrendered to the darkness of the ravine. Mother's saddle-bred horse weathervane was spinning and slowing there by the vegetable patch where she'd tried and failed to grow cucumbers and peppers last summer, and the swings on the old set were floating and starting with the pulse of the breeze.

There at the edge of the property where the land dipped into the common gulch Marissa saw a strange movement. She chanced moving the shade over a full inch or two and focused on the grainy vision. There was something at the edge of the ravine, moving in time with the wind like a car stuck in a snowbank.

It was a trash can, caught between two trees and a wedge of prickerbushes, hence the odd metallic clunking sound. Marissa was about to laugh at herself for actually mistaking a trash can by the gulch for an extension ladder clunking up against the house when there was a sudden pop from the corner of the room, deep in the structure. Her hands flew to her mouth and she spun around, choking down the scream that had come up through her core, knowing it was one of those settling cracks but unable to deny it had scared the living shit out of her. Almost in answer then, as if the place were coming up with its own lullaby for Marissa in order to reintroduce her to the sacred sounds and hymns of the place she'd been reared, there was a muted rattle and hum from the belly of the house, and the familiar coda of the heat coming up.

Marissa sat on her bed, pictured her parents sleeping comfortably down the hall, and wept harder than she ever had in her life.

EARLY BIRD

An extension ladder, asshole? Tumbling trash cans and swings in the wind? By 11:43 p.m., I was back at the shop working against the clock, putting shit together as quick as I could so I could get the fuck out of there before Reynolds came in at 6:30 a.m. to open things up, long before if I did things just right. Then I'd call out from the road, just two sick days in a year, not bad for a part-timer, eh?

First, there was the lolly column I had to disassemble. The threaded shank was a flat-top measuring nearly two feet across, and while it was perfect for helping to budge concrete slabs from their underside it wasn't gonna do dick for me unless I could make it into a cutter of sorts. I knew I didn't have time to measure everything out perfectly 'cause we didn't even have a caliper with jaws that big, but when I took the shank to the lathe I did a pretty good job reshaping the top end into a threaded cone. For torque I needed a three-prong crankshaft that could bear a shitload of foot-pounds, and the cropping and welding took me longer than I'd expected.

The next part made me want to hurl shit around and trash the place I helped organize, since cancelled backorders weren't my job and Schillinger had buried all his mistakes somewhere so the boss wouldn't ride his ass for ordering specialty material without having the customers pay in advance. I wasted about forty-five minutes looking in all the shop cabinets, out behind the forklifts at the back of the warehouse, along the far edge of no-man's land in the corner where they stacked all the wet vacs and pallets of sweeping compound, and I finally found his little hiding place in shipping and receiving, down on the floor under the table by the loading dock where they had the packing tape, the label maker, and the box cutters.

Bingo, bitch.

Right there behind a pile of flattened cardboard with the other specialty garbage lying on top of old invoices were those diamond bandsaw blades twined up in their figure eights.

In about an hour I'd have them welded onto the screw threads, and while they might not have been the perfect bond for the base material I needed for them to cut through, they'd do. And a water source? That one made me laugh out loud actually.

By 2:45 in the morning I'd completed work on the apparatus for all but the trimmings. By 3:15 I'd taken the roll cage for the 4000-watt Coleman generator and cut and rewelded the bars to make an offset brace-rack for the machine, complete with a couple of stainless mounting brackets.

I thought of skateboarders and the X Games and how little we all respected that dumbass bullshit and I thanked those useless bastards for the concept, as I tore apart the bottom of a mop bucket nobody was gonna miss and welded on the multi-directional casters. Last was the safety harness I raped for its belt latch.

I looked at my creation and saw that it was good.

I went into my office, got on the computer, and made the adjustments that would bury the lolly jack, the diamond band-saw blades, the generator, the safety harness, an exterminator's ¼ × 12 carbide bit with an SDS shank, a cordless rotary hammer from rentals, a nylon and elastic four-way barrier unit city workers normally put up when they were fixing a water main, a couple of removable sleeve anchors, a wrench, and the last piece I still had to grab. Then I threw the scraps outside into my trunk along with my creation, careful not to bump and burr the threads I'd so carefully crafted. The sun wouldn't be up for a couple of hours, plenty of time for me to get back and do what I still had to do.

Cleaning up inside was a familiar chore, and I spot-checked everything twice before making my last warehouse walk, straight down aisle seven again where they stocked the safety equipment. Three-quarters in about ten feet down from the harnesses on the shelves and hanging off J-hooks, I saw what I needed there on the second rack from the bottom. The icing on the cake, asshole, the exclamation point.

I just had to find one my size.

And add the decals you could get at any neighborhood dollar store.

CHAPTER THIRTEEN

Marissa awoke the next morning, threw on a pair of sweats, and dashed out into the hall. There was a glorious aroma of coffee coming from the kitchen, and she raced down the short set of carpeted stairs.

Daddy was in the den working on her device, wearing his jammy bottoms that were so long at the feet he had to cuff them, a T-shirt, and his favorite plaid robe. His silver hair was sticking up on top and it proved that he hadn't taken the time to groom before coming down to dutifully continue with what was most important to his daughter. She squealed, ran over, and hugged him.

"Whoa, easy there, Shane!" he said, brimming with obvious pleasure. She held on just that extra second before letting go and sat right there on the floor at his feet.

"How's it going?" she said.

"How was the old room?"

"Sweet. What you got there, anyway?"

He turned to stare back through the magnifying glass at the mechanism in his other hand. It looked as if her trigger-killer had been burst inside out, with wires, springs, coils, and tabs poking and dangling.

"I have here a project," he mused, "with interesting formulaic inconsistencies I hadn't accounted for in my original calculations, yet wonderful opportunities for discovery."

"Daddy, in English! Success or setback?"

"Oh, right." He snapped it all together like a magician fitting a chainsaw, garden shears, and a live rabbit back into a top hat and set the thing into the slot at the base of what appeared to be a small charger.

"It will be ready sometime today, honey. I had to readjust for a cross-up in the circuitry I didn't expect and . . ."

He looked at her over the rim of his glasses and smiled.

"Long story short, I substituted and improvised, making it so you'd be up and running sooner than later." He stood up and placed his hands in the middle of his back. Then he motioned her over, indicating that they should both lean in so that Marissa could see the dot of red light on the side of her reconstructed device.

"That's actually a miniature light bulb," he said. "I had to remove your old warning indicator and go micro, one millimeter in diameter, probably a world record."

"I'll call Ripley's and Guinness myself," Marissa said. "What's the deal?"

They both straightened.

"When the red starts flickering you're close, and when it goes green you should get your patchwork back."

"Totally unjammed?"

"Totally."

He moved past and made his way for the kitchen.

"I have a cup of autumn blend going in here if you want any," he said. "Cinnamon and pumpkin."

She followed in tow with a smile.

"Mother doesn't like that froo-froo kind of thing."

"Yes, but I had a feeling you might be craving an old treat and I stopped on the way home yesterday." He poured. "One cup, no waiting."

She sat at the table and, after she added the cream and the Splenda, he took a chair across from her. He sat, palmed his hands around his own drink, and stared at the affair for a moment.

"Your mother tells me you're not happy at school."

Marissa looked off to the back window that had a bar of sunlight coming through making a glare on the countertop. She blinked and knew that if Mother was in the room she would surely give her an impromptu speech about wearing sunglasses so much that she'd made herself into a light-sensitive cripple.

"I'm not," she said finally.

"Do you want to come home?"

She shrugged.

"Well, think it over," he said. "Offer's on the table."

She eyed him directly. That was a firm proposition, no baloney. He must have made Mother agree or he wouldn't put it out there like that. Clearly he'd been working on multiple projects last night and this morning.

"I decided last night that I'd ask you," she said, "but in the light of day in my old barren room it didn't seem so realistic. I mean, what if it didn't work out? What if it turned into a thing where Mother could just string together one lecture after another about how I'm supposed to make something of myself, and break out on my own, and reach self-actualization and all that?"

Daddy smiled back mostly with his eyes, and then let his glance fall to the table in front of him.

"I remember when you first asked me if Santa really existed," he said.

Marissa put her cup down.

"I thought it was Mother who shattered that particular dream."

He pursed his lips for a moment and shook his head.

"No, actually that was my unexpected responsibility. It was during the PECO shutdown and we were all working overtime, putting in crazy hours, trying to manage an abundance of geopolitical and economic concerns that had us seeing double." His face had gone flat with the memory. "We thought we might lose the company." He took a drink and rested the cup back on the table. "Anyway, I come home from a particularly hard day at work, and Mother is in the kitchen making stir fry, my comfort food. I barely have my coat off and you jump into my arms and make me go to the picture window and watch the snow that started falling about an hour ago. So we go to our special place on the sofa, knees pressing into the cushions, and you say, 'Daddy, is there really a Santa?' Of course, I have no idea what to say except the God's honest truth, so I reply, 'Marissa, Santa is more like a feeling than a real person.' Now your eyebrows are up in those questioning arches, and you say, 'So you're the one who brings the presents?' I sigh and say, 'Yes, but listen, this is important. You can't go telling all your friends there's no Santa. I mean, some kids wait for him all year.' So you take it all in, nod, and reach up to touch my sideburn like you always used to do. Then you say, 'Why do they tell us there's a Santa if there isn't one?' At that point I'm stalling because I'm preoccupied with the mortgage and the job and a whole universe of issues you'd never understand, and I say, 'They tell us there's a Santa so there's something to hang on to. It's nice to believe in something. I guess we make stuff up for the people that need it the most. Kind of like the Eagles, you know? We always believe they can win a Super Bowl even though they never do.'"

He paused for emphasis.

"So I come home the next afternoon from another particularly difficult day at the office, and there's something waiting for me on the coffee table. See, it's this green clay paperweight shaped like a football—uneven laces, misshapen edges, a hairline crack starting to cut its way through the middle. There are letters and numbers colored like candy canes affixed to the top ridge with Elmer's glue, and they spell out '2001 CHAMPS.' And the card underneath reads clearly in my five-and-a-half-year-old daughter's clumsy printing, 'Merry early Christmas. Love Santa.'"

He looked up at Marissa and his eyes had gone moist.

"Yes, you could already read and write at that tender young age, and no, you hadn't developed the patchwork just yet." He folded his hands and spoke back down at them. "Some things aren't about lessons and lectures, honey. Sometimes it's just about family."

"Sorry to spoil the Kodak moment," Mother said. She was dressed and carrying Rusty under one arm. There was a silk scarf on her head and it worked for her, making her classic and pretty. "I'm going to walk the dog. With the three of us living under the same roof again, someone is going to have to do all the work around here." She winked, and Marissa breathed a sigh of relief. That was as close as she was going to get to a coming-home party, and everything was going to be just fine. In a strange kind of way this beast, whoever he was, had opened up possibilities for Marissa Madison, and she couldn't wait until her handicap was remedied so she could finish this thing. Start anew. Grow into who she was going to be at a pace she could handle.

Mother took Rusty to the front door to put on the leash and body harness, and Marissa shuffled behind, peering into the den and looking at her trigger-killer sitting there in its charger, little red light staring back at her stubbornly. The heater kicked on in the basement, and Marissa was standing in the spot where you could actually feel a slight vibration accompanying the muffled knock and clatter. It was like an old song that was part of the soundtrack of your life, and it grounded her, comforted her, and let her know she was finally home.

PHONE TAG

Oh yes, asshole. It was all about home being where the heart was, about abandoned construction sites, quarter-inch pilot holes, nylon tarpaulin barrier tents, and clattering heaters. It was about rivers and crankshafts and concrete and gulches and a bunch of other things no one ever bothered to think about until the toilet backed up or the stoplights went dark or the computers froze or the subways stopped running.

The boss tried calling my cell a couple of times that morning, thinking I'd be stupid enough to pick up.

By then I had long started getting into the dirty work.

CHAPTER FOURTEEN

There was a buzz Marissa felt in her back pocket, and a thrill ran up her spine. There weren't too many people ringing her cell phone on a regular basis, since she had so few friends and confidants calling just to bullshit and talk about all the "drama." Her patchwork had weeded out that field a long time ago, and it was pretty much limited to her parents, the bursar's office, Verizon, and her advisor.

That meant that Jerome might be returning her call, and she was thankful she had switched it off ringtone as a precaution last night. She and Mother were reorganizing the linen closet in the hallway between bedrooms on the landing, and Marissa was the one on the floor. Mother was up on the chair, and if it had been the other way around the woman might have heard or felt the vibration, making Marissa thank goodness, as odd as that particular personification seemed at the moment. They had pretty much cleared out the disaster on the bottom shelf they normally treated like a throw-away area with the family packs of Charmin and tissue boxes crammed atop three plastic tubs spilling over with bags of cotton balls, Q-tips, light bulbs, old makeup cases, rubber stops for Mother and Daddy's bed that kept rolling away from the wall, combs and brushes, and a million carry bags from the dentist with extra toothbrushes and floss. Marissa jumped to her feet, reached around, and grabbed from the second shelf some contour sheets that had been in the household since before she was born. In her haste yanking them out she almost knocked Mother off her chair.

"Honey! Careful!" she said.

"Sorry," Marissa said. "These old things should be in the basement. Groundcloths for painting or something. They're an eyesore up here."

Mother put her hands on her hips.

"You're starting to sound just like me. Go ahead, dear, put them in the basement."

Marissa almost tripped rushing them down the stairs to the living room. She didn't even steal a glance over toward the den to check on her trigger-killer, because she'd peeked in there five times in the last hour and she'd promised herself she wouldn't "watch the pot trying to make it boil" anymore, at least until noon. She moved through the kitchen and had that awkward, silly moment where she actually couldn't find the doorknob for the basement because the pile of sheets in her arms came up past her chin blocking the view, and she felt around for the damned thing like a blind woman.

It was a trick getting the lights on, closing the door, and finding the first step without going ass over teakettle, and in the process of doing all this Marissa scolded herself for taking so long trying to save a second as we so often did when it was best just to slow down and restructure the stage blocking. Finally, she settled for tossing the rumple of sheets over the railing, and she took the rest of the stairs two at a time.

It smelled faintly of rust or something down here, and she had it in the back of her mind to suggest that they next straighten the mess under the stairs and sweep behind all the cabinets, a full makeover and a triple dose of Febreze. OMG, she *was* starting to sound just like Mother! She got out her cell phone, holding her breath like a child.

There was a message, and she recognized the number. She hit her voicemail and put the phone to her ear.

"Hey," his voice said. "Call me."

This was it. Marissa hit call-back and peered cautiously back up the stairway. Could Mother hear her through the closed door, up two floors in the middle of the house? Probably not. Though Marissa spent more time down here than did her mother, she couldn't recall ever being able to hear anything even from the living room or the den coming from this area except the rattling heater. Just in case Mother had followed her to the door, however, Marissa moved to the middle of the room, cradling her cell and crouching over slightly, cupping her hands around the whole deal to deaden the audible.

He picked up, and her heart raced.

"Hello," he said.

"It's me, Marissa."

"I know," he replied. "Why are you talking so low-toned and funny?"

"Why are you doing the same?"

"I'm in the library."

She straightened her posture. Even without context this thrilled her. She also knew that sticking contour sheets in the basement wouldn't take too long, and she had to hurry.

"I'm . . . not going to be a nurse," she stammered. "I never wanted to be. I'm moving back home and possibly quitting college, at least temporarily."

"Then I wish you good fortune with these new endeavors," he said, and she almost laughed aloud, knowing that if she let it slip it would be a double whammy, possibly alerting Mother and at the same time making Jerome uncomfortable with his improved vocabulary. Her response was, "So what's up with you?" and right after saying it she closed her eyes tight with embarrassment. Could she *be* any more simplistic?

"Can't you tell what's going on in my life from your psychic connections?" he said.

That was a good one, actually.

"It's shorted out," she said. "I can't read the patchwork at the moment."

There was a pause, but it didn't seem to be one of indecision. It felt like timing.

"Stay that way," he said finally. "If you do, there's an 'us.' Think it over. Call me."

The line went dead.

Marissa let her arm drop to her side. Numbed and listless, she treaded back to the stairs. Like father like daughter now, she was faced with one of those paradoxes he so enjoyed with that calendar project he was never going to finish. But this was no difficult pleasure. It was the lesser of two evils, lose-lose, pick your poison.

She closed the basement door behind and made her way to the kitchen. Her chest was tight and her throat hurt and she opened the fridge absently, closed it, and walked through to the living room to take the step-down into the den. There, so delicate and complicated, was her trigger-killer, angled back in its charger, bare and coated wires curly-cueing out of it and winding back to other small contact points in a complicated, organized tangle. Its tiny light at the bottom right was straight red, ready to go winking at any moment now on a countdown to green.

If it went live, she and Jerome would never be. If she pulled the plug right here and now they had a chance. The problem was that her premonition of winning this thing seemed contingent on the patchwork mapping her a route, and there was no indication she could survive it without her best stuff.

Of course she could unplug the damned thing and get right back on her cell phone, this time dialing 911. Then of course, the wedding bells she might hope for would be forever tinged with the trailing screams of the girls from here on in who'd fallen off the radar.

Marissa stared at the little red light.

And couldn't decide for the life of her.

A hand closed on her shoulder and Marissa almost screamed, turning sharply, both hands up at her mouth.

"Couch," Mother said. "Now."

From the expression Marissa saw in her eyes this was going to be a planning session, tough love, heart to heart, and this time Mother wasn't going to throw in the towel, walking away damaged and bruised just because her daughter threw back a potshot or two. Marissa hesitantly padded into the living room and settled down on the sectional where she could keep her eye on that trigger-killer.

Mother sat across from her and folded her legs up and under.

"You know," she said, "in every family, every relationship, there is someone who comes to the plate and gets things done even when it's unattractive to do so. I think of it as a custodial function, and while I don't like to think of myself or my own daughter as janitors, we sometimes have to clean things up."

"We . . ."

"Did I stutter?"

A silence played out between them, and Marissa's eyes were the first to drop.

"So I'm a custodian."

"No, dear, look at me. You are more of an internal decorator, and with that patchwork going you're one step ahead of the owners, architects, and groundkeepers, that's all." She took a moment for repositioning, slipping her feet to the carpet and webbing her hands around her knees. "When it comes to Jerome Anthony Franklin," she said finally, "you have to understand that you didn't just fill his heart with first love. You rearranged the furniture of his entire life and put him in a place of extreme public scrutiny."

At first Marissa thought that Mother had actually been on the other side of that basement door, and she panicked, thinking that in her "best interests," the woman would try to ground her for life now, take her cell phone, monitor all the computers, buy a chastity belt on eBay. But just in case it was a lucky guess at the right time, Marissa responded as if the last time she'd spoken to Jerome was months ago.

"Thanks, Mother. You know just how to make a girl feel good about herself."

"It wasn't your fault."

"We've said these things already."

"But you don't believe it even after working it through. You blame yourself for that poor young man falling on his face out there, when all you did was lead him to drink from the well of his own potential. The patchwork wasn't given to you so that you could sing for people and write music for people, and eat, drink, and sleep for them."

"Then why am I cursed with it?" Marissa said, a bit louder than she'd intended. "What good did it ever do me or anyone else?"

"There are a lot of businesses and townspeople around here that could make you a list, dear, but none of us ever felt you needed that kind of verification. Do you? Is that what this is about?"

"No."

"Then what is it?"

"I'm still in love with him."

"You're not, baby, not really."

Marissa stood up.

"Please don't tell me how I feel, Mother."

"Then you tell *me,*" she said, standing herself. "How could you possibly be in love with a young man you hardly even know anymore? You're obsessed with an image you erected from his skill set, not his past, his family, his heart, and his soul."

"So now you know whether or not I feel love? *God,* Mother, you are annoying sometimes!"

"No, Marissa. Like you, I'm just a custodian, trying to avoid another spill around here."

"I thought you understood . . ."

"I do, only too well. I know that love is intensive, something women oftentimes feel on a deeper level than men, and I've mostly kept silent because as the kids say nowadays, 'I feel you.' But there's nothing there but misery, darling. When it comes to your livelihood, it's your choice, not mine. College is the best way to go, but your father and I will support you either way. In terms of Jerome Anthony Franklin, take my advice and don't call him. Let it go. Please."

Marissa sat back down and pulled up her knees and hugged them, looking off to the den, trying not to cry in front of her mother. In a way she was relieved in that the woman would have given a different sort of dissertation if she'd actually heard her calling Jerome in the basement. This was precautionary, and a small part of her wanted to laugh at how close Mother was to reading what was actually going on here. You didn't need patchwork to possess a certain uncanny Madison sonar, and she hated her mother for it and at the same time despised herself for agreeing with her, at least in the part of her mind still governed by common sense. She walked out of the room and made for her bedroom. She was going to curl up in a ball under the covers and think about things. Take a nap. Wake up with a new perspective.

But when Marissa awoke she was no better off than when she'd shut her eyes with the quilt pulled over her head. She loved Jerome Anthony Franklin more than anything she had ever known. It was like falling, like dying. But she just couldn't bring herself to unplug that trigger-killer. If she did she was dead, and if she dialed in a distress call to the boys in blue there would be another girl soon taking her place. Then another and another.

Her digital said 11:43 and it freaked her, since it was almost that time when she'd laid down for a nap and it was clearly not Friday morning anymore. The darkness in here painted a thick, strange picture. She'd slept through the entire day and into the night, and while it wasn't so surprising that her parents had let her hunker down with this Jerome thing and sleep it off, her digital had, of course, read exactly 11:43 last night when she'd woken up disoriented, mistaking tumbling trash cans for serial killers. The coincidence was weird and it made her feel that this echo was a precursor to something huge and terrible.

Her trigger-killer. Was it working? It had to be by now, hadn't it? Daddy promised.

She turned on the lamp by the bed and it hurt her eyes, making her squint. She sat up and folded her arms, her face feeling puffy. Pouting, she reached for her hand mirror on the end table next to her cell. She had those sheet-line impressions on her right cheek and her hair looked like shit. She sighed. Her trigger-killer couldn't be working yet because there were no flashes whatsoever, and suddenly she had a horrible thought.

What if Daddy's theory was wrong? What if her patchwork wasn't buried in a blown circuit, but gone forever?

Marissa grabbed her cell and looked at it blankly. No messages, but she hadn't expected any. She got up and the floor creaked. She was still wearing the jeans and Chase Utley Phillies T-shirt she'd put on earlier, and she suddenly had the feeling the killer was waiting for her out in the hall.

But he couldn't be. One of her parents would have set the downstairs alarm before coming up here; it was so ingrained in them to do so floor to floor it had become ritual, like flushing the toilet or hanging up your coat or sticking your cell in your back pocket so you could jump right on it if something came up.

Marissa pushed out into the hall and felt for the light switch. Usually it was one-two-buckle-my-shoe, but she hadn't been here for long enough that she had to paw around. If a hand closed over hers she'd scream to wake the dead. If the lights came on and there was a man standing there by the linen closet she'd have a heart attack. If there was a figure waiting in the downstairs closet . . .

She found the switch, padded down the short flight of stairs, and set off the motion detector, the beeping keypad giving its gentle countdown they were all so used to hearing in the distant background that if one of them got up in the night for a drink of water it didn't even wake the others anymore. She walked over to the pad by the front door, put in the code, took a step back toward the den, and something changed. It was the lighting, the visual tone of the shadowed living room.

There was something coming across the carpeted floor now, something off-kilter, and it took a second for Marissa to register that it was a mechanized illumination going on and off, lighting part of the space and then leaving it in darkness.

She ran into the den.

Her trigger-killer was there on the table blinking red, and she stood before it, mouth ajar, strange light playing on and off across her face. It would be any second now. Like so many things in life, the decisions that would affect it the most had to be made on the spot, like right now, no tomorrow.

She reached for the contraption, ready to rip it apart and take her chances with the beast. Yes, that was the answer. The patchwork had indicated she would win, and maybe it was just her assumptions and faulty projections that made her think she needed a psychic aid to beat this bastard. She would defeat him somehow and then continue on as a "normal person," dating Jerome, getting to know him all over again, loving him, immersing herself in him.

But then again she just couldn't.

In the end, she hated living inside what felt like a cloud, as if one of her senses had been taken from her. Without the patchwork who was she? Who exactly did Jerome want?

The flickering upped in tempo and Marissa Madison was staring into a strobe light. Her eyes widened. She was frozen where she stood, and the rapid blinking suddenly stopped.

The tiny light turned solid green.

Patchwork burst into her so hard she sat down with a thump right there on the carpet. It was almost too blissful, as if the flood had been building behind a dam and here was the glorious torrent.

She saw in her mind that Daddy had taken a glass of warm milk before bedtime because he'd had an upset stomach worrying so much about his daughter's future. Mother had it on her list to call Marissa's landlord first thing about severances, deposits, and refunds, though she was holding off on Widener because she was sure she could get Marissa to change her mind at least about that part.

Nothing about a serial killer.

Marissa stood up and actually swooned with the next thing that hit her. It didn't make a bit of sense, but it was the strongest premonition she'd ever had.

No. Not premonition. Instructions. Spelled out letter for letter.

Marissa made for the basement, digging her cell out of her back pocket. It didn't hold together in any way, shape, or form, especially since there was no reason to contact Jerome at this point, but everything in her being cried out to her in an absolute urgency to do this thing.

Now.

She keyed in the alarm code for the first floor there on the pad by the basement door and heard the muted sixty-second countdown on the other side of it as she hustled down the stairs.

She was compelled to send Jerome Anthony Franklin a text.

And the words were nothing but poetic gibberish.

Despite all this, Marissa stood at the edge of her television area and typed in the words, letter for letter as they had appeared in her mind. She checked it. Hit send.

Something was wrong, something moving at the edge of the basement, there by the wall where there was bare space for all but the rug Daddy had set down for the poker table he'd never got around to setting up.

The rug was moving. Something was pushing it up from underneath, which was impossible. This was a concrete floor, and from over the lip of the rug there was a hand pawing up and over, a yellow gloved hand feeling about, doubling the piece of rug backward on itself, and then an arm making a flat L-shape over the fold, and then another hand and arm doing the same, and he pulled himself through and Marissa was frozen there where she stood.

It was the rubberized flying dude from the Pacifico Ford, yellow head squared off with small pieces of torn caution tape like streamers dangling from the top and sightless cartoon eyes staring above that wide apple-slice grin.

After planting his feet he straightened and grew and grew, seeming to rise clear to the ceiling, and his long shadow played across half the basement. He was humongous, six foot five at the least, and as he came for her the patchwork slammed home, giving her splintered pictures of who this guy was, his cold evil, his terrible genius.

His name was Deseronto, and he was wearing a hazmat suit (hazardous materials for you dumb fucking homeowners), and he'd done a complicated dance over the last twenty-four hours, all based on the storm drain he'd noticed out in front of the Madison residence and the twin brother he'd discovered back on Dartmouth, where they were renovating that house and the job had been stalled. When Marissa was worrying about tumbling trash cans, he was busy creating an apparatus that could manually cut through concrete, a big diamond screw thread in a roll cage, you just needed a man strong enough to turn the crankshaft and a distraction loud enough to cover the wrench and grind, like a rattling heater coming up intermittently.

The ADT stickers hadn't bothered him in the least, since it wasn't often folks rigged their basements where the egress windows were always padlocked. Everyone thought the access was covered upstairs, so once the hole was cut he'd camped out there in the storm drain, listening to Marissa make her phone call, learning her secret "get-away" and waiting for nightfall. If she hadn't come down to sneak a communication tonight, he'd known there was always the weekend. He was smart and he was patient.

His strides covered a lot of ground, and he was on her in an instant. Marissa recovered from her phobic shock and terror just enough to try for that mask, but she wasn't tall enough. Her nails clawed at his chest area, and he reached out with those huge yellow mitts that palmed both sides of her head in what almost appeared a gesture of affection. They smelled of the rust and decay of the storm drain, and he gave a sharp twist, snapping her neck.

She heard it pop, felt herself break in what felt like two pieces. Her head lolled and she crumbled, and he yanked her under his arm, walking her back to the wall like a sack of meal.

Marissa was pinned to him and her head was bobbing, but she was alive. For a bare second he had to stomp on the fold in the rug to keep it from yawning back and covering the hole, but it was only a second, and he was swift about shoving her down through the opening, banging her head on the rim with a meaty thump she heard more than she felt.

He laughed from under the mask and Marissa heard him think to himself, *"That's gonna leave skin and hair tufts,"* and she felt him loving the idea that her DNA didn't matter worth a shit, and even though he was leaving behind clues with this one, there was no one in the great wide world who could connect all the dots. Not unless things went suddenly unlucky. And luck had always been his favorite bitch.

She landed in a heap and had a sideward, tilted view of the storm drain while he pushed through above her with a boot propped on either side. The long cylinder was dank and filthy and flaking, and she was lying in a runnel of ice-cold water that wasn't quite as big as the maroon stain on both sides of it cutting down the center of the pipe. It stank of corroded steel and rotted leaves, and just past a small nest of twigs was Deseronto's apparatus.

She kicked at it just as he crouched down, the rug slowly folding back over above them, and the bulky mechanism was heavy as hell and it was stuck on something, it had to be, for she had connected with it hard enough to send it rolling down the pipe. She concluded that he must have put a stick or a rock as a stopper in front of the wheels, and she heard him grunt in frustration, amazed that she was still alive and more amazed that she'd had the power to kick at his machine. Marissa was impressed too. Even in this dire circumstance she was still joking with herself just as Mother would if it were her down here in the pipe, thinking she had to Google this immediately and add somewhere in Wikipedia that you really could move significantly with a broken neck.

She kicked again, and the wheels stumbled over their obstructions, whacking and stuttering and taking that evil contraption down the rusted chute.

"Fuck!" she heard, and he struggled to jump past her, a thicket of arms, legs, and torso scrambling over her in the dim glow that was shadowing over as the rug settled up there.

"Yes, *fuck,*" she thought, "*fuck you!*" This could screw him big-time. Through the patchwork she saw that it was hell getting that thing up here to start with. It fit through the manhole cover up on Dartmouth well enough, and he'd ridden it like a sled down through the back end of the ravine, but dragging it up at the halfway point had been a chore even for him. It was only half a block or so, but the streamlet of storm water was gritty as hell, like sandpaper, and while he did indeed manage to haul his creation up to New Ardmore Avenue, there was no way he was going to backtrack it, hit the T-joint at the halfway mark, make the hard right, and doggie-crawl all the way to the park creek blocks away even though it was all on a downhill slope, not in these tight quarters with a dead body, no sir.

Suddenly he was back, and he was straddled over her and she hadn't heard him coming. He ripped off his helmet, a chalky blur with black eyes.

He let out a guttural roar and clamped his teeth to the meat of her face. He was sunken to the gums all around her nose, and he snapped his head back and forth like a mad dog. She felt pain and a hot greasy wetness, and he ripped free and she was cold and he reached down and wrenched her head around so hard her neck dishragged and her chin twisted straight back between her shoulder blades in a straight 180. It was a bright bolt of agony, and she thumped face first into the churning water. Then she was removed, watching the scene from the side in third person. It was the patchwork providing her a dissociated view, fading at the edges as it slowly shut down.

She saw him drag her rumpled form down the pipe to the apparatus he'd retrieved. She saw him settle on it, position himself on his back and pull her atop, next strapping the both of them tight. Next he was grunting, pushing with his palms, starting the toboggan, or more accurately, the two-man luge.

She watched Jonathan Martin Delaware Deseronto lying back, holding her like a small child, rolling through the storm drain, banging the hard right at the "T" and clattering down the long stretch cutting through the hills of the neighborhood. They were picking up speed he could barely control now, thundering down for the creek that zigzagged through the park five blocks away, deep in where he'd pulled off the drain grate and parked his Toyota just off the bank.

They shot through the opening, and the final descent was longer than he'd remembered thinking it would be. They landed in a foot of water with hearty splash and shuddered with the impact, sliding and stopping by some big polished rocks. He hurt his back, but not that much. He'd banged an elbow, but not all that bad.

It was all fading, the scene getting smaller as the circle of perception was shrinking at its circumference.

He hauled the apparatus up the bank, pressing it overhead so it wouldn't leave marks though he knew the cops would have his boot size. Tiny loss for a greater gain. By the time he got it in his trunk with his hazmat suit and went back for Marissa, the entire vision was down to the size of a basketball. She knew he had one more stop before hitting the road back to the shop for the cutting phase, and she also knew he doubted very much that anyone on Dartmouth Avenue at midnight was going to notice a guy wearing sunglasses, a hard hat, and a reflective vest stopping to gather up the blue nylon tent structure propped around the manhole cover of the storm drain.

Deseronto got in the car and put on the reflective vest and the hard hat. Sunglasses could wait: after all, he had to drive out of here with his lights off and it was dark as shit. He started up the vehicle, thinking himself ultimately clever for backing in here with the trunk side facing the bank of the creek. It had made the loading far easier.

He pulled out slowly and didn't hear the crunch and tinkle of the broken beer bottles Gary Fey and Danny Santo had scattered at the edge of the creek, smashing them after partying hard a week ago Thursday. Deseronto had backed over the litter of glass with his rear tires coming in, and he ran over all of it again on his exit, the latter rendezvous more profound than its predecessor. The rubber didn't puncture immediately; he had good Firestones.

He pulled off the curb at the edge of the park and did so carefully so he wouldn't scrape a fender. Then he sped back to Dartmouth. It was going to be another long night, and the moon was suddenly buried in cloud cover.

Chop, chop.

There was a rain coming on.

PIT STOP

That's right, asshole. All things considered it was a good stalk and kill, chock-full of chance cards, community treasures, positioning, and playing pieces like a live fucking Monopoly game. Enough twists and surprises for ya? Scared to pass "Go" now?

Speaking of which, it's my turn. Didn't want to see Mama's ghost up there in room 457, I'll give you that much, but now that I've relived the moment for moment in Marissa Madison's head as Marissa Madison we'll call it dead even.

So why do I keep talking to you, the nobody? I guess it's something I've always done, as if you were my private little audience member bound and gagged and tied to your chair, forced to submit and witness my gospel. But time's a wasting and, to be real, I'm still standing here in the Motel 6 archway holding this icy-cold dead-alive thing face to face like a Siamese twin connected at the forehead, and I'm tired of it. I smell something familiar and realize my nose ain't been bit off, it was just some symbolic bullshitty payback that was part of the package, part of living in Marissa Madison's shoes for a hot minute, and to tell you the truth the chomping was the only thing she did that had me half interested. At least it took some balls, and don't fucking laugh 'cause I ain't in the mood for your punning.

So what now? The rewind is dead because Madison is, and like her dear sweet parents might have said, "It's time to move forward."

Tell you where I'm headed, asshole.

I'm gonna find a way to get off this jobsite and I'm gonna make my way across the street and up the hill to that BP gas station. I'm gonna find me two tires, roll on out of here, bury this bitch stitched or in pieces, and go home to get a good sleep.

"Not quite yet," she croaks from behind that wet hanging hair, and her breath is thick and smells awful familiar.

And then I get it. It's the smell. Pungent and specific and familiar as hell. Symbolic bullshit, but this time with meaning, with punch, and a huge set of balls.

See, the cutting phase at the shop went well (except for that moment her hair bunched up in the mouth guard of the Sawzall skidding the wood-cutting blade straight up her cheek), and in a matter of minutes I had her sectioned and packaged like chicken parts in one of those big aluminum-loaf flimsy-tins we used to soak gears in. I had the tools cleaned, rinsed, and sanitized before you could say "boo," and even though I had to refill the sprayer's gun reservoir with another dose of concentrated industrial acid cleanser to blitz the floor and squeegee all the waste down the drain, I was resetting the warehouse alarm and locking up by 1:15. It was smooth sailing until I pulled out of the parking lot, reached in the glove compartment just to check, and brought out the crinkly bag that was empty for all but some shitty busted-up crumbs at the bottom.

See, we all know the other stuff, asshole. I drove to the usual entry point for the dumping phase back in the cul-de-sac where Skinny Jimmy Whalen used to live, but there was an Upper Darby cop sitting there with his lights off parked at the curb. Come to think of it now I didn't even see anyone there in the cab, but I wasn't gonna take any chances.

Don't you get it? I blamed the sudden bad luck on the fact that I didn't have my munchies. 'Course we all know I wound up on 476 with two flats in a rainstorm, but the part I forgot to connect here was that I made a small pit stop before heading up to the highway. For luck. And I was in the neighborhood.

I stopped at the 7-Eleven on 69th Street.

For my El Sabroso Hot and Spicy Pork Rinds.

CHAPTER FIFTEEN

Jerome Anthony Franklin was on break working the graveyard shift and he was bored and frustrated, hanging out in the back room with the dry stock and trying to figure out how to use the electric pallet jack. There was some dumb rule that you couldn't bring the heavy machine onto the sales floor because of customer liability, but there was an issue here for worker's rights as well, having to lug fifty-pound boxes one by one to the racks, and he made a mental note to look it up in the library tomorrow. Maybe he'd contact regional and start a petition. Maybe . . .

"Jerome! Mr. Franklin!"

It was Balbir, and every time the man barked out orders in that accent laced with polite desperation Jerome was perturbed at those who would see the man as no more than cliché, a Hindu originally from Bombay who was running an inner-city 7-Eleven. There was nothing cliché about making a living and nothing stereotypical about a man from a foreign country trying to better himself, a man who liked watching soccer and brewing homemade green tea, a man who had a daughter married to a guy who owned a breakfast truck in Center City and a son who was studying to be a pharmacist, a man fighting the good fight and who'd always treated Jerome more than fairly. He opened the door and stuck his brown head in.

"Jerome, my friend!"

"Yes, boss."

"I have a customer to attend to and someone just left without taking his receipt."

"No problem," Jerome said, grabbing his coat, which he'd tossed on top of the 2 for $2.00 snack cartons. He took the slip from his manager and smiled in passing. Balbir hated it when business wasn't properly completed, and while it was anal to chase someone down to offer a record of transaction for a pack of gum or box of Tic Tacs, it was his thing. And the pallet jack wasn't going anywhere anytime soon.

Jerome jogged down the front aisle and, while sidestepping to avoid a pallet of bottled water, he almost ran into the Slurpee machine. Outside he was a few seconds too late, for there was just one car at the edge of the front lot, waiting at the exit ramp for the cross-traffic to clear. It was a Toyota with fumes of exhaust threading up into the rain, making mystic reflections under the street lamp.

"Your back tires are low," Jerome thought. Then he shrugged and got his cell out of his jacket pocket to check the time.

There was a text from Marissa. His heart kicked up a notch, and he moved back under the overhang. This was from a couple of hours ago, and he hadn't checked for her reply because he hadn't expected one. Marissa Madison wasn't going to give up her gift. And even though it hurt to admit that to himself, he'd committed to moving forward the moment he'd suggested the ultimatum.

Strange.

Her message didn't make sense.

It said:

"Follow Cinderella with the two busted slippers so the ghosts won't cry anymore."

He frowned and turned back to the store, slipping the phone in his pocket and wondering why he'd considered getting back with her at all. She was crazy. Always had been. He had the door half open and stopped right there in his tracks as something connected. It was a statement that one of his favorite all-time race car drivers, Emerson Fittipaldi, had made back in the mid-nineties when he lost an Indy race. He'd referred to his car as a "she" and called the faulty tires "her shoes."

He looked back with a start, and the Toyota with the low back tires tried to cut into traffic, having to screech to a stop. The driver laid on his horn and pulled back up into the lot a few feet because his nose was sticking out. The rain was coming down hard.

Jerome stuck his head back into the store.

"Boss! I gotta go! It's an emergency!" He turned and took off, splashing over to the side lot where the Malibu was parked, as he and Grandma shared it when they both worked the night shift—picking each other up and dropping each other off as a way to keep in touch. He had no idea what Marissa's message really meant and less of a clue what he would do if he managed to confront whoever was in that vehicle. But all the connections were more than coincidence, and he'd never doubted Marissa Madison's relative powers. He only questioned her ability to follow through with her visions.

But he was suddenly compelled to do this, all in, right now.

For Marissa.

For crying ghosts.

He couldn't quite catch up. At Manoa it looked as if the guy had gone left and Jerome followed him, just catching the glow of his tail lights cutting down Reed Road. He was nearly positive that he saw a receding flicker of red heading left on Springfield at the top of the hill, and at the first stop sign he thought for sure the guy had done a quickie right/left to head for Route 1. But at the fork in front of the Marple Crossing Shopping Center he had to make a decision. Was the mystery man with the Cinderella tires continuing on the same throughway or making for 476?

Jerome could have sworn he saw something flash for a second way up past the overpass where there was a sign for Chester left lane, so he kicked it in and swung onto the merge for the bigger of the two highways as fast as he dared without hydroplaning. The rain was coming down in buckets and his wipers weren't that great. He was lucky to have this ride, but really, Grandma, hit the auto parts store, will ya? He chewed at a hangnail. He'd risked his job to go on this wild goose chase, and he had to admit to himself that it was insane.

But there was something about that message. Something desperate and sad and important. And he loved Marissa Madison. As bad as she was for him.

He thought he saw the lights of another vehicle way up ahead a few times, but in this kind of downpour everything seemed like a mirage. At the Swarthmore exit an eighteen-wheeler going way too fast shot by in the passing lane, but besides that it seemed no one was out here. Jerome slowed down despite himself. He wanted to help, to figure out the puzzle, to come up big for his ex, but it wasn't going to do anyone any kind of good if he wound up driving off a cliff or down an embankment. Enough was enough.

He was about to double back when he came around a long yawning bend and saw something. Up ahead there were lights, but they weren't hanging low on a shitty Toyota. It was a state trooper parked in the breakdown lane with his flashers going. Jerome approached, slowed, and stopped next to it.

There was no one in the car. And just past it there were scrapes in the road, as if someone had peeled out dragging his back end.

Jerome pulled over just past where the scrapes were and put on his emergency blinkers so he could think. What was this? Why had he been summoned or whatever Marissa would call it? She scared him and saddened and thrilled him. Still. But this had everything to do with trouble and bad endings. Though there wasn't anything he could fathom worse than the Citrus Bowl, a vacated cop car, skid marks, and an isolated highway in the rain had nothing to do with magic slippers and fairy-tales. Besides, he was pretty sure that he'd lost the guy back on Springfield Road. He'd been going on faith.

I'll give it a mile more. Maybe two.

He put the Malibu in drive and slipped back to the highway. He passed under a bridge that was pitted and water-stained on its underside, and it imposed upon him a feeling of dread he couldn't substantiate. Exit 6 was coming up on the right. He took a look farther up the road and thought he saw traffic.

He hit the gas and continued up Route 476, driving straight into the teeth of the storm.

THE UNVEILING

Ha!" I spout right into Marissa Madison's dirty tangle of hair. "I said *ha!* Your nigger-boy drove right past the exit! Just like the Citrus Bowl, he failed you! Just like in the Mustang trying to give you a poke, he fell short! Just like with his grandma and his teachers and his buddies in the lunchroom, he dropped flat on his face! Oh, you sure can pick 'em. Thanks for the show!"

She laughs back at me and it sounds harsh, as if it's coated with the dirt of the hole I'm still planning to bury her in. Her breath still reeks of pork rinds and she's holding my neck tight with her fingers interlocked behind it, in turn forcing me to keep my bucket hold beneath her dead naked ass.

"Before we finish this business," she says, "I want to run some numbers by you. Like a parts breakdown you'd see in the shop, or one of those bids from the Navy Yard where you look at the graphs and figure out the ratios."

I shut my mouth and she says, "I want to discuss the mathematics of visions, Jonathan. You have certainly not been standing here in the archway of the Motel 6 watching movies, but the scenes you've experienced took up literal segments of time, not much, but enough to become real 'substance.' While a lot of the presentations actually skipped time, or rushed through it like a montage sequence, like paraphrase, even those events occupied certain precious seconds. There were a number of scene clips where you briefly lived in the younger versions of yourself, while there were flashbacks inside of flashbacks which by default took up absolutely no time at all, like my meeting Jerome in the stairwell and then his rap battle in the lunchroom, both displayed during the larger scene where I was walking into the mall. And even though the outer scenes were never played out in full linear minutes, like the string of highlights illustrating Jerome's following you down Reed Road to Springfield Road to the fork in front of the Marple Crossing Shopping Center, my exhibition as a whole took *time,* measurable *time,* just not real time, ya dig, Johnny-boy? Ya gettin' my drift?"

I never let no one call me "Johnny" except Mama, so I squeeze her hard enough to flop her head against my collarbone, and she grunts all pissed off.

"Careful, jerk! Someone broke my neck, it's sensitive!"

"Sorry," I say. "So what's your fucking point?"

She puts her forearms against my chest and pushes off so I'm facing that awful tangle of hair again.

"The point is that altogether," she says, "considering all the scene partials, I managed to hold you here on this jobsite for sixty-six minutes. Sixty-six. Time for Jerome to go back to his grandmother's house in Broomall and sit in the living room while she continued on her night shift. Time for him to put two and two together and get back on the road. You see, her place is right near an exit to Route 476, and Jerome just needed time to think and a place to do it. He always just needed time."

She places her hands on both sides of my head, and her voice comes through in a whisper now.

"And he's no loser," she says. "You are. Asshole."

She changes, she breaks and crumbles, and I'm standing in the archway of the Motel 6 with an armload of body parts. The rain is sweeping in from the east and the moon is making reflections all along the puddles of the walkway that dance and jump with the pellets of the rain. All seventeen pieces of Marissa Madison tumble out of my arms, splashing in the puddles gathered at my feet, her head making a meaty thump on the pavers and rolling. It bumps off the base of one of those disassembled luggage rollers and settles facing upward, the eyes glassy and the nose area nothing more than a dark, stringy void.

Shadows move above her and then they're pushed off by a creeping sort of light fingering along the ground, snaking in and out of the crevices and edges cut into the darkness by the jobsite machinery.

Headlights.

Jerome Anthony Franklin here to find Cinderella and quiet the ghosts.

I think about running off right toward the new construction and the storage units. I think about moving back to the inner darkness of the motel, but I don't. Instead, I watch him sweep his brights across the front end of the jobsite down there in the public lower parking area, checking the semicircle of office trailers up on blocks and when he sees that everything's dark and vacant, sure as shit he's gonna advance those headlights to bumpier ground. Up here.

I think about the possibilities, and I wonder how everything could have actually fallen into place so perfectly. I consider

Marissa Madison and the creepy way her powers have stretched out past the span of her lifetime, like echoes, like vapor, and I remind myself that echoes fade and stench dissipates. In the end she was just a girl. A girly-girl who thought coaxing her boyfriend to a showdown was gonna solve things. Like the schoolyard. Like the movies.

I feel the corners of my mouth tent-pitch upward.

Then I run out into the rain, sneakers slapping along the brick pavers of the entrance walkway. I can hear Jerome Anthony Franklin working through the various ruts and divots down left, revving the engine and spinning his tires in the mud here and there along the incline, and out the corner of my eye I can sense the jagged points of light reflecting high off the exposed steel in the broad skeleton of the motel's residence quarters stretching along to the west. I am pretty sure there aren't any shadows jumping off me as I splash through the puddles over here, and as I shove between the luggage racks and Rubbermaid push-dollies filled with reusable scrap, I know my cover of darkness ain't gonna last all that long. Twenty seconds until Franklin makes it up the washed-out access road, takes the dogleg, and floods the area with light. Twenty-five, maybe.

I dodge through the checkerboard of jobsite equipment, slip on a pile of wet rebar that shouldn't have been lying across the makeshift walking path to begin with, and bark my shin on the edge of a Big Tex trailer hitch. I slide a bit, sidestepping, arms windmilling, still smiling and grimacing, telling myself, *"Don't rub it!"* and next I'm sloshing through the mud as fast as I am able without doing a face plant and belly-slide right here in this open stretch leading straight to my car.

Wish I had time to look for a wrench. It would come in handy when I make to remove the license plate.

See, I have to get it off the back before Jerome Anthony Franklin enters the fold, lights up the world back here, checks things out, and makes his "discoveries." So he'll think there's a blank spot.

So he'll believe I got a reason not to kill him.

CHAPTER SIXTEEN

Deseronto used the dead cop as a buffer and went in sliding on his knees in the mud. Air burst out of the corpse sandwiched up against the low fender, and it smelled like chicken. That one almost made Deseronto crack the fuck up, but he wasn't usually a laughing sort of fellow and his protruding knucklebone was killing him. He set to work on the license plate, wet hair dangling in his eyes, and at first it seemed it was going to be lickety-split. The left set-bolt spun off in a heartbeat, but the right was stubborn, rusted and frozen. Jerome Anthony Franklin was getting close to the turn, brights pointed up at the storm clouds like those Hollywood victory spotlights because he was at the base of the last part that had looked steep, almost a drop-off. With any luck he'd get stuck there for a second, back off, and reroute, moving around through the weeds.

Deseronto switched it up and went ass-first into the mud. He planted the soles of his sneakers above the dead cop, fingered behind the plate on both sides of the fastener, and leaned back, yanking with all his strength and his weight. For a second he got nothing, and then he heard the gritty "pop" of a bolt-thread being forced past the base material wedged around it. Then another "pop" and another, and when it finally came free the momentum threw him backward, almost smacking the back of his head flat into the mud.

By the time he pushed up to his feet the lights were coming around the corner.

Deseronto scrambled back for the cover of the scattered machinery, ducking behind a large yellow compressor angled up on one side off its tow-wheels just as Jerome Anthony Franklin drove up bumping and bobbing. The kid moved cautiously by the Toyota, slowing and parking just past it, pulling in rear to rear leaving a car's space between.

Perfect.

Deseronto had a good view from around the back of the compressor and down a path made by two dozers and a stack of concrete block. Jerome turned off his lights and shut the car off. When he got out and made his way around the front side of it there in his pathetic 7-Eleven uniform he looked hesitant and vulnerable, not alarmed and razor-sharp, so Deseronto concluded that he hadn't yet seen the dead cop wedged in partially beneath the lowered back fender of the Toyota. He hadn't had the angle.

More perfect.

Jerome passed his front passenger door, moving carefully through the mud, staring at Deseronto's opened trunk. When he got to the rear corner of his Malibu he saw the cop lying at the base of the sunken Toyota. He stopped there in his tracks.

And Deseronto called out to him softly.

FOREPLAY

When he hears me call his name it chills him straight to the marrow. I can see it plain as day, asshole, and I know how easy this is gonna be. And fun too. He's wire-tight, looking all around trying to pretend he ain't looking, but the sound is tricky with all the weird echoes and the rain. He can't pin me down, and that's the point.

"Jerome . . ." I singsong again. "There's a dead man laying there in the mud, for real—for real, ain't no drill, and if you don't wanna join him you're gonna do everything I tell you. Now hold on. Don't even think it. No wild horses or crazy roadrunners. You ain't gonna come back in here like a cowboy looking for me in the clutter. I know everything 'bout you but you got nothing on me, and while I could be some skinny runt like you, I think you're smart enough to know not to chance it. I got no reason to lie to ya, 'cause tell the truth I could kill ya even if I was some skinny little runt, or running little cunt, or whatever you think you might be able to handle. But the fact is I'm over six feet tall, and I could snap you like a twig."

He's frozen right there, left hand splayed out, right hand in a fist still holding his car keys. Then I use what folks might call my Injun talents passed down by generations of warriors hunting in the brush, and I move silently to another spot, this time behind some big plastic barrels filled with steel rakes and pick axes.

"And I know what's running through your head," I say. Then I almost laugh aloud, because he jerks there in his spot, freaked by the way I seem to be throwing my voice all over the jobsite. "So don't you go listening to your street sense or whatever the fuck you'd call it back in the hood, 'cause there ain't gonna be no making a break for your ride, hitting the gas, and kicking mud back into my face. You don't know how fast I can come on, so you'd best recalculate whether or not you could get back around to the other side of your car, get in it, and drive out of here before I could stop you and break your little chicken neck. Go on, work the numbers. First you gotta account for slippage. In the mud. I've been here for over an hour getting used to the way you gotta make your way around here, and I guarantee you'd lose a second on your starting burst no matter how subtle you tried it, like Bugs fucking Bunny bicycle-pedaling his feet with that fuck-tard tin drum soundtrack, you see what I'm saying? Then you might skid going around the corners, and even if you jump across the hood you have to account for how close you parked to that big concrete pipe. I saw your door hit it when you got out, and it's gonna be a chore getting back in. To be honest with you, I could throw down some strides out here without even half trying and you wouldn't even make it to the door, let alone have time to push up the proper key from the bunch you've got there in your fist. So first things first: why don't you take them keys, walk 'em over to your trunk, open it, and then put those bad boys on the roof of my vehicle, right in the middle where they'd be a real pain in the ass to get to if you suddenly got itchy through the process and thought you could make a run for it."

I watch him comply, and once he's got his trunk open I tiptoe hunched over alongside a big roto-tiller and sneak around the back edge of a 65-horsepower walk-behind saw. Now I have a view off to the side of him, and he's just tossed the keys up on the roof of my Toyota.

"Over here," I say, and he can't help but jump and snap his head around despite himself. His hand instinctively makes a motion toward the side of his jacket, and I stop him, saying, "Nah, nah, nah. Bad boy. Let's put an end to all that mystery right now. Empty them pockets nice and slow, and then turn 'em inside out like goat's ears so I can see."

He takes out his cell phone, a big flat black one.

"Hold it by the edges, boy. You touch the face of that thing and try to record something it'll be the last thing you do. That's right. Now let it drop in the mud and stomp on it, real good so I can hear the glass crunch and the plastic crack."

He does it and right after he says,

"My pockets don't turn out. They aren't sewn like that."

"How you know?"

"Because I'm smart."

"All right, smart-ass. Take the coat off and toss it as far away from you as you can. That a boy, nice and easy."

The wind picks up on his follow-through and I see him trying not to flinch. He's cold now. I use the moment to duck behind one of the Bobcat front-end loaders, and I'm trying my best not to snicker to myself as I do it because Jerome Anthony Franklin is about to get colder.

"Let's talk about the piece now, Jerome, the hardware you're packing."

"What piece?" he says.

"That .32 Beretta you're hiding somewhere. If you left it in the glove compartment you're stupid as shit, but I agree you're smarter than that. See, I know you went back to Grandma's house, and it wasn't just to get your thoughts together. You dug into that box with the yarn spinner and the old pictures in it. Figured you'd bring some protection."

"I don't have a gun."

"Take off that smock, prick. And toss it as far away from you as you can. Your shirt underneath that as well. C'mon, let's have a contest. See if you can throw that stuff as far as the jacket."

He does it all, nice and slow, and he has that moment afterwards where his arms are crossed up at his bare chest like a middle-school girl carrying her books. He's shivering.

"Pants too," I say. "Go on, get naked all the way down to your drawers. When you're done I'll let you put your sneakers back on. Time to see if you got fancy with an ankle holster, like I thought you should have snagged the minute I knew you were working there late at night under the El."

"I can't afford an ankle holster."

"Yeah, but you can buy sweat socks. Off with the sneakers and pants—do it."

I watch carefully as he slides off his kicks, then unbuttons and rag-rolls down the denim.

"Pull 'em off," I say. "Sit right there in the mud."

When he complies I see the spirit go out of him, shoulders sagging, knees pointed, Fruit of the Looms buried in sludge. He pulls his feet through and stuffed into his tube sock there's a shape.

"Nice," I say. "Now here's the deal. A, you can shoot at my voice, waste your bullets, hope to get lucky; or B, you can point the barrel out in front of you playing Navy Seal, stalking in through the maze where you thought you last heard me, trying to pin me into a corner. But I know the lay of the land back here. I'm gonna wear me a shadow, wait for you, and wrench your head around like a steering wheel, you feel me? Option C is much, much better, so think about it real hard for a second. You can always throw the gun, toss it like a grenade into the machinery and the shadows, and I'll consider not crushing your skull with a shovel. How do you like that?"

"I don't."

"Didn't really need an answer, boy."

"It was rhetorical."

"Whatever. Toss the gun."

After the slightest of pauses, Jerome Anthony Franklin throws the .32 into the dark scatter of machinery, actually around fifteen feet over to my left. It makes a muted sound, hitting off something cementous, and then there's a splash with a particular sort of resonation, as if it landed in one of those fifty-gallon steel drums filled with rainwater. Shit. Hard for me to get to it now, but no matter. Didn't need it anyway. Guns were never my thing. Too easy, like cheating. Back out front, Jerome Anthony Franklin is hugging his knees, shaking with the cold, head buried in his forearms.

"Stop your quivering," I say, "and put your Keds back on."

"Can I have my jacket?" he says, all muffled.

"No."

"Then what's the difference with the sneakers?"

"Forty-five-millimeter offset, and a 5 × 100 bolt pattern, that's what."

He looks up sharply, trying to pinpoint me with everything he's got, but of course he's off by a bunch.

"Why are you throwing those particular numbers at me?" he says.

I laugh.

"Because the Chevy Malibu and the Toyota Corolla are similar makes and models and the Firestones and Goodyears are all universal. Because you don't have my plate number. Because you've been lucky enough not to have gotten a look at me, and your cell is in the mud, prick. You need sneaks, but trust me, you won't need a jacket to warm on up. Not for long. You'll be too hot and busy. See, I want your back tires, *Jerome*. I want you to fix my two flats."

CHAPTER SEVENTEEN

The cop was heavy, already stiffening, and Jerome slipped twice trying to drag him away from the fender. Also, Deseronto had made it clear that he didn't want the kid dicking around in his trunk, said his roadside emergency kit was incomplete anyway, so Jerome had to use his own hardware, jacking up both cars with the same tool, one after the other. By the time he had completed the first half of this dog and pony show his fingers had pruned and his briefs were sooty black like his sneakers. He had a scratch down one leg and he'd taken the skin off two of his knuckles when he'd scraped the back of his hand along the concrete pipe Deseronto's car was wedged up against, working the wrench to force off a bolt that had burred. He'd just crankshafted the Malibu up with the scissor jack a second time, and on the final turn with the long handle his tender knuckles dragged down through the mud deep enough to hit firmer substance.

"Fuck," he seethed.

"Now, now," Deseronto said. "One down, one to go. And the first was the hard one considering the close quarters, so you should pat yourself on the back for a job well done. This is the home stretch now, boy. Easy street. Let's get a move on."

Jerome brought over the wrench and started on the first lug nut.

"I still don't see why you don't just kill me," he said.

"Don't be so sure I won't."

"Why haven't you?"

"Too much fun seeing you do my dirty work." Deseronto moved silently off left to fresh ground behind a pile of corrugated sheeting. Now that the gun was out of the picture, the omniscient voice wasn't really all that necessary, but Deseronto liked the effect, the way it seemed to unnerve this rather stoic, no-nonsense young man. In fact, Deseronto wanted to break him, cut him down emotionally, total him and leave him speechless. Jerome put the last lug nut in the hubcap he'd pried off and rolled the tire through the mud to the Toyota, leaning it there at the rear. It took him only a second or two to go back and jack down the Malibu, and he moved the lifting apparatus back over to Deseronto's vehicle, reaching under the fender, searching for the hole.

"Whoever you are, the game is up," Jerome said, probably in some weak, self-defeating attempt at trying to lure his captor into illuminating his true intentions. "It's over. I've seen your car."

"Like the thousands of other Toyotas in the area."

"I saw some of the stuff in the trunk."

"Shit that can be easily removed."

Jerome pulled off the flat, switched it with the one he'd taken from his own car, and tightened the nuts, smacking the wrench with the flat of his palm until they squeaked as he'd been told. He hefted the ruptured tire back across the mud, and after returning to lower the Toyota on its fresh set of Firestones, he shuffled back to stick the damaged tire onto the rear axle of the Malibu. Finally, after tightening down the last nuts, tapping the hubcap back into place, and executing the final lowering process, the operation was completed. He was soaked and filthy as if he'd just run naked through a coal mine. Deseronto's voice came from the far right then, out by where there were a couple of Knaack boxes stacked on top of each other.

"Wrench and jack go back in the pouch, boy, and I want you to stick them in your trunk. Next, gather the broken parts of your cell phone and your clothes. They join the wrench and the jack, and then you shut the lid. Chop-chop. Miss a beat and I'll kill you, I'm not playing. Night's still young."

Jerome followed orders. He found the remains of his cell phone and held them up so his tormentor, wherever he was, could see. He fished his pants, shirt, smock, and jacket from the mud and put them in his trunk as well. He closed the lid and gave it an extra push for show.

"Good," Deseronto said. "Very good. Now, Mr. Dead Cop goes back where he belongs." Jerome looked over toward Deseronto's opened trunk.

"You're kidding."

"I kid you not."

"He's kind of heavy—"

"Work it out. Move."

Jerome walked to the vehicle mechanically and bent to it. He struggled. Took him three tries, and he eventually had to stand the corpse up face to face and press to him body to body to nudge him up over the lip. When done, Jerome was shaking, blood smeared across his forehead and along his right arm. He pointed to where he thought Deseronto might be hiding.

"You won't get away with this," he said. "And you won't be able to pin it on me. They'll find you. Hunt you down like a dog."

Deseronto made a snorting sound, and it came from behind the luggage racks now, where the brick pavers were patterned.

"They ain't gonna care about the ghost driving the mystery Toyota, Jerome. They're gonna have their man."

"But why on earth would I kill this 'missing' cop?"

"You wouldn't. But after a bit of investigating they'll conclude he was collateral damage, knowing that you had every reason on earth to want to kill all the white bitches."

Something flew through the air, and Jerome backed off a few steps. It landed, skidded through the mud, and came to rest at his feet.

It was Marissa Madison's head.

Jerome Anthony Franklin put his hand to his mouth. He fell to his knees.

And he broke down there in the mud.

FORESHADOW

Look at her, Jerome. Stop cheating."

He shakes his head, eyes squeezed shut, bottom lip poked out like a kid who don't want to eat his asparagus. I soften my tone.

"She's a peach, son. Be brave. She loved you, so prove right now you loved her. Go on. Show it wasn't just skin deep. Have some respect."

I know I've really broken him then, because he falls for the bullshit psychobabble I just took straight out of my drainpipe. I don't have a good view of her down there facing away at ground level, but I see him clear as day firming up his backbone, letting his eyes flutter open, and taking in the sight of her, absorbing it, cupping his hands around her cold cheeks and mumbling sweet nothings. I know she looks ghost-pale and amphibian-like at this point with her nose ripped clean and her eyes rolled back showing their whites. It's a nice moment, but I bore pretty easy.

"Put her head in my trunk, Jerome. We're almost finished with this business together, but I always take a trophy. The rest of her is back in here, and I'm sure you'll find it all soon enough."

He don't even argue. He's how you would say, "resigned" to it all by this point. He stands, still cupping his precious artifact between his palms, and he walks her over to my trunk nice and slow like it's some sacred religious ritual.

And now it's over. One more thing to do. One more piece of business.

"Jerome," I say, "last scene, pal. Get the keys off the top of my roof, open your passenger door, and sit on the seat sideways. Put your hands between your knees down toward the ground all the way to your ankles, and keep your head lowered and your eyes shut tight. I'm gonna come out from back in here, make my way to my trunk, and get a length of manila rope I've got in there. I'm gonna tie your wrists to your ankles and have you lie back on the floor in that little space in front of the seat, right there on the floor mat with your feet and hands sticking up. I'm gonna close the door behind you and drive the fuck out of here, got it? By the time you figure out how to get to the knots and pull yourself up, I'll be long gone. But you gotta keep your eyes shut, Jerome. It's a matter of trust now. If I see you get a look at me I'll have to kill you, and we don't want that, do we?"

He goes and does what I told him to do. He has to climb on my front hood to get to his keys, but he hurries along as best he can. He even goes a step further like he's trying for extra credit or something, 'cause when he opens his passenger door and sits on the edge of the cushion, he don't just put his wrists up against his ankles like I told him. He sticks his hands all the way down into the mud like he's grabbing the bottom of his feet.

Kiss-ass.

Teacher's pet.

Cocksucker.

I come out from behind the luggage racks and the Rubbermaids, walking slowly but deliberately, and I ain't veering left 'cause I ain't going for any manila rope in my trunk. I know he's well aware deep down that when it's all said and done I ain't banking on some half-baked attempt to frame him for the murder of a cop and thirteen young women. I know he's certain that these are the last breaths he's ever gonna take, and I figure he's wondering where I'm gonna fit his body with the trunk being so full and all.

Well, I got a back seat, brutha.

And my Toyota needed detailing anyway.

I stride out into the open space, and while I'm closing in I see him talking to himself with his eyes still squeezed shut, just in case I suppose, maybe mumbling prayers up to God or something. There's a runner of snot going from his nose to his cheek and bright white spit at the corners of his mouth.

"I found some rope back there on a roll of tarp," I say, walking up. "Honest. It ain't as good as what I got in my trunk, more like the stuff they give you when you get a Christmas tree and they tie it to your roof, but it'll do. Put your feet and hands closer together for me. It'll be over before you know it."

He gathers everything in close, hands still sunk into the mud, and he looks like some African farmer fixing to pull up a stubborn root. His eyes are still pressed shut and he tilts his face upward.

"You don't respect musicians," he says.

I stop about ten feet from him. Don't make sense. If anything, I would have thought he'd have used his last words to tell me I was way over the top, playing the charade that I was gonna keep him alive too long for anyone to believe with the Christmas rope horseshit and all.

"What you mean?"

He smiles, eyes shut.

"You have a rhythm," he says. "A certain amount of beats that go down when you speak and a similar number of measures you utilize for movement. I'm a musician, and I've identified your patterns."

"Yeah, so what?"

He shrugs, and that string of snot is starting to bug the living shit out of me, swinging there between his nose and his cheek like a loose clothesline.

"So nothing," he says. "It's just something I picked up on in the last half-hour or so. Something you couldn't care less about, but something you should know just the same."

I step closer. Enough. Time to end this.

"Wanna hear a book on tape?" he says.

Again, I stop.

"What the fuck you talking about?"

"A gift," he says. "Left from Marissa. After I stopped at my grandmother's place it was on my car stereo, playing all the way up here. I didn't understand it. Couldn't quite figure the context. Then I couldn't turn the thing off. It was on a loop, just drawing me in. Listen."

I take another step forward and I hear something through the open door. It sounds familiar, but faint enough that I can't pin it down. Then I step in even closer and I realize I'm hearing my own voice, narrating to myself around sixty-six minutes ago about being stuck out on 476 with two flats.

"I lean back into the trunk and force myself not to start throwing shit around. Last time I had the jack out, I think I threw the tire iron back by the dented tin that once had three types of popcorn in it. I should have tucked the little black bitch away in the triangular leather pouch that goes in its place under the false-bottom particle board covering the tire well. But I didn't, and it was irresponsible . . . I lean back into the trunk and force myself not to start throwing shit around."

"See, it was always about the hardware," Jerome says.

"Last time I had the jack out, I think I threw the tire iron back by the dented tin that once had three types of popcorn in it."

"But your tire iron wasn't 'by' the dented popcorn tin," Jerome says. "It was inside it."

He jumps up out of his squat faster than I would have expected, a flurry of knee-bones and dirty elbows, and while he's raising up the piece of steel that he'd had hidden there in the mud I wonder which specific intervals he used to sneak over to my trunk, root out the popcorn tin, take out my tire iron, and bury it while I temporarily had my eyes off him, doing my own sneaking behind the machinery making sure I didn't snag a toe and go headlong. I think about how clever this son of a bitch has been, making his moves while I was making mine, then slipping back into his role changing the tires as if he'd never altered that numb and sluggish prisoner's march.

His eyes are wide open bursts, lips curled back in a scream, and he brings down his weapon like the Hammer of God. I hear it hiss through the wet air.

And all I feel is the nothingness.

CHAPTER EIGHTEEN

Jerome Anthony Franklin struck Jonathan Martin Delaware Deseronto square between the eyes and buried the flat edge of the tire iron three and a half inches into his skull. The sound was thick and meaty like a hatchet head sunk in wet timber, and the monster's arms flapped spasmodically, his big feet backpedaling. He was dead before he splashed down into the mud.

Deseronto looked at himself lying there on his back, hair plastered and straggled down one side of his face, forehead stoven down to a bloody groove, both of his sightless eyes crossed in at skewed angles. Standing over him, Jerome Anthony Franklin was hunched over, breathing heavily, face dead set in that he believed he had done the right thing.

And like fumes of exhaust, Deseronto got a whiff of the future, probably some after-effect left by the ghostlike presence of Marissa Madison still lingering in the air space. He saw Jerome Anthony Franklin in a midnight-blue Amosu designer suit defending himself in a court of law, not only against charges for the bludgeoning but also an aiding-and-abetting scenario, as if the two had been a team all along like the Maryland snipers. Deseronto saw television cameras, newspaper clippings, and Internet postings claiming that the young man's defense was, in fact, the most powerful judicial presentation ever given on American soil by someone without a law degree, and his brilliant closing broke viewing records on YouTube. The verdict was innocent on all charges, and Jerome Anthony Franklin was named "Philadelphia's Favorite Son," referred to as "The Man Who Got Deseronto" and offered full scholarships to Stanford, Duke, Princeton, and Harvard.

The image of Jerome's future was fading, but Deseronto was granted a final look, a "montage sequence" showing the young man slightly older, running for office, marketing himself as a self-made American man and promoting a platform supporting the underprivileged, the forgotten, the underdog, and the plea that the greatest American ideal was founded upon the principle that we all deserved second chances, that our country loved those who got back on their feet after failure, brushed themselves off, took the hard road through personal industry, and finally made something of themselves. His campaign was launched with television ads featuring inner-city children achieving great things in scholarship, civic activities, music, and sport, and each was backgrounded by his old hit, "You Made Me a Memory."

The future vision finally winked out when there was a scene portraying a forty-something Jerome Anthony Franklin, as governor, unveiling a street sign replacing the one at the corner of West Chester Pike and New Ardmore Avenue in Broomall. It said "Madison Lane."

Jonathan Martin Delaware Deseronto turned and left his dead body lying there in disgrace.

There was someone calling for him back at the motel.

It was his mother, up in room 457.

AFTERLIFE

I'm standing by my mother's death bed in room 457. The walls are striped green and maroon and there's a Bible on the end table. There's a TV, a sitting chair, a mirror, and a bathroom off to the left.

Mama's lying there making bony shapes under the sheets and she has the breathing mask on, partially askew with the funnel out so she can whisper to me in tones of the dead. I'm standing there and I hang my head, letting my spirit-hair dangle in front of my face.

"I tried to warn ya," she says, voice holding on to that last bit of strength, "but in the end I don't think it would have made any difference."

She coughs, and I look up through my hair a little. Her slight frame convulses, and her knees come up in points. She gets it together and turns back to me slowly, one red eye staring dully through the black buckled strap bands.

"You killed the wrong bitch, Johnny," she says. "She's big up in here."

"What you talking about?" I say.

"You always was slow. Listen. There ain't no heaven or hell for us, Johnny. There's just here. This place. Where I get to watch you pay your debt and do what you were born to do. I helped create you, and now I'm the asshole strapped to the chair digging your gospel."

"I still don't see what you mean," I say.

"Then shut up and pay attention. You're a sociopath, Johnny. An emotionless beast who doesn't understand where feelings come from. You're a cold receptacle. And now that you're dead you can start."

"Start what?"

"Your job, Johnny. You're a swallower now. You're here to greet the dead one by one, and swallow down their two most profound memories, their very best and their very worst. Once you live through the scenarios you'll take 'em for keeps, that is if your patrons decide to sacrifice their moment of glory to be relieved of their misery. That cop you killed, his name was Billy McNichol. His best memory was the day he made the force, throwing his hat in the air at the war memorial with the rest of them and seeing his old Pop there in the bleachers dabbing the corner of his eye with a hankie. His worst memory was watching a YouTube video, one minute and thirty-three seconds of it in the situation room with three other officers, a detective, and a representative from the DA's office, all of them studying the bumpy and shaky footage there in the lacrosse equipment room at the high school with gray lockers in the background, a weight bench, and a wall poster that preached exercise as a way to conquer obesity. The three assailants had their sweatshirt hoods pulled drawstring tight over their heads, scrunching their faces into alien ovals they thought would be harder to identify, and they'd formed a rough triangle with Billy's sixteen-year-old son Steven as the pinball, shoved repeatedly between them, head snapping back over and again with the force of their punches, later to go comatose in the hospital and pass quietly, all because Billy had told him the day before to stand up to the tall one named Conner Wexman, stand up to him good and don't come back into this house until you've learned to be more of a man out there."

My cheek twitches.

"And then there's the girls, I suppose."

Mama caws like a crow and then she's coughing again. After a sluggish recovery, she moves the mouthpiece farther up her cheek with frail, shaking fingers.

"Yeah, there's the girls," she says. "Ain't difficult math, Johnny. Don't take a genius to figure that you'd be obligated out of the gate to swallow the best and worst experiences of your victims—Becky Lockhart, Sarah-Jean Kennedy, Veronica Kimbel, Meghan McGillicutty, Rennatta Rogers, yadda-yadda, that is if they opt for the trade-off. Even though there are a few souls out here that prefer to take all their baggage with them into the beyond, there are far more that would rather be free of it."

I squint down like a Chinaman.

"Good amount? More? You mean . . ."

Mama licks her dry lips.

"You're gonna be a busy boy up in here, Johnny. This here is the junction point. Like a toll booth. And you're the operator behind the glass."

"How many altogether?" I say.

She looks at me with that blurry red eye and says,

"Go to the window and see."

I move across the room and pull over the thick cloth curtain, and it smells of dust making me know that even in death my senses are primed and ready for bear.

Outside it's still dark, but not so dark I can't see. I'm looking at the embankment I drove my Toyota down, but from a different angle. And it's flooded with people, standing and staring up at my window, and all of them are wearing what they died in. It's an ocean of people standing and waiting on the hill, and while the front of the line snakes around the corner of the motel out of sight toward the entrance, there's a back side of that line going up and beyond the embankment as far as the eye can see, all along the lip of the Exit 6 ramp and leading off toward the highway.

"It's infinity, Johnny," my mama says.

And then there's a knock at the door.

ABOUT THE AUTHOR

Michael Aronovitz is the acclaimed author of two short story collections, *Seven Deadly Pleasures* and *The Voices in Our Heads*, and a novel, *Alice Walks*.